"Snappy dialogue, a well-drawn supporting cast and an irresistible canine companion all add delicious flavor. Gulp this book down or savor it, but consuming it will guarantee a sustained sugar high."
—*The New York Times Book Review*

"With a one-of-a-kind heroine and a plot that's just as addictive as checking Instagram, *Two Parts Sugar, One Part Murder* is a fresh take on the cozy genre. I couldn't help but root for influencer Maddy Montgomery whether she was trying to solve a murder or just not burn the cake. The Baker Street Mysteries has already become one of my favorite series! #MorePlease."
—Kellye Garrett, Agatha award winning author of *Hollywood Homicide* and *Like a Sister*

"A lively series launch, with an edgier heroine than the baking-framed novels by Jenn McKinlay and Joanne Fluke."
—*Booklist*

"Valerie Burns sweetens the pot for cozy mystery fans with this debut in her new series. City transplant Madison Montgomery finds her small-town tribe and new strengths in a delicious story of baking, backstabbing, and murder."
—Maddie Day, author of the Country Store Mysteries

"Everyone is a suspect in Valerie Burns's entertaining new mystery, filled with surprising twists, suspicious characters and a mastiff named Baby who will win your heart. Top that off with humor and delicious recipes and you have a delight of a cozy."
—Valerie Wilson Wesley, author of *A Fatal Glow*

MURDER IS A PIECE OF CAKE

"This fun culinary cozy mystery is the perfect beach read."
—*Modern Dog*

"Burns proves that a girl and her mastiff can't be defeated."
—*Kirkus Reviews*

Books by Valerie Burns

Baker Street Mysteries
TWO PARTS SUGAR, ONE PART MURDER
MURDER IS A PIECE OF CAKE
A CUP OF FLOUR, A PINCH OF DEATH
ICING ON THE MURDER

Books by Valerie Burns writing as V.M. Burns

Mystery Bookshop Mysteries
THE PLOT IS MURDER
READ HERRING HUNT
THE NOVEL ART OF MURDER
WED, READ & DEAD
BOOKMARKED FOR MURDER
A TOURIST'S GUIDE TO MURDER
KILLER WORDS
BOOKCLUBBED TO DEATH
MURDER ON TOUR
THE NEXT DEADLY CHAPTER

Dog Club Mysteries
IN THE DOG HOUSE
THE PUPPY WHO KNEW TOO MUCH
BARK IF IT'S MURDER
PAW AND ORDER
SIT, STAY, SLAY

Published by Kensington Publishing Corp.

VALERIE BURNS

Icing on the Murder

Kensington Publishing Corp.
kensingtonbooks.com

KENSINGTON BOOKS are published by

Kensington Publishing Corp.
900 Third Avenue
New York, NY 10022

All Kensington titles, imprints, and distributed lines are available at special quantity discounts for bulk purchases for sales promotion, premiums, fund-raising, and educational or institutional use.

Special book excerpts or customized printings can also be created to fit specific needs. For details, write or phone the office of the Kensington Sales Manager: Kensington Publishing Corp., 900 Third Avenue, New York, NY 10022. Attn. Sales Department. Phone: 1-800-221-2647.

KENSINGTON and the KENSINGTON COZIES teapot logo Reg US Pat. & TM Off.

ISBN: 978-1-4967-5340-3
First Trade Paperback Printing: August 2025

ISBN: 978-1-4967-5341-0 (e-book)

10 9 8 7 6 5 4 3 2 1

Printed in the United States of America

The authorized representative in the EU for product safety and compliance
Is eucomply OU, Parnu mnt 139b-14, Apt 123
Tallinn, Berlin 11317, hello@eucompliancepartner.com

ACKNOWLEDGMENTS

Special thanks to my editor, John Scognamiglio at Kensington, and literary agent, Jessica Faust at BookEnds. Thanks to Alex Savage and Stephen Kotow for sharing your Navy expertise, and John Fortunato for letting me pick your brain about the FBI. Thanks to Michael Dell for editing, and Erica Reddick for consulting. Thanks to Melinda Bandy, Patricia and Kay Lillie for sharing your yummy recipes, and to Tammy and all of the Halls (Tim, Ben, and Sofie) for test baking and tasting. Thanks to Christopher and Carson Rucker for their fashion expertise. Thanks to Kellye Garrett for all of the sprints. Most of all, I want to thank Debra H. Goldstein for sprints, pep talks, advice, moral support, and the friendship that helped me get from the start to the end.

Icing
on the
Murder

CHAPTER 1

"Ladies and gentlemen, all the way from New Bison, Michigan, it's time for the main event. Army versus Navy in the battle of the century." Tyler Lawrence paused dramatically before continuing. "Now, let's get ready to *rum-bullll*!" He drew the last syllable out for a long time in his best impersonation of Michael Buffer, the wrestling and boxer announcer.

I wasn't a fan of either sport. Having grown up on a naval base surrounded by sailors, even a fashionista like me recognized the phrase. I was surprised by Tyler's performance. He was normally a quiet man of few words, but ever since he took on the added responsibility of acting mayor in addition to his shop, he's been much more outgoing.

With his fist to his mouth as if he were holding a microphone, Tyler Lawrence moved around the large dining room table and stood in front of Michael. "In this corner, at six feet tall and weighing in at . . . ?"

"Two hundred five pounds." Michael stretched his neck to the side in the way I'd seen professional athletes do in preparing to compete. His neck cracked, and he grinned across the table at me.

"We have Army veteran and renowned local veterinarian, Dr. Michael 'The Man' Portman." Tyler cheered and smacked Michael on the back.

My head baker and friend, Leroy Danielson, stood behind Michael and massaged his shoulders like a trainer preparing a boxer to enter the ring.

Tyler went back around the table. "In this corner, at five-feet-four-inches tall and weighing in at . . . ?" He stuck his fist in front of my face.

"None of your business," I said.

"Representing the Navy in this battle, we have the daughter of Navy Admiral Jefferson Augustus Montgomery. Fashionista, social media influencer, entrepreneur, and owner of Baby Cakes Bakery, Madison 'The Squid' Montgomery." Tyler cheered.

"Don't call me Squid."

April Johnson was the sheriff, my tenant, and, most importantly, my friend. She chuckled and reached over and fluffed my hair. At nearly six feet tall, with gray eyes and dark wavy hair, she was stunning. April often downplayed her beauty by pulling her hair back into a bun and wearing very little makeup. On the rare occasions when she allowed herself to be a normal human instead of a sheriff, and wore makeup and flattering clothes instead of a uniform, she was a knockout. Today was Sunday. April was off duty and looked like a model.

"This is a lot of foolishness," Hannah Portman said. She sat at the head of the dining room table and sipped her coffee.

Hannah was Michael's grandmother and one of the Baby Cakes bakers. She had been best friends with my Great-Aunt Octavia, who started Baby Cakes and from whom I'd inherited it.

"April, don't encourage this nonsense," Hannah Portman said. "If we're done with our Sunday meeting, then we can go and let Maddy and Michael work out the details of their budget without an audience."

"But we were just getting to the good part," Tyler said.

Hannah Portman was an older Black woman who had mastered "the look." She fixed her gaze onto him, and he immediately stopped. "Did you hear me?"

"Yes, ma'am." Tyler dropped his hand with the invisible microphone, rose, and started to clear the table.

Leroy Danielson snickered. Big mistake.

"And you can take Baby outside to do his business." Hannah put one hand on her hip. Her look dared him to argue.

Thankfully, both Tyler and Leroy knew where to draw the line.

Leroy patted his leg. "Come on, Baby."

Baby had been trained by Great-Aunt Octavia. He took a moment to stretch but then trotted next to Leroy, lining his right shoulder up with Leroy's leg and sitting patiently while staring up at Leroy for his next command.

Leroy smiled down at Baby. "Baby, heel."

Baby kept his shoulder lined up with Leroy's leg and adjusted his gait to match. The two walked out of the dining room, and I heard the door open and knew they were outside.

"Humph," Hannah said. "Now, you two have work to do, and you don't need an audience to do it." Her gaze moved from Michael to me. Then, she picked up a pitcher of orange juice and a plate and left.

April rose and picked up a casserole dish and the remaining plates. "I'm going before she comes back."

When April had run for sheriff of New Bison, Michigan, she wasn't a trained policeman. In fact, she actually entered the race more from a need to prove that she could. The desire came after she'd entered the race. Her experience in beauty pageants and the support of Great-Aunt Octavia propelled her to victory.

When she won, she went through training and learned the job. It turned out well. April found her calling and turned out to be a great sheriff, even though she lacked confidence. So each Sunday, Great-Aunt Octavia invited April and her other close friends over for brunch, and they discussed any hard cases. The New Bison version of Sherlock Holmes's Baker Street Irregulars was born. Now, even though Great-Aunt Octavia was gone and it was a weekday, the group still met whenever there were difficult problems to be solved.

Today's problem wasn't a crime, but figuring out the budget for Michael and my wedding might lead to bloodshed.

"Okay, Squid," Michael said. "What's the big problem?"

"What are you talking about? And don't call me Squid."

The various branches of the military had a number of names for one another. Most were benign. Michael and I often tossed them around as we bickered. *Squid* was his favorite term of endearment, and I didn't mind it any more than he minded when I called him a *grunt* or *dumb Joe*. However, while engaged in tactical negotiations, I wasn't ready to concede anything, yet.

"I had hoped we could spend this afternoon doing . . . other things." Michael grinned, and a wave of heat rose up my neck.

"We have business to take care of first, soldier." I squinted. "So, keep your mind focused on the mission at hand, and maybe we can get to some of those . . . 'other things' later."

Michael snapped to attention and saluted. "Sir. Yes, sir."

"There's a bridal expo at the casino, and I plan on attending. You'll never guess who's going to be there."

Michael raised a brow. "You're right. I can't guess, so you better tell me."

"Serafina," I whispered as though afraid someone would overhear. I waited for a reaction. When none came, I repeated myself. "*The* Serafina."

Michael shrugged. "Should I know who that is?"

I pulled out my phone. "You have got to be kidding. Everyone knows Serafina. She's only the biggest, most amazing wedding planner on the planet. She's planned weddings for celebrities all over the world." I held up my phone and showed him photos. "She's planned weddings for Austrian royalty, A-list celebrities, an Arab sheik, and even two past presidents. Last year, she planned a wedding at an ice cave in Greenland, and the year before that, she planned a wedding on an active volcano."

"What does any of that have to do with us? We agreed that we'd have a small wedding, right here in New Bison. No ice caves. No volcanoes."

I leaned forward. "Rumor has it that she's looking for a new challenge."

"Rumor?"

"You remember Jessica Barlow? She's Carson Law's assistant. Well, she heard on the down-low from a friend who does Serafina's makeup that she is planning to pick a winner at one of her bridal expos and do a reality wedding—"

"No!"

"But you don't even know what I'm going to say."

"It doesn't matter. I don't want a live-streamed, reality-TV spectacle wedding." Michael frowned. "Frankly, given what happened the last time you were engaged, I wouldn't think you'd want to go through that again, either."

I rose, but Michael was there to stop me. "Maddy, wait. I'm sorry." He tilted my chin up to force me to look in his eyes. "I'm really sorry. I didn't mean to hurt you."

"I didn't say I wanted a live-streamed wedding. I don't."

"Okay, what do you want?"

I took a deep breath. "I've dreamed of my wedding day since I was a little girl. It's the one day when you get to be Cinderella . . . a princess."

"Can't you be a Cinderella without a live-stream video feed?" Michael rubbed the back of his neck.

"I can, but according to *Great Lakes Bridal* magazine, we have to establish a budget. So, here's what I was thinking." I slid my phone over, showing him the spreadsheet I'd worked on all night.

Michael sat down, picked up his coffee cup, and then skimmed over the numbers. He stopped and stared, and a red ball rose up his neck and onto his face. His eyes bulged. "You want to spend *how* much on a wedding dress?" Michael had only seconds earlier taken a sip of coffee. The shock must have forced the liquid down the wrong pipe. He broke into a coughing fit. His eyes watered, and his face got red—not an easy feat for a Black man.

I pounded him on the back. "Am I supposed to slap you? Or put a paper bag over your head?"

"Neither." Terror flashed across his face, and he slid off his chair and increased the distance between us. He reached over and grabbed a glass of water. After taking a few sips, his coughing slowed down. "Putting a bag over my head? Are you trying to suffocate me?"

"How am I supposed to know? You're the doctor, not me." I shrugged. "Maybe you're supposed to breathe into a paper bag."

"That's an old trick for hyperventilation."

"Just the thought that I might put a bag over your head worked, didn't it?" I grinned.

Michael leaned back in his chair and stared. "And slapping me? What was that supposed to do?"

"Isn't that what you're supposed to do for shock?"

"Another antiquated idea. You should never slap someone, especially someone who's hysterical."

"Good to know. Although it's what they always did in movies."

"And for the record, I wasn't hysterical." Michael reached over and pulled me into his arms. After a few moments, he pulled back and gave me a hard stare. "Maddy, listen. I know that you've lived a life with very few limits where money was concerned. Your dad was extremely generous."

"You think the Admiral spoiled me?" I pulled back and searched his face.

"I prefer the term *overindulged* rather than *spoiled*. *Spoiled* implies something has gone bad, and I don't believe that. But, we're going to have to live within our means. Between my veterinary practice and what you make at Baby Cakes, that's it."

"But, the Admiral is willing to pay for the wedding. We could—"

Michael was shaking his head before the words were out of my mouth. "Absolutely not."

I folded my arms across my chest. "Why not? He wants to do it. It'll be our wedding present."

"You're twenty-eight, and I'm thirty. We're not kids just out of college who need their parents to pay for an entire wedding. Besides, spending the kind of money you're talking about is just wasteful."

"It's our wedding—the only one we'll ever have."

"It better be," Michael joked.

"Don't you want it to be memorable? Special? Something that fifty years from now, when we're old and gray, we can sit in our rocking chairs on the front porch and look back at the memory of our special day with pride?"

"Yes, but fifty years from now, when we're old and gray, I don't want to still be paying for the wedding either."

"But—"

"Maddy, I'm not suggesting we get married at a fast-food restaurant with paper plates and plastic forks. Although, I'd be fine with that by the way."

"Well, I won't." I frowned.

"I know." Michael laughed. "I didn't fall in love with a plastic fork kind of girl." Michael placed his forehead against mine. "Can we compromise?"

"How?"

The Army and Navy went to work. We put our heads together and came up with a plan that would have put the Treaty of Versailles to shame.

CHAPTER 2

"You look worn out. I can't believe you and Michael spent three hours coming up with a budget that both of you could agree on." April sat at the kitchen table sipping coffee.

"Congress has an easier time coming up with the annual budget for the entire country, but we managed it." I stretched.

April reviewed the spreadsheet on my phone. "How'd you do it?"

"After the first couple of hours, we weren't gaining ground. So, I took a lesson from the Admiral and decided to regroup. We each wrote down our deal-breakers. Michael's list was easy."

April scanned down. "No live-streamed wedding."

"That was a piece of cake. After everything I went through last time, I'm fine without having millions of strangers watch. So, *check*."

"Chocolate Soul Cake?" April looked up at me. "Everyone loves the Chocolate Soul Cake, but I thought you wanted to try some other flavors."

"I do. That was another area of negotiation. We're going to

have multiple tiers. Michael agreed that as long as one layer was Chocolate Soul Cake, then he didn't care what the rest of the cake was."

"That's good." April smiled. "Leroy would be so disappointed if he didn't get to try out some of the new flavors he's been experimenting with."

"I've been looking at pictures, watching videos, and surfing the web for everything I can find on the new trends for wedding cakes. Some of the top cake designers have been trying different flavors and decorating techniques that we need to try. I mean, I do own a bakery. So, the chocolate cake is fine. It's on the inside. No one will see it. The important part is really the outside of the cake, and I think we can make it look beautiful no matter what flavors we come up with."

"You're getting really good with watercolor cake painting. I saw the video you uploaded last week."

"I studied art history in college. I guess a bit must have rubbed off. Plus, it's fun, and if I mess up, I can always scrape it off and start over or just eat the mistakes. So, at least one layer of Chocolate Soul Cake. *Check*."

"No penguin suit? Seriously, you aren't going to make him wear a tux?" April held out her hand and checked my forehead to see if I was running a temperature.

"I'm not sick. That was actually the easiest concession to make. Both the Admiral and Michael are active military and can wear mess dress."

"What on earth is mess dress?"

"The formal attire that all branches of the military are allowed to wear instead of tuxedos to formal affairs. The Admiral will be in Navy mess dress, and Michael's will be Army, but that won't matter. Both branches have a blue option, so it'll be fine. Michael's pants might be lighter blue than the Admiral's, but both branches are allowed to swap the pants for white. That means if we go with the white pants, the wedding will need to take place before Labor Day. *Check*."

April stared at me with awe. "I had forgotten that Michael is in the reserves, so still active duty. Good call." April stared at the list. "What was on your list?"

"I want a wedding planner to help with the decisions, and Michael was okay with it as long as I stayed within budget." I pointed to the line with the budget amount.

April's eyes expanded. "Can you do that?"

"I can with one other concession." I paused for a beat. "The Admiral's wedding gift will be my dress. He wanted to pay for the entire wedding, so he will save a ton. Plus, I won't have to buy a wedding dress from Walmart."

"One of the biggest expenses is the wedding dress. What was your dress like before? You know, the one you had for Elliott, if you don't mind talking about it."

Before coming to New Bison, I had been engaged to who I thought was the man of my dreams—a doctor. Elliott, the man I thought was Dr. Right, was actually Dr. Completely Wrong. It turned out I was more in love with the idea of marrying a doctor than the actual person. Elliott wasn't interested in marrying me either. I learned that when he didn't bother showing up for our live-streamed wedding. That humiliation led me to look for an out-of-the-way rock that I could hide under until the social media attention died down. Nothing else could have convinced me to leave the excitement of my life in L.A. to come to the obscurity of New Bison, Michigan. But, when Great-Aunt Octavia died and left me her house, bakery, and two-hundred-fifty-pound English mastiff, I saw my chance and jumped at it. Moving to New Bison turned out to be the best thing I could have done. This is where I met and fell in love with Michael Portman, whom I love with all of my heart. In the end, it worked out well.

"The Admiral spent a small fortune on that dress. It was handmade in Paris and had a fifteen-foot train. It was gorgeous."

"Wow. Couldn't you wear—"

"Nope. No way. *Nein. Certainement pas. Ni za chto. Za nic w świecie!* Absolutely not. That dress holds too many bad memories. Wearing it again is out of the question."

April held up her hands in surrender. "Point taken."

"Besides, it's too elaborate for New Bison."

April scanned the spreadsheet. "I still don't see how you plan to stay within budget."

"That's because I have a secret." I grinned. "The Admiral always said you never go into a conflict without an ace up your sleeve."

"Okay. What's your ace?"

"The venue. Carson Law is going to let us have the wedding at the Carson Law Inn."

"OMG!" April gasped. "Brides would kill to have a wedding at the Carson Law. I mean, it's the nicest place in New Bison. Which room is she giving you?"

"She's booking the entire inn." I grinned.

"Wow! Just wow!"

I turned to Baby, who was curled up in his dog bed in the corner. Baby was a big boy, and his dog bed was bigger than a toddler bed. In fact, it was about the same size as a twin bed, but Baby loved it, and that's all that mattered.

"She loves Baby, so I think I have him to thank for that."

"She's pretty fond of the Admiral, too." April wiggled her eyebrows.

"They did hit it off well, didn't they?" I sipped my coffee.

"Maybe she'll do your veil? She could do some type of veil-hat combo."

"That would be so cool. We'll see." I sighed. "Anyway, that just leaves the food, flowers, and all the other details . . . so many details."

April reached across and patted my hand. "You'll do fine. I know you think you can't make decisions, but you are fine making decisions when they're important."

"There are just so many decisions." I scrolled on my phone until I found what I was looking for. "Look at this checklist. There are eleventy-seven-million things that you have to pick." I pointed. "I have to decide how I want the napkins folded. Are you kidding me?"

April smiled. "Look, you've got this. And, I'll help . . . if you want me to."

"If? Are you joking? Of course I want you to. You're my maid of honor. I'm relying on you and Candy."

"Was Candy upset that you picked me as your maid of honor?"

"No way. She knows you're my bestie. Plus, she's the bridesmaid. It's going to be a small wedding with just the two of you as attendants. She gets all of the attention without any of the extra maid-of-honor work." I sighed.

"That was three sighs in less than five minutes. You're really stressed about this. Maybe you should take Michael's suggestion and elope."

"What did you do when you got married?"

April didn't like talking about her marriage to the late Clayton Jefferson Davenport, but she stopped scrolling through my phone and thought for a few minutes. "I was so young and inexperienced when I met CJ. And he was . . . well, he was so sophisticated, confident, and rich. I felt like a backward schoolgirl when it came time to arrange a wedding that would impress his friends and business associates. I had about as much class as Elly May Clampett from *The Beverly Hillbillies*. So, when CJ suggested we hire a wedding planner, I was relieved." She gazed into the past for a few moments, and a smile touched her lips but never made it to her eyes. Eventually, she shrugged. "It was a beautiful wedding, but I felt like I was attending someone else's wedding, not mine. From the dress to the food, everything was decided for me."

"Didn't you get to pick anything?"

"Oh, I was asked if I wanted red roses or yellow orchids, but if I made a suggestion that I really preferred carnations, then there were snorts or the condescending looks that signaled that I'd made the wrong decision, again. Eventually, I stopped making decisions. If anyone asked my opinion, I merely said, *I can't decide. Which one do you think?* Nothing was personal to me. Nothing was special."

"I think I'd be okay with that as long as the wedding planner had good taste. A wedding is the biggest, most important day of a woman's life. The last thing I want is to make the wrong decision."

"Maddy, you are the most fashionable person in New Bison. Everyone loves your style." April reached over and patted my hand again. "If you pick what you want, it will be the right decision."

"You sound like Michael."

"Maybe because he's right?"

"Hmm. Maybe, but I had help. My last wedding planner was tougher than a naval company commander. She helped me pick my wedding dress. She told me what I liked and what would look best. Even now, I have a particular style. I know what designers I like. But, I also have a stylist who helps me. I don't have to make a lot of decisions alone."

"I don't think you're giving yourself enough credit. You may have a designer who helps you, but ultimately it's your choice. I've seen the style boxes that your personal shopper sends. Plus, you didn't have help when you told Tyler how to rearrange things in his yarn shop to attract more customers. That was all you. And you were the one who got rid of the dusty area that Miss Octavia was using to sell gadgets and turned Baby Cakes into a hip bakery with a demonstration area."

I chuckled. "I didn't have much choice about renovating the bakery after the fire."

"You could have just had them reconstruct it as it was."

I thought about that for a few seconds. I opened my mouth to object, but April wasn't done.

"It was you who got Baby Cakes internationally recognized with close to a million followers on social media, thanks to your pictures and videos and hashtags."

"All the credit for that goes to Baby." I looked over at my big slumbering pooch. "He's so photogenic, everyone loves him."

"They do love Baby, but he didn't take those pictures himself. You did. Stop selling yourself short."

"Thanks, but it's not the same thing. If I goof up a pie or a video, well, I can just post a funny hashtag. I'm good at making fun of myself. Over the years, I learned if I make fun of myself first, then no one else can make me feel bad about myself. But, this is different. It's not just my wedding. It's Michael's, too." I paused. "I just don't want to mess this up."

April reached over and squeezed my hand. "You won't mess it up. Michael loves you. He wouldn't care if you wore blue jeans and a T-shirt."

"He doesn't care now, but will he care fifty years from now?"

April shook her head. "Honestly, I doubt if Michael Portman or any other man really cares, but especially Michael."

"Well, I'm determined to be a good wife and a credit to him. He's a doctor . . . a veterinarian, but that's a doctor. He's a prominent person in this community. I don't think I could live with myself if I ever embarrassed him or if I disappointed him. So, I intend to do everything I can to make sure that doesn't happen. Serafina won't bite her tongue. If I pick something that's tacky, she'll speak up. That way, I can feel confident that the wedding will be perfect. If I could get Serafina's help, then I know I can pull off a wedding that will be beautiful and that both Michael and I can be proud to look back on fifty years from now."

"Okay." April sighed. "I understand. How can I help?"

"I want you to go to the bridal expo with me."

"Done." April narrowed her gaze and stared at me. "Why do I feel there's something you're not telling me?"

I focused on an invisible piece of lint for several moments. Then, I dragged my gaze up and met hers. "I might have actually already entered the contest."

She raised a brow. "Might have?"

"Okay, I entered the competition."

"Without telling Michael?"

I nodded.

She revved up to give a lecture, but instead, she shook her head. "Okay, fine. How can I help?"

I clapped. "First, I need you and everyone at the New Bison Police Department to vote for me on Serafina's website." I picked up my phone and sent her a link. Typically, the sheriff's department and the police were two separate entities, but New Bison was a small town and April's predecessor had combined both departments. The sheriff was an elected official with control over the New Bison Police Department.

"Fine. What else?"

"I'll need moral support at the bridal expo."

"That goes without saying. What else?"

"Help me take out the competition." I grinned.

April narrowed her gaze. "Maddy, I'm the sheriff. I can't condone any behavior that is against the law."

"All's fair in love. War. And winning a bridal reality competition."

CHAPTER 3

After April went downstairs to bed, I let Baby out to take care of business and then went to bed. However, sleep was elusive. At least it was for me. Baby snored and drooled as soon as his head hit the pillow. I watched the rise and fall of his chest as he slept. After a few minutes, I snapped a picture. **#BabySleeping-LikeABaby #CleanConscienceGoodSleep #MyBabySnoresLike-ABuzzSaw #MastiffLove**

Ever since I heard Serafina was going to be in this area, I'd been stalking her online. Stalking in a good way, but according to Michael, it still amounted to stalking. *Whatever*. She was in Chicago doing a talk show and opening a new bridal store on Michigan Avenue. If I didn't have to open Baby Cakes tomorrow, I would have driven over to do some reconnaissance. Meet her assistants. Get inside intel. Production assistants and camera crews were always willing to talk, especially when filled with cake, cookies, or pastries. Baked goods were better than money when it came to getting people to talk.

When my life revolved around posting on social media, and the Admiral took care of all of my financial concerns, I would have cyberstalked Serafina. Now that I had inherited a house, Baby Cakes Bakery, and Baby from my Great-Aunt Octavia, I had to embrace adulting. Great-Aunt Octavia's will stipulated that in order to inherit, I had to stay in New Bison, live in the house, run the bakery, and keep Baby for one year. I looked at my snoring mastiff. Keeping Baby was the easiest thing ever. Although, when I first laid eyes on the massive dog, I confused him with a small pony. The house was outdated, but it had good bones. I loved that it backed up to Lake Michigan and had incredible views. The hardest part of Great-Aunt Octavia's will was to keep the bakery running. A few months ago, I couldn't bake anything. Even now, I wasn't a natural baker. However, I am a quick learner, and I can follow directions. Thankfully, Great-Aunt Octavia left me her recipes and two great assistants in Leroy Danielson and Hannah Portman. Leroy was a natural baker, and he had worked side by side with my great-aunt for years. One of my first actions was to promote him to head baker. Turns out it was also one of my best decisions.

Miss Hannah and my great-aunt had been friends for more years than I'd been alive. She too was a natural baker. She was also my fiancé's grandmother. Sadly, Miss Hannah was suffering from early-onset dementia. Most days she was fine, but sometimes, when she was overly tired, she had memory lapses. Interestingly, even during memory lapses, she could still bake. It was something she loved and did almost on autopilot. Coming to the bakery every day and doing what she loved was good, and we planned to let her do it as long as she could. Right now, when she had a lapse, we found that resting often helped. However, we knew that wouldn't always be the case. She was taking medication that seemed to be helping, but we both know it was simply delaying the inevitable. It worried Michael. It worried me, too. In just a few months, I had grown to love Miss Hannah dearly. Thinking about Miss Hannah sent a tear down my face.

"No point in borrowing trouble is what Miss Hannah would say." I wiped the tear away. "I just need to enjoy each and every minute that I have with her. Right, Baby?"

He opened an eye at the sound of his name but must have decided that no further response was needed because he quickly closed it and continued to snore.

Tomorrow, I will open Baby Cakes and put the finishing touches on the display cake I was decorating for the bridal expo. Thanks to a patron who loved Miss Hannah's lemon squares, I managed to snag a booth for Baby Cakes in a prime location. We would also make some cake samples. The day after was the expo.

My phone rang. It was the Admiral.

"Hi, Dad."

"Hi, honey. I wasn't going to bother you, but I saw your post about Baby and knew you were awake."

I smiled at the thought of my dad following me on social media. "I'm just working on a list of things I need to do before the bridal expo." I spent a few minutes and filled him in on the results of my negotiations with Michael.

My relationship with my dad was complicated. After my mom's death, he was physically present but emotionally AWOL, unable to cope with his grief, a blossoming career in the Navy, and a small daughter. He compensated by providing all of the material things I could ever desire with none of the emotional support or boundaries. It's only in the months since moving from Los Angeles to a small town in the Midwest that I've learned to stand on my own two feet and not lean against my dad for support and direction. I still struggled with making decisions, but as a business owner, I learned to trust my instincts.

"Wait. Are you telling me that instead of paying for an entire wedding, I've only got to pay for your dress? Wow. I knew I liked Michael. Even if he is an Army Joe." The Admiral chuckled.

It's amazing that even at twenty-eight, living on my own and running my own business, I was still filled with pride knowing that my father approved of my choices. Especially when it came to something as important as selecting the man I'd chosen to spend my life with. "He's stubbornly independent, but I love him. Is that okay? The dress?"

"Absolutely. Although, if memory serves, your last dress cost enough to feed a small third-world country, but I can sell blood and a few internal organs that I'm not using, and I'll come up with the money somehow."

"No organ sales will be needed. We're going to have a simple but elegant wedding." A thought flickered in my mind. "What was your wedding with Mom like?"

The Admiral rarely talked about my mom. However, since his recent visit, he'd opened up a bit more. He paused for a few moments. I could hear the smile in his voice. "Your mom was beautiful. She wore an off-white dress and looked like an angel that had just stepped down from heaven." He chuckled.

"Do you have any pictures?"

"I'm sure we have some around here somewhere."

"Would you send me a picture? I'd love to see what she wore. I don't suppose you know where she got it? OMG, do you know where the gown is? Did you keep it?" In the Navy, my dad learned to travel light. Only the necessities would fit in the lodgings available on base. I'd certainly never seen a chest stashed away with mementos and keepsakes. But, pictures were different.

He rubbed his neck. "We weren't rich. She didn't have an expensive gown from Paris. In fact, I think someone made it for her."

"That doesn't matter to me." It had mattered a great deal not that long ago. But a lot had changed in the nine months that I've been in New Bison. I'd changed.

"If you really want to see your mom's wedding dress, you may have better luck finding it than me."

"What do you mean?" I sat up in bed.

"It's been close to thirty years ago, but your grandparents weren't enthusiastic about your mom marrying me. They had someone else in mind. When your mom made it clear that we were getting married, well . . . I just didn't feel good about asking them to pay for the wedding." He paused. "I dug my heels in and refused to have them pay for anything."

"Sounds like someone else I know."

"Hmm. You might be right. Maybe the Navy and Army aren't that different after all." The Admiral sighed. "I'm sure your mom was disappointed, but she never said one word."

I'd failed. I hadn't taken Michael's wish to pay for our wedding ourselves without comment. Darn it. Focused on my shortcomings, I missed my dad's comments. "What was that?"

"I said, Octavia may have the dress. She packed up and removed your mom's things after the funeral."

I scrambled out of the bed, slipped on shoes, and padded down the hall.

After a few moments, I heard Baby following me.

"Octavia knew someone who sewed well, and I think whoever this person was made your mom's dress."

"In New Bison?"

"I believe so. Maybe Miss Hannah will remember."

"Or maybe Great-Aunt Octavia kept the gown."

I'd been through every room in this house, and I hadn't seen a wedding dress. However, there was one place I'd never searched. The attic. I made my way to the garage. I stared up at the cord that hung down from the ceiling. When I'd first seen the cord, I planned to cut it. Fortunately, April explained that the cord was needed to access the extra storage in the garage. *Who knew?* When pulled, that cord lowered a set of stairs that led up into the attic.

I stood in the garage and stared at the cord. As much as I wanted to yank that cord and pull down those stairs, I couldn't.

"What on earth are you doing?" April put her service revolver on a nearby shelf and stared.

"Hey, Dad, I gotta go. I'll call you tomorrow. Don't forget to send pictures." I hung up and turned to April. "Trying to get up the courage to go into the attic and see if Great-Aunt Octavia kept my mom's wedding dress."

I quickly filled April in on what I'd learned from my dad, including my hope that Great-Aunt Octavia had not only held on to some of my mom's things but that she might have kept her wedding dress.

"I don't suppose checking the attic could possibly wait until tomorrow?"

I shook my head.

April sighed. Then, she pulled the cord and lowered the stairs. She grabbed a flashlight from the toolbox that Great-Aunt Octavia kept in the garage and that Michael made sure included what he called *the essentials*. She headed up the stairs but stopped at the last minute, came back, grabbed her gun from the shelf, and stuck it in her waistband.

"What's that for?" I asked.

"Nothing." She climbed the stairs mumbling something that sounded like *rodents*.

"Baby, come," I ordered.

He lumbered over, stood on his back legs, and put his front paws around my neck. He yawned, and I nearly passed out.

"Sweet Mother of God, Baby. What have you been eating?"

He licked my neck.

"Remind me to schedule your dental cleaning first thing in the morning."

We stood that way for several minutes. I heard a loud thump and swearing coming from the attic.

"You okay?" I asked.

"Tripped over a box. Hey, I think I found something."

"Is it the wedding dress?"

"No idea." She huffed. "I'm coming down."

There was a loud sliding noise, and then April backed down the stairs dragging a large chest.

Between the two of us, we got the chest down the wobbly stairs. We each grabbed a handle and carried it into the kitchen.

Covered in dust and spiderwebs, April took a towel and cleaned herself off. Then, she gave herself a shake like Baby after a bath.

The chest wasn't old, but it had my name taped to the top in a spidery scrawl that I recognized as belonging to Great-Aunt Octavia.

TO BE OPENED BY MADISON MONTGOMERY IN THE EVENT OF MY DEATH

CHAPTER 4

"Wow." I stared at the note.

Great-Aunt Octavia had left notes, letters, and VHS tape-recorded messages for me to find, so I recognized the hand-writing.

"Are you going to open it?" April asked.

I took a deep breath and lifted the lid. I expected a musty, mildewy odor, but the aroma of lavender and something else wafted up to my nose. I took a deep breath. "Lavender and . . ."

"Rosemary."

I spent a few moments gazing in wonder at the treasure trove inside. There were packets of letters tied with ribbons, pictures, lace tablecloths, a quilt, and a box.

My heart raced at the sight of that box. One part of my brain wanted to rip into it like a two-year-old opening Christmas presents. The other part of me wanted to savor each and every moment. That part won. I pulled out my phone and took pictures.

The first packet of letters I picked up were dated two years before my birth and addressed to Seaman Recruit Jefferson Augustus Montgomery. I resisted the urge to open the letters and devour each word. I photographed them and stacked the letters in chronological order for reading later. The pictures were of a beautiful woman and a sailor.

"Is that your mom and dad?" April asked.

I swallowed the lump that filled my throat. "Yes. This must have been not long after they met."

"How can you tell?"

"My dad's uniform."

"He looks like he should be in that musical with Gene Kelly and Frank Sinatra."

"*On the Town.*"

"Is that the one where they sing 'New York, New York'?"

"Yeah, but the uniforms don't look exactly like that." I took a few minutes to point out all of the differences between the uniforms from 1949 to 2000. "I don't suppose most people would recognize the difference."

April chuckled. "Nope. They wouldn't."

"Although, the military really needs to think about upgrading their uniforms again. They are so 2024. I mean, I know they have to be practical, which is why they redid them a few years ago. Plus, thankfully, someone got the bright idea to make them flame-retardant. Duh. But seriously, I hate camo. I don't care if it's blue and gray, green, or beige. *Yuck!* No one looks good in those. And honestly, what exactly are you blending into with that?"

"How many different uniforms are there?"

"Every sailor is issued six uniforms in their seabag." I ticked them off on my hand. "There's a PT or physical training uniform, which is the gold T-shirt and navy blue shorts. A service dress white uniform, which is the typical sailor outfit. And can you believe the women's uniform doesn't even have belt loops or pockets? Archaic, right? There's a service dress blue uniform, a working uniform type three, coveralls, and the Navy service uniform."

"That's a lot of uniforms."

"Some of the designs haven't changed since the 1800s, and it shows." I shrugged. "I guess the history is nice, and I know they need to be functional, but it's the twenty-first century. We should be able to have style and function."

We flipped through the photos. Most of them must have been taken by my mom. She would write the date on the back and what was going on. She sent pictures of herself dressed up for church or sitting at home painting. *I didn't know my mom liked to paint. This was something we had in common. I never knew.* Later, she sent pictures of me as a baby. There were a few pictures of my parents together and fewer still of all of us. However, when I did stumble across one of those pictures, I was awed by the love that I saw reflected in the way my parents gazed at each other.

I pulled out a handmade quilt. I held it up. "It's a beautiful quilt. I wonder who made it?"

The quilt was a patchwork of brightly colored squares and appeared to be hand stitched. It was lightweight and delicate, and some of the lighter-colored squares were yellowed with age. There was a red border around the outside and a white square with red stitching.

April held up a corner. "What's this?"

On the underside of the quilt, someone had stitched names and dates. There was a note pinned to the quilt from Great-Aunt Octavia.

"Want me to read it?" April asked.

I nodded.

"Maddy, This quilt has been passed down from mother to daughter. From one generation to the next since 1845. Your great-great-great-grandmother Emma Watts made this quilt. She was born into slavery. Your mom researched our family tree and found records showing she was purchased. Lord have mercy for that blight on humanity.

Anyway, her name is written in the front of that big Bible I keep on the bookshelf in my library. Well, Emma gave the quilt to her daughter, Callie. Callie gave it to her daughter, Pearl. Pearl was my grandmother. They used to call her Dixie. Grandmama Dixie gave the quilt to my mother, Willie Mae. Willie Mae gave it to her oldest daughter, Henrietta. Aunt Henrietta died and the quilt passed to your mom, Leah. I knew she would want you to have it, so when she died, I packed it away for you. I pray that one day, you'll pass it on to your daughter. I know you probably can't sew, but if you talk to Sister Sylvia from the church, she can teach you how to add your name to the quilt. Sister Sylvia takes her ushering seriously, and she looks mean enough to bite the head off a nail. But, can't nobody sew better than that woman. That's why we asked her to make your mama's wedding dress. I wrapped that up, too. Your daddy didn't know what to do. He probably would have thrown it out if I hadn't got there. Anyway, it's all here. It ain't no fancy stuff like those highfaluting folks you wear, but it was made with love. Take care of it, Baby.

Love Octavia."

CHAPTER 5

"This is amazing," April said.

I was stunned speechless.

"Say something."

My brain was rattled from all of the information I'd just learned. I couldn't process anything except, "Sister Sylvia can sew?"

April chuckled. "She looks mean, but I guess she has hidden talents."

"Well hidden. Buried deep down inside."

"The quilt is great, but why do you look like you're going to burst into tears?" April came over and put an arm around my shoulders and gave me a sideways hug.

"I need a cup of tea." Before putting the quilt away, I laid it out and quickly snapped a picture.

#FamilyHistoryOnFabric#PassedFromMother2Daughter 4Nearly200Years#FromSlave2BusinessOwner#We'veComeALong WayBabyCakes

I posted my picture. Then I folded the quilt and placed it back inside the chest and closed the lid.

I took a few minutes to get mugs and pulled out the English Breakfast tea I knew was April's favorite. I used the single-cup coffeemaker to get hot water. When the tea was ready, I sat down and collected my thoughts.

I took a sip of tea and gazed into my mug while I arranged my words. "I never knew my mom or any of her family. When I was small, I spent time with my grandparents, but they died when I was young. I don't remember a lot about them, and the older I get, the hazier the memories. I have snatches of conversations or flashes of events that I think must have happened, but it's almost like a smoke vapor. It rises and then dissipates into the atmosphere. I knew that Great-Aunt Octavia existed, but I don't remember ever spending time with her. Most of my life, at least the things that I remember, are of the Admiral and me. Now, I find out about my great-great-great-grandmother and family traditions. It was just a bit . . . overwhelming."

"I can't believe you haven't ripped that box open to look at your mom's wedding dress. Is something wrong?"

I tried to find words that didn't make me seem shallow. "What if I don't like it?" I looked up at my friend, expecting to see disappointment at my shallowness. Instead, I saw understanding and amusement.

"I think that would mean you're normal."

"But, aren't you supposed to *want* to wear your mother's wedding dress? That's why women kept them, right? They passed them down from one generation to the next. Just like that quilt."

"Maddy, my mom was married in a gown that looked like she'd just stepped out of a Grimm's fairy tale. She had a bow stuck everywhere one would fit. It was a mermaid-style dress, so it was fitted close at the top and through the hips and then flared out at the bottom. It was so tight, I couldn't lift my leg to walk. I had to shuffle like an old woman. I hated that dress." April laughed. "There was no way I was wearing that."

"Was your mom disappointed?"

"Are you kidding? She laughed harder than me. She was seventeen when she married my dad. She worked at a soda shop all through high school to pay for the dress that she found in the Sears Roebuck catalog. She said she felt like a royal princess. I'm sure all of the bows, lace, and flowers were all the rage in the 1970s. In the twenty-first century, it was ridiculous."

I didn't have any experience with mother-daughter traditions. And, a naval base full of sailors wasn't a great place to learn. "So, she didn't expect you to wear her dress?"

"If I remember correctly, she suggested I burn it." April chuckled.

"You didn't. Did you?"

"No. I donated it to a charity that deconstructs old gowns and creates prom dresses. They sent me a picture of the before and after. I was amazed." April shook her head at the memory. "Anyway, I don't think anyone will be surprised or disappointed if you don't wear it. You have a reputation for style. It's okay if you don't like the dress."

I took my courage in my hands and walked over to the chest. I opened the lid and pulled out the box. It wasn't a large box. My mom must not have liked big, elaborate ball gowns. *That was a good sign.*

I took a deep breath and opened the lid. Inside, the dress was folded inside acid-free paper for protection.

The dress was an off-white floor-length gown with a silk underdress and what appeared to be a handmade lace overlay. It was old-fashioned and beautiful.

"Wow." April asked tentatively, "What do you think?"

"I think it's beautiful."

"Me too." April tilted her head to the side and stared. "But you don't seem enthusiastic. It's okay not to like it."

"No, I like it. It's just not what I imagined."

"Did you have something in mind?"

Reluctantly, I pulled up my phone and swiped until I came to the picture of the sleeveless, asymmetrical ruched mermaid gown with an oversized bow in the back and layers of tulle that I had been dreaming about for weeks. "It's by Hanifa, and I'm obsessed."

April stared at the picture. "It's beautiful. I could totally see you wearing that. Holy cow, is that the price?"

"Yes, but honestly, that isn't bad. It's a lot less than my last wedding dress. Besides, my dad will be paying for it. Remember?"

"Right. I forgot. I mean, it's an amazing dress. If you like it. You should wear it. I—"

"But . . . I like my mom's dress, too." I stared down at the delicately crocheted gown. "I mean, it was my mom's, and I don't have anything that belongs to her. Aren't you supposed to wear something old, something new, something borrowed, and something blue for good luck?"

"Yes, but the old doesn't have to be your mom's wedding dress. This is your special day, and you should wear the gown you love."

I heard the words, but they weren't getting through to my head. "I love my mom's dress."

"I'm so glad you love it." She clapped. "Are you going to try it on?"

I placed the dress on the table. I pulled out my phone and zoomed in to get a closeup that showed the intricately crotcheted overlay.

#HandcrotchetedWithLove#DontMakeThemLikeThisAnymore #MyMomLikedLace

I uploaded the photo and then pulled off my pajamas, which consisted of one of Michael's old black-and-gold Army T-shirts and shorts. April helped me slip the dress over my head. There were a million buttons that started around the middle of my butt and went up to the top of my neck.

My mom was obviously taller than me. The dress puddled on the floor around my feet. I was barefoot, but even with my tallest Bottega Veneta heels, the dress was miles too long.

I tossed the bottom of the skirt over my arm and headed to my bedroom to get a good look at myself in the mirror.

Apart from the length, the dress fit well, although it was a bit snug across my hips.

"My mom must not have had junk in the trunk." I looked over my shoulder at the way the dress bunched over my rear.

"That's only because she was taller than you." April pulled the dress up around my waist. "See, your torso isn't as long as your mom's, so it doesn't fit you right, but I'll bet if you got it tailored, it would fit you like a glove."

I went to my closet and pulled the two pumps with the highest heels—an off-white muted pair of square-toe Loewe leather Toy pumps and a similar-colored pair of Bottega Veneta leather knot pumps. I held them together. Both were about three-and-a-half-inches tall, but the Bottega Venetas with the gold knot heels seemed more fun, so I put them on. "Still too long."

"I would break my neck if I tried to walk in those heels now," April said. "I used to be able to not only walk in heels but twirl a baton while wearing nothing more than a bathing suit and a smile." She spun around and mimicked the routine she went through while competing in beauty pageants.

"I once ran through Paris's Charles de Gaulle Airport in heels taller than this with two carry-ons, and yes, I made my connection."

April chuckled. "I don't know if I'm more impressed with the fact that you ran through an airport in four-inch heels or that you only had two carry-ons."

"I'm sure you won't be surprised that my luggage was over the weight limit, and I had to pay a fine."

"Not surprised at all." April laughed.

"Mom was very conservative. This dress is nice, but it's so . . .

covered. Floor-length. Long sleeves. High neck. I feel like I'm just a head sticking out over the top of a mile of lace." I spun around.

That's when the trouble started.

My heel got stuck in the lace that was pooled on the floor.

Baby watched the drama unfold from his perch on the bed.

Arms splayed, I tried to prevent a fall, but went crashing onto the bed, face first.

Baby must have thought my fall was an invitation to play because he stood up, bowed down with his butt in the air, and then pounced.

In addition to his nearly eighth of a ton hitting my back, his nails caught in the lace overlay.

April yelled, "OMG! Baby, no!"

I rolled over in an attempt to dislodge the mastiff and heard a loud rip.

CHAPTER 6

It took both of us several minutes to unravel the mess that had once been my mom's wedding dress. I sat half-naked on the bed and stared at the pile of yarn hanging from the bottom of the dress. "I can't believe this dress survived for thirty years, and I managed to ruin it in less than one hour."

"Oh, Maddy. I'm so sorry."

"Not your fault." I glanced at Baby, who was sitting beside the bed staring up at me with his large, soulful eyes.

"It's not your fault either, boy."

Baby rested his muzzle in my lap as two large strings of drool hung from his jowls.

"Maddy, you can't blame yourself, either. It was an accident. It could have happened to anyone."

I gave her my *you have got to be joking* look.

"Well, it could. The dress was too long. You didn't intentionally get your foot caught in the bottom. You didn't intentionally trip and fall onto the bed. And Baby didn't intentionally pounce on your back . . . well, maybe that part was intentional, but he didn't intentionally snag his nails in the lace." She sat next to me and placed an arm around my shoulder. "I know you're sad, and it's going to take some time, but eventually you'll know I'm right."

April might be right, but right now all I could feel was frustration, disappointment, and a hole in my heart for what I'd done. To punish myself, I took a photo of the ruined lace and uploaded it. #ItWasAnAccident #HeartBroken #DelicateLaceNot 4TheClumsy

Every time I looked at the dress, a cold hand squeezed my heart, and a tear dropped from my eye. Eventually, the flood of tears was too great to stop. April hugged me until the flood stopped and I had no more tears to shed. I was exhausted.

"Would you like me to take this?" April asked.

I nodded and then lay on the bed.

April replaced my shame in the acid-free paper and put the lid back on the box. Then, she went back downstairs.

My phone rang. I wasn't in the mood, especially at—I glanced at the time—two in the morning. Normally, seeing Michael's face would make me smile, but I was too exhausted to force my lips upward.

"You okay?"

"No."

"You want company?"

"No."

"Anything I can do?"

"You got a time machine? I'd love to go back in time about two hours, before I ruined my mom's wedding dress."

"It was an accident. Your mom would understand."

"Maybe. Or maybe she would say, *You've got all the grace of a rhinoceros wearing roller skates.*"

"Based on what your dad told me about your mom, I doubt that."

"You and my dad talked about Mom? When was this?"

"When he was here. We talked about a lot of things. Mostly,

we talked about how much you remind him of her. And how proud he is of you and the woman you've become."

"That should make me feel better, but I actually feel worse because I know I must have disappointed him, too."

"That's not true. The Admiral didn't strike me as someone who is overly sentimental. I doubt that he even knew what happened to your mom's wedding dress."

"Just because that's true doesn't make me feel better."

"Seriously, Maddy. I'm here if you need a shoulder to cry on."

"Thanks, but I've cried all of the tears I have, and I'm exhausted. However, I'll think up some ways that you can comfort me tomorrow."

"Oh, I can provide comfort tonight. Give me twenty minutes."

I could hear the smile in his voice, and it brought a smile to my face. "Thanks, soldier, but I'm tired."

"Remember this day, Squid. Never let it be said that the Army wasn't ready, willing, and able."

CHAPTER 7

I was exhausted, but sleep eluded me. When the sun rose, I stopped pretending. I got up with a massive headache. In college, all-nighters were common. At twenty-eight, my body had forgotten how to bounce back.

Baby continued to snore while I showered and dressed. He was not a morning dog, and I liked that about him. When it was time to go, no amount of red eyes from my favorite coffee house, Higher Grounds Coffee and Tea Shop, would be able to caffeinate me enough today. Still, I pulled out my phone to place my daily order and noticed a message from the owner, Candy Hurston Rivers.

Sorry you had a rough night. Two triple-shot red eyes will be waiting for you.

I replied*, Aww. Thanks. You know me so well.*

She sent a heart emoji along with a cup of coffee, a dog panting, and what appeared to be a cup of whipped cream. Those last two emojis were a message for Baby that his pup cup would be waiting, too.

Candy was my next-door neighbor's daughter. She had also

been married to New Bison's mayor. After his murder, she turned the hardware store he owned into a coffee shop. The store's placement next to Baby Cakes Bakery was ideal for patrons seeking sweets and caffeine. The fact that I was addicted to coffee made the location perfect for me.

Normally, I would have spent extra time on my hair and makeup, but today was going to be tough. I needed to finish the cake for the bridal expo, help Leroy and Hannah bake, and work on my strategy for winning the bridal competition. Plus, I still needed to beat myself up for at least two more days for ruining my mom's wedding dress.

Baby Cakes was on the corner of Main and Church Streets, which was one of the three blocks that made up downtown New Bison. I drove around back and pulled into my parking spot. There were only two parking spaces behind the building. Great-Aunt Octavia had a sign installed in front of the spot that was closest to the door. It read, OWNER, DON'T EVEN THINK ABOUT PARKING HERE! Even after nearly nine months, I still smiled every time I saw that sign. It was mine. I was the owner of Baby Cakes Bakery.

Baby was less impressed. He got out of my Rivian SUV, walked over to the dumpster, and hiked his leg.

We went inside. The first thing that always hit me when I entered Baby Cakes was the aroma. Sugar, vanilla, and freshly baked bread were the first scents. I paused, closed my eyes, and took a deep breath. I inhaled the glorious smells, which felt like a warm blanket and represented home.

"You just gonna stand there sniffing? Or did you come to work?"

"Good morning, Miss Hannah." I swallowed the smart-mouthed retort that immediately came to mind. "I'm here to work, but I need coffee first." Even in my sleep-deprived state, I knew better than to smart-talk an older Black woman. Especially when that woman was my fiancé's grandmother.

"Humph. Too much caffeine ain't good for you. That stuff is about as addictive as crack."

Leroy came out of the kitchen. "Miss Hannah, what do you know about crack?"

Miss Hannah snorted again. "I can read."

Leroy handed me a cup of coffee.

I took one whiff and then tossed it back like a tequila shot.

"Wow. That was impressive. All you need is a little salt." Leroy struggled with his lips, but the smile he wouldn't let them relax into was in his voice.

"I needed that. Thanks for picking it up for me."

"I'm not the one to thank. I found it on the counter in the kitchen."

"Might need to start locking that closet at night," Miss Hannah said. "Anybody can walk up in here whenever they want." She walked back into the kitchen.

"What's got her in such a bad mood this early in the morning?" I said. "The tunnel only connects these two buildings together."

"As far as we know," Leroy said.

A few months ago, Candy discovered a tunnel that connected Baby Cakes to her building. Since then, she often slipped in to talk. Since her discovery, we learned that this area of Southwestern Michigan was full of tunnels and underground caves. These secret passages had once provided shelter and a sanctuary for slaves following the Underground Railroad, as well as hidden storage for bootleggers and smugglers using Lake Michigan to transport stolen or illegal goods. In fact, April was still doing double duty, serving as New Bison's sheriff while also investigating an art smuggling ring she'd been assigned a few months earlier by federal authorities.

I removed my coat and hung it on the hook by the back door. "Is she afraid someone will break in to steal thumbprint cookies?"

"You might be surprised." Leroy wiggled his eyebrows.

I stopped and stared. "You can't be serious."

"I've been propositioned and offered some amazing items in exchange for the secret recipe for Great-Aunt Octavia's Chocolate Soul Cake and thumbprint cookies."

Something in his voice told me he wasn't joking.

"Like what?"

Leroy was tall and thin with shoulder-length dark wavy hair, which he pulled back into a ponytail. His brown eyes were hidden behind a pair of thick black-rimmed glasses. His face flushed, and he dropped his gaze to avoid eye contact. He was a horrible liar. "Nothing."

I moved in front of him to block his path, folded my arms across my chest, and waited.

Silence was a great tool. Most people couldn't handle it and were compelled to fill it. Leroy was no different.

"It's nothing big. I mean, people know that you've shared the Soul Cake recipe, and they think I'd spill it. Which I wouldn't."

That wasn't it. He was still avoiding eye contact. There was something more. I waited.

Leroy took a deep breath. "I was offered a job."

"Baking?"

Leroy nodded.

"Where?" Baby Cakes was the only bakery in New Bison. April's late husband, CJ Davenport, had threatened to open another bakery across the street, but when he was murdered, that ended the danger of Baby Cakes losing its baking dominance. With a population of 1,600, New Bison was smaller than most of the naval bases where I'd lived. If you subtracted people who were gluten intolerant, dieting, or just didn't like sweets from the 1,600, there weren't enough people left to split between two bakeries.

Leroy's cheeks went from light pink to rose red. Eventually, he lifted his gaze. "St. Joe."

St. Joseph was more than five times larger than New Bison. There was a large appliance company, and tourists flocked to its shores like bees to honey every summer. There was also more than one bakery.

"Wow. So, how did this happen? I mean, did they just call you up and make the offer? Is it a good offer?" I kept my voice neutral and forced a smile while I did a mental time check to determine if I had enough time for a nervous breakdown before the bakery opened in thirty minutes.

"I wasn't looking for another job. Honest! I was just here doing my baking demo."

"Macaroons?"

"Yeah, and these two people who were sitting and watching in the demo area came up to me after class." He shrugged. "I didn't go looking for them."

"I didn't mean to imply that you did. I just wondered if you weren't happy here because—"

"That's not it. I'm very happy. I'm the head baker." He winked.

My first official duty as owner of Baby Cakes Bakery had been to promote Leroy to head baker. After all, he knew a ton more about baking than I did. Even someone like me, who struggled with making decisions, could see that was a no-brainer.

"Well, that's good because—"

A loud knock on the back door interrupted my thoughts. Baby heard the knock and came trotting back from his dog bed to see who was entering. Based on the wag of his tail and the fact that he wasn't trying to leap through the door like Cujo, whoever was knocking must be a friend.

I opened the door.

A large man with a big smile greeted Baby.

"Hiya, Baby. How are you doing, big boy?"

Baby wagged his entire back end.

I'd learned to accept second billing behind my dog and waited.

Eventually, the man looked up at me. "Where do you want 'em?"

"Where do I want what?" I stared.

Leroy smacked his forehead. "Holy cow. Is it that time of year already?"

"What time of year?"

"Apples," Leroy and the big stranger said together.

"I didn't order apples." I turned to Leroy. "Did you order apples?"

"Miss Octavia ordered them," the man said.

Great-Aunt Octavia was dead, so unless she was placing orders from the grave, this had to be some type of error. "How?"

Leroy turned to me. "September and October is apple season."

The big man nodded. "Our season starts around the second week in September." He leaned forward and whispered, "But October is the best time to pick. Miss Octavia had a standing order for ten bushels."

"Ten bushels?" I said. "That sounds like a lot of apples."

"Yup. Where you want 'em?"

I could think of a couple of places where I wanted to tell him to place ten bushels of apples, but none of them would have been dignified.

"What's taking y'all so long?" Miss Hannah walked back to where Leroy and I were talking. "Good Lord, is it that time of year already?"

"Sure is. Where you want 'em, Miss Hannah?"

Unlike me, Miss Hannah didn't think twice. "Kitchen."

The man turned and went outside.

Before I had time to ask Leroy and Miss Hannah what on

earth we would do with ten bushels of apples, the man was back, wheeling a pallet full of apple crates stacked one on top of the other.

Leroy and I took several steps to allow the man to pull his flat cart through the narrow back hallway, around the corner, and into the kitchen.

I watched from the doorway as he unloaded the crates and placed them on the floor. When all ten crates were unloaded, he turned, tipped his hat, and wheeled his cart out the back door.

Nearly every surface was covered with apples.

"What on earth are we going to do with all of these apples?" I asked.

"Eat them?" Leroy joked.

I picked up one of the apples. It wasn't until I picked it up that I noticed it was different from the others.

"What's up? Why are they so different?" I scanned the various crates. "These look more yellow and these are bright red."

"Different types of apples." Leroy pulled an apple from several of the bushels and placed it on the marble counter. "This is a Honeycrisp apple. It's sweet with a crisp bite." He held each apple up to the light and modulated his voice as if he were a wine critic. "It's got a pleasant aroma and a nice bouquet." He held up another variety. "This is the McIntosh. It is a juicy apple with a tart flavor that makes it great for applesauce, cider, and pies." He picked up another apple. "Now, this is the Paula Red. It's a pleasingly tart little apple with a good aroma." He took a sniff. Then, he picked up the last one. "Red Delicious. This is the most popular apple in the United States. It's known by its bright red flesh and has a full-flavored sweet taste and a crisp texture." He bit into the apple and grinned as the juice dripped down his chin.

"How do you know so much about apples?" I asked.

Leroy grinned, but before he could take credit as an apple connoisseur, Miss Hannah pointed to the front of the crate where each variety was labeled, including a description. "He read the labels."

"Which one is the sweetest?" I asked.

He pointed to the Honeycrisp. "Try that one."

I picked up the one he identified. It wasn't large, and the skin wasn't as bright red as the one he'd bitten into. Still, it was firm, and there were no blemishes. I hated bruised fruit. I wiped it off and prepared to bite into the flesh.

"Hmm, you better be careful," Miss Hannah said. "Apples are dangerous."

"Why?"

"Look what a mess we're in after Eve ate the apple in the Garden of Eden. Plus, they didn't do much for Snow White either. Best leave them alone, if you ask me." She grinned.

CHAPTER 8

We didn't have time to linger over the question of what to make with a bazillion tons of apples. Nor did I have time to get the scoop on whether I was about to lose my head baker. I was too busy moving the apples around so that they weren't blocking every flat surface in the kitchen.

Baby Cakes wasn't large. However, one side of the bakery was where we had all of the display shelves and where we did the majority of our business. There were a few bistro tables, but that was it. When Great-Aunt Octavia ran the bakery, she had used the other side of the building to sell bakeware and gadgets. The bakery was separated from the sales area by a wall. After a fire forced a remodel, I had the wall removed. It opened the bakery up and brought in a lot more light. I got rid of the bakeware and turned the sales area into a space for cooking classes. It wasn't huge, but it had a galley-style design with a large island, an oversized double oven, two sinks, a built-in refrigerator, and plenty of seating. I'd had mirrors and cameras installed overhead to help those in the viewing area see everything that Leroy did.

Leroy didn't have a cooking class today, so apple crates were piled on the floor behind the island. When it was done, I couldn't help snapping a photo.

#WhoKnewThereWereSoManyDifferentVarieties?#WhatWill WeMake? #AppleSeasonAtBabyCakes

I posted to social media, ran next door to Higher Grounds, and picked up two more red eyes and Baby's supersized pup cup. By the time I returned, there was a crowd outside waiting to get in.

According to my watch, we still had ten minutes before we opened. That's when I noticed those waiting weren't our usuals. All of my gray cells weren't fully caffeinated yet, but reality dawned on me. "Sorry to keep you ladies waiting." I unlocked the door and held it open.

Tomorrow was Saturday, Baby Cakes' busiest day of the week. Hannah, Leroy, and I would be busy attending the bridal expo. I'd never attended a bridal expo before and wasn't exactly sure what to expect. Candy Rivers was the expert and had not only come up with a plan for the expo but had suggestions for helping Baby Cakes stand out. Because I would be focused on things related to the wedding, she suggested I hire helpers for our booth. The women waiting outside had signed up to help.

I wasn't surprised to see my next-door neighbor, Alma Hurston. Alma was also Candy's mom. No surprise there. Leroy's mom, Fiona, wasn't a surprise either. She was a house-keeper at the Carson Law Inn. She'd switched her highly sought-after day shift for a night shift, more to spend time with her son rather than to push cake, but I wasn't complaining. The faces that I hadn't expected to see were those of Kay Lillie, a VP at New Bison Savings and Trust, and high school student Holly Roberts. Through an arrangement with the high school, her work-study job enabled her to serve as the part-time secretary for acting mayor Tyler Lawrence, and she was the daughter of Michigan State Policeman Trooper Bob.

Candy signed up the helpers and arranged for them to be on-site today to learn about the bakery business. Personally, I thought it was a bit of overkill, but I wasn't an organizer.

Inside, I handed each of the women one of the newly designed Baby Cakes oxford shirts, with Baby's face embroidered over the pocket, and an apron.

Holly held up her shirt. "These are cute."

"I assumed we'd be wearing T-shirts," Kay Lillie said.

"I'm not really into T-shirts. I prefer for our brand to be a bit—"

"Booshie?" Hannah said.

The others giggled.

"Upscale," I said. "It's an event. We want people to think of Baby Cakes Bakery for their wedding, not just their toddler's birthday."

Hannah snorted.

"Anyway, it's just a plain cotton button-down shirt. Does everyone have a pair of black slacks?" I waited, and when everyone nodded, I continued. "Great. That's the wardrobe. Black slacks and these white cotton oxford shirts. Plus, your navy blue Baby Cakes apron."

"What's that inkblot thing on the front pocket of the apron?" Alma asked.

"That's a QR code. If anyone has questions, all they have to do is scan it with their phone. It'll show them our website and allow them to sign up for an email or a call from me or Leroy."

"That's pretty cool," Holly said.

"Thank you." I was pretty proud of myself for thinking of adding the QR code to the aprons. I had business cards with it, but those are pretty easy to lose. This would make it easier.

Kay Lillie raised her hand. "What kind of shoes? It's been years since I've had to wear heels, and I don't think I could—"

I shook my head. "Any nice flat shoes are fine."

Holly held out a foot. "Tennis shoes?"

She was wearing a pair of black Converse Chuck Taylor All-Stars. "Those are fine."

She squealed and clapped. "I'm so excited."

Her enthusiasm was infectious. Everyone was excited to help. Leroy explained that most of them would be walking around and offering free samples of cake, but there may be times when he would need help.

"I've made a video that will play on a monitor in our booth showcasing the different cakes we can make. I'll stop by periodically to check in, but it's a big expo, and I'll be busy."

"Is it true that you're going to be in that competition?" Fiona asked.

"Yes, and I hope all of you will vote for me . . . and Michael to win the Serafina wedding package."

Everyone nodded.

"All of my friends at school have voted multiple times," Holly said. "That will be so exciting if you win. I think I would die. Won't you just die if she picks you?"

"Let's hope no one dies, but I would be thrilled to get an expert like Serafina's help when making decisions."

"Famous last words," Hannah mumbled.

I wasn't sure if she was talking about my desire to get Serafina's help or my hopes that no one would die. Either way, I got a chill down my spine.

CHAPTER 9

Just as we were finishing up, my cell phone vibrated. It was Jessica Barlow, a Southern belle aspiring designer. Jessica was also an incredibly talented photographer and artist. When she found herself in New Bison a few months ago with my arch nemesis, Brandy Denton, I managed to make some headway in breaking through her mean-girl façade by getting her an interview with world-famous milliner Carson Law. The two had hit it off, and based on what I'd heard from Mrs. Law, Jessica was a wonderful personal assistant.

"Hi, Jessica. What's up?"

"Listen, you hooked me up with Mrs. Law and totally did me a solid, so I owe you. You didn't hear this from me, but you're in."

"In what?"

She sighed loudly, and I could almost see the accompanying eye roll through the phone. "You're in. I'm at the Carson Law Inn, and I overheard Serafina talking to her two toadies. Geez! I thought working for Brandy Denton was bad. Serafina makes Brandy look like Mother Teresa."

I walked toward the kitchen and away from anyone who might overhear my side of the conversation. "Are you saying I made it into the first round of the wedding competition?"

"You got it, Sherlock!"

I swallowed the scream that rose in my chest.

"But, if you tell anyone I told you, I'll cut out your heart and serve it to that big hairy mutt of yours."

"You're just as lovely as ever. Most people would just deny it."

"Yeah, I'm not most people," Jessica said, but I could hear the smile in her voice.

"That's awesome. Thank you."

"Don't thank me too soon. Based on what I'm seeing of Serafina, you may regret ever entering that contest."

"What do you mean? She's the best. She's arranged weddings for everyone who's anyone. People would kill to have Serafina plan their weddings."

"Hmm. The question is who would they kill?"

"What do you mean? She can't be that bad. They say all geniuses are a bit . . . quirky."

"Look. Call it what you will. All I can say is that I thought I was in hell working for Brandy Denton. Based on what I've seen of Serafina over the last twenty-four hours, I was wrong. Brandy was a lightweight tyrant wannabe. Serafina is Satan's spawn, but you do you. I'm out. Good luck and go with God." Jessica hung up.

Go with God? I shook my head like Baby. Jessica was an artist. Everyone knew artists had a tendency to be overly dramatic. I needed Serafina. She could make all of the little decisions that I'd never be able to make. No way was I backing out of this. It was a contest, and I intended to win it, no matter if it killed me or who I had to kill.

CHAPTER 10

I did a happy dance in the kitchen.

"Umm. Is that the way the Navy dances?"

I whipped around and stared at Michael as he laughed at my moves. I was too happy about making it through the first hurdle of my quest to win a Serafina-planned wedding to care about the embarrassment at being caught doing my rendition of the Carlton.

"You think the Army can dance better than the Navy?" I joked. "Bring it on, GI." I put a hand on my hip and waited.

Michael shook his head. "Is that a challenge?"

"Yep. Let's see your moves." I raised a brow and impatiently tapped my foot.

"Perhaps if there was music?"

I hadn't even realized that there was no music. We stared at each other for several seconds and then burst out laughing.

"What are y'all doing?" Hannah came into the kitchen and stared at us as if we'd lost our minds.

"Nothing," we both responded in unison and then laughed again.

"Customers are backing up out here. So sober up and bring another tray of those thumbprint cookies out here." She walked away shaking her head.

"Did she just say sober up?" I asked.

Michael nodded. "She did."

"What brings you here? Not that I'm not happy to see you, but aren't you supposed to be saving New Bison's pets?" I pulled a tray of thumbprint cookies from the trolley and placed them on the counter while I waited for his reply.

"Do I need a reason to come by and see you?" He put his arms around me and nuzzled my neck. "Maybe I missed you?"

"Hmm . . . maybe I missed you, too." I turned around and kissed him thoroughly. After a few minutes, I pulled away. "Okay, GI. What's up?"

"Wow."

"If I don't get these cookies out there soon, your grandmother is going to come back in here. Now, what can I do for you?"

"Two reasons. First, Baby has a grooming appointment today."

"Darn it. I forgot about that. I want him looking his best for tomorrow. Okay, what's the second reason?"

"Who is Serafina?"

I felt the heat rise up my neck and turned to focus on the thumbprint cookies. "Serafina? Why do you ask?"

"I'm asking because I got a text message congratulating me on my upcoming wedding." He tilted his head to the side and tried to make eye contact, but I avoided it.

"That was nice of her to congratulate you. I mean, I've been getting a lot of congratulations."

He folded his arms and stared down at me. "She also said she wanted to meet with me and my fiancée about the competition we entered for her to plan our wedding."

Darn it.

I took a deep breath. "Serafina is a wedding planner. She's going to be at the bridal expo that I'm going to tomorrow. Along with a lot of other vendors . . . you know, even Baby Cakes is going to have a booth. Everyone associated with weddings will be there. Photographers, wedding planners, caterers, it's going to be huge."

"What competition? You didn't say anything about a competition, and we agreed no live-streamed wedding."

"No live-streamed wedding." I took a deep breath. "Many of the vendors are offering free giveaways to attract attention. We're giving away a free cake. So, the brides leave their contact information. It's really just a way to build your lists. I'm not planning to call people, but some vendors will. They get your email or telephone number and then they start sending emails offering discounts. It's just marketing. Serafina is offering her wedding-planning services for free for one couple," I said as nonchalantly as possible. "I entered us in everything I could. You never know what we might win. There's even a honeymoon giveaway to Hawaii."

"That's it? It's just a giveaway?"

"That's it." I crossed my fingers and put them behind my back.

"Okay, well . . . I guess that's okay."

I released the breath I was holding. Winning a wedding by Serafina would only be beneficial to her if she could maximize her exposure via all forms of social media. But, Michael didn't need to know that. Not yet anyway.

"Madison Renee Montgomery," Hannah yelled.

"I better go." I grabbed the tray of cookies. "Baby!"

Baby walked back to the kitchen. He saw Michael and got on his hind legs and gave his face a lick.

"Glad I got my kisses in first." I smiled.

"Come on, Baby. I think we both need a bath." Michael opened the back door and took Baby for his grooming appointment.

After they left, I walked out of the kitchen and back to the main area of the bakery.

The bakery traffic was busier than usual. Fridays were always a busy day. If there was one day when people were likely to bring treats into the office, it was Friday. I encouraged it by offering specials. Today's special was a buy-one-get-one deal on Leroy's croissants. I'd also passed the word that the bakery would be closed on Saturday, so anyone needing a sugar fix for the weekend would need to come today.

A couple of our volunteers hung around and helped with the crowds. Most of the customers were regulars. They knew what they wanted and so did we. Those transactions went quickly.

The volume slowed down to a trickle an hour before closing. We sent each volunteer home with a box of goodies. Leroy went to the kitchen to bake, and Hannah manned the counter while I cleaned.

The bell over the door tinkled, but I didn't bother turning around. Whoever it was, Hannah would take care of it.

"Maddy."

I turned around and was blinded by lights, cameras, and what felt like a crowd of people who had descended on the bakery. I blinked to regain my sight after the flashes temporarily blinded me.

"Madison Montgomery, you entered the competition for a Serafina Dream Wedding, and I'm excited to tell you that you made it into the second round." A small woman with big hair and big teeth flashed a smile that nearly blinded me.

For a split second, I had no idea what was going on. Then, I caught sight of Serafina. My memory flashed back to the days when I was a social media influencer and received products that I was expected to unbox and hype. I flipped the switch. *Lights. Camera. Action.*

I screamed, "Oh my gosh! Oh my gosh! Seriously?" I jumped up and down and clapped like a seal. I squeezed tears out of my eyes and screamed. "I can't believe I'm going to have a chance to meet Serafina. I might pass out. I think I'm going to pass out." I fanned myself like a Miss America contestant trying to avoid crying.

Serafina reminded me of an aging Hollywood actress who had had so much cosmetic surgery that she looked more like a mannequin than a human. Her hair was jet black. Her skin was pulled so tight, moving her mouth to eat must have been a challenge. Her lips were life preservers, and her eyelashes were so long, they reminded me of Mr. Snuffleupagus from *Sesame Street.*

I screamed again.

Serafina forced her lips upward and smiled. That was the reaction she wanted. Adoration. She stepped forward. "Hi, Maddy. I'm Serafina. Are you excited?"

I screamed some more.

Serafina rubbed her ear. "I guess that's a yes." She chuckled. "Is your fiancé here?" She scanned the room.

The only other male in the room was Leroy, who came out of the kitchen to see what the excitement was.

"No. He's working. He's a veterinarian. But, he's going to be so excited. This is just the most amazing thing ever. I love your work. I have admired your weddings for years, and I never dreamed that I would have the opportunity to possibly win a Serafina wedding." I screamed and jumped up and down.

"You're familiar with my work?" Serafina asked.

"Absolutely! I saw pictures of the wedding you did for that

Brazilian soccer star who married that French model last year. And the pictures from that wedding you did in Iceland for that billionaire who married the Italian opera singer was A-MAZ-ZING! I can't believe I'm actually standing here talking to *the* Serafina!"

"Well, you are." She glanced around the bakery. "Is this your . . . shop?"

My shop? Hmm.

"Yes. Welcome to Baby Cakes Bakery."

"How quaint."

Quaint? Was she looking down her nose at my bakery?

Before I could respond, Candy rushed from the back. She must have taken the tunnel from Higher Grounds to Baby Cakes. Candy screamed like a fan seeing her favorite rock band. She rushed up behind me. "OMG! Serafina is here. The biggest name in wedding planning, here in New Bison at Baby Cakes Bakery! Holy freakin' cow!"

"Who do we have here?" Serafina asked.

"This is Candy Hurston Rivers. Owner of Higher Grounds, the best gourmet coffee shop in New Bison." *No need to tell her it's the only gourmet coffee shop in New Bison.* "She's also one of the bridesmaids." My cheeks hurt from forcing them to smile. Geez! I used to do this fawning, super-excited act all of the time. I was definitely out of shape.

"What brings you over? And will you be attending the bridal expo with Madison tomorrow?" Serafina pushed the microphone into Candy's face.

"I picked up my dog, Daisy, from the groomer, and when I saw that Maddy's dog, Baby, was there, I picked him up, too." Candy smiled.

"Baby?" Serafina asked.

Uh-oh. She said their names and summoned the demons.

There was a loud crash in the kitchen, and two huge English mastiffs trotted in from the back.

Daisy was first. She had Baby's favorite toy, a stuffed lamb chop, in her mouth. Baby followed.

I stepped in front of Serafina in an effort to shield her from the train wreck I saw approaching.

Too late—the mastiffs saw Serafina and the camera crew. Almost as if in slow motion, the mastiffs hit the brakes, but the floor was too slippery. First, Daisy slid into one of the camera crew and dropped the toy, and then Baby slid into the back of Daisy.

One of Serafina's assistants stepped up and made the mistake of reaching for the lamb chop.

"No!" Candy and I both shouted simultaneously.

Baby growled.

The assistant dropped the toy and retracted her arm.

Daisy grabbed the toy and took off in a version of keep-away, with drool hanging from her jowls and a look of pure joy on her face.

Baby Cakes wasn't large, but with Baby's two-hundred-fifty pounds and Daisy's smaller one-hundred-sixty pounds in full play mode, racing around the bakery, followed by Candy, me, two of Serafina's assistants, and a cameraman, it felt like a closet. Just when Baby got close enough for me to grab his collar, he ducked, dodged, and ran.

In all of the confusion, one of the microphone or camera cords got wrapped around Serafina's legs, and down she fell.

Leroy joined the fray and positioned himself like a catcher trying to block home plate.

The agile dogs skirted by, dripping drool like tinsel.

Leroy lunged and missed. His momentum carried him to the right while his feet slipped on the slimy drool and went left, taking out the cameraman, who crashed to the ground and twisted his body to protect his expensive equipment.

A loud voice shouted over the chaos, and Hannah stepped

out from behind the counter. She put her hands on her hips and yelled, "Daisy and Baby, sit down, NOW!"

Baby and Daisy recognized the voice of authority when they heard it. To my utter amazement, the mastiffs skidded to a halt inches from Hannah's feet. Both dogs pushed their butts to the ground and gazed up at her as though she'd just said the magic word, *cheese.*

Hannah wasn't done. She narrowed her gaze at Daisy and commanded, "Drop it."

Daisy opened her mouth, and the drool-soaked lamb chop fell to the floor.

It took me a split second to collect my wits and get Baby and Daisy by their collars.

Candy came up next to me and grabbed Daisy so I could focus on Baby.

Serafina let out a string of expletives that I hadn't heard since I'd moved off the naval base with my dad and a few thousand sailors.

"Turn that blasted camera off, you moron. Do you think I want my fans to see me flat on my—"

"Serafina, we're live," a mousy woman whispered loud enough for everyone in the bakery to hear.

If looks could kill, the mousy assistant would have dropped dead. Instead of instant death, she shrunk into herself and shriveled up like the legs of the Wicked Witch of the East after Dorothy's house fell on top of her.

Serafina turned to the camera, plastered a smile on her face, and said, "Folks, we've gone to the dogs. Tomorrow, we'll be at the New Bison Casino with our top five finalists. One lucky bride and groom will win an all-expenses-paid wedding of their dreams completely designed by yours truly!" She smiled broadly and batted her lashes at the camera. Given the length, that alone must have taken remarkable eyelid strength. "So, be sure to check out my channel online where I'll keep you all posted. Remember, *Your happily-ever-after starts with Serafina.*"

Long pause.

"And we're clear."

The lights were cut. The cameras were off.

Serafina's smile vanished just as quickly. She whipped her head around and glared at her assistant. "You're fired."

The mouse's lower lip quivered, and she was two seconds away from a meltdown.

The other guy present was a big burly man with bushy eyebrows and a five o'clock shadow. He extended a hand to help Serafina, but she batted it away and pushed herself up on her feet.

Serafina glared. "You're fired, too. All of this is your fault. You should have prevented that moose from ruining my shoot."

"Yes, Serafina. Sorry," he mumbled.

Serafina huffed. She turned her gaze in my direction, raised an accusing finger, and opened her mouth. That's as far as she got.

Baby turned his attention in her direction and growled.

Serafina swallowed whatever comments she planned to make, turned, and marched out of the bakery.

The big burly man who'd tried to help Serafina stand walked over to me. "May I use your cell phone? I can't seem to get good reception."

"I'm sorry about . . . everything." I handed him my phone.

"Do you mind if I . . . ?" He stepped over to a corner.

"Of course not." I hurried to the other side of the bakery to give him a bit of privacy. Candy was nearby. "That poor guy lost his job," I said.

"I feel awful," she said. "I should never have brought Daisy and Baby back here."

"Well, that wasn't your fault. Baby is here every day. He's never done anything like this before. I have no idea what got into him." I scowled at the mastiff.

The burly assistant came back over and returned my phone. "Thank you so much."

"I'm sorry about your job and that poor girl, she—"

He waved away my apologies. "It's fine. Serafina fires one or both of us at least once every day." He shrugged. "I've worked for her for two years, and I'm used to it, but Lucy's only been with her for a couple of months, so she still takes it hard."

"Seriously? So you didn't lose your jobs?"

He grinned. "I doubt it. Serafina's got a reputation for being hard to work with. No one's beating down the door to replace us. Don't worry about it."

The mousy assistant stuck her head back in the door. "Luke, hurry."

Luke thanked me and then rushed outside.

With Serafina and her entourage gone, the bakery felt desolate. It had only been five people in total, but when they were gone, it felt like a movie theatre after the credits have rolled. The only thing left are empty seats, trampled popcorn, and candy wrappers cemented to the floor by the sugar from dried-up soda.

I glanced around at the few people who remained. Someone gave a nervous laugh. As though everyone took a collective breath, the normal hum of activity returned. People laughed. Talked. Ate. We'd had a commercial break and now returned to our regularly scheduled program.

"Baby! How could you?" I glared.

He had the decency to bow his head and avoid eye contact.

"You were a very bad boy."

Hannah turned her gaze to me. "He was not, and you stop saying that right now."

"How can you say that? You saw what he and Daisy did. They ruined my video with Serafina. They knocked her down. They ran through the bakery like—"

"Like dogs?"

"Like poorly behaved, untrained dogs."

"Maybe so, but that doesn't mean that he is bad. He isn't bad, and I'm not going to stand here while you call him names. He didn't know you were doing a video, and I don't think I like that . . . Serafina person anyway. It's a wonder she can open her eyes with those creatures on her lids." Hannah pursed her lips. "I'm not saying Baby and Daisy were right to knock her over, but they aren't bad."

Baby must have known he was the topic of our conversation because he sat perfectly still while his gaze moved from Hannah to me.

Daisy slid down on the floor in a sphinx position and gazed up at Candy.

If I had hoped for support from Candy, I was disappointed. She squatted down on the ground and immediately started cooing and petting Daisy while mumbling gibberish as if talking to an infant. "That's mummy's lamby-kins. Sweet girl."

Leroy stuck a finger in his mouth, indicating the baby talk was making him gag, but not before he finished doing something on his phone.

My cell phone was in my pocket, and it immediately started vibrating and dinging. I prayed. "Please tell me you didn't . . ." I should have saved my breath and my prayers. Leroy had managed to snap a photo of Serafina as she fell. There were blurry images of two mastiffs, and me staring with my mouth open.

#SerafinaMeetsMastiffs #BabyCakesGreetsCeleb #HeadOver Heels4Mastiffs

"Leroy! How could you?"

"It's already trending. Check the numbers." He grinned.

He was right. People loved bloopers, especially when they involved celebrities, and she was a celebrity.

"Serafina doesn't strike me as the type who will appreciate the public laughing at her."

Candy nodded. "Based on the daggers she shot at her assistant, you'd better watch your back."

CHAPTER 11

"How could you? You entered us into a social media competition?" Michael alternated pacing and yelling.

"I told you about the competition."

"No, you said it was a giveaway. You didn't mention video cameras and some larger-than-life reality star. Besides, I thought we agreed. No live streaming."

"But our wedding won't be live streamed. This is a competition for the chance to win the services of a wedding planner. It's no different from the hundreds of other drawings I'll be entering at the expo tomorrow."

"Somehow, I doubt it." He rubbed the back of his neck.

I wrapped my arms around him. "Trust me."

He gazed into my eyes.

Was that doubt? Didn't he trust me?

I dropped my arms and pulled away, but he pulled me close and kissed me hard.

When we came up for air, all doubt was erased from his face, and we both were hot and bothered.

"My offer to elope still stands. We can be in Vegas in a couple of hours and—"

I was shaking my head before the words left his mouth. "No way, soldier. You're not getting away that easy. We are not going to elope. We are going to stand in a church before God and all of our friends and family and declare our love publicly."

"God is everywhere. He's in Vegas, too."

"What about our friends and family?"

"Video?"

"I didn't think you wanted a live-streamed wedding?" I chuckled.

"Maddy, I'm serious. Is that really what you want?" Michael studied my face. He must have found his answer because, after a few moments, he sighed. "Okay, then a formal wedding in a church with all the trimmings it is."

"Will it bother you to have a formal wedding?"

"As long as I get to marry you, I don't care where or how." He pulled me close and kissed me.

I pulled away. "Okay, I have work to do before tomorrow, so you better go."

"Work? What work?"

"I still need to finish painting the top layer of the last sample cake. I thought I'd have it finished already, but about halfway through, I changed my mind and had to start over."

Michael looked at the cake. "It's beautiful. You're a talented painter."

My heart skipped a beat at the compliment. "Thanks, but I'll be pushing things to the wire to get this finished in time. So, you need to go. As it stands, Leroy will have to assemble it at the expo. But he says it'll be easier that way. He'll just take the skewers and do it on site."

He picked up several of the wooden skewers we used to secure the tiered layers of the cake together. He gently touched the end. "Ouch! These things are dangerous."

"Not if you don't touch the pointy ends," I joked. "Now, seriously, I have a lot of work to do, and you are distracting me." I kissed him.

"Are you sure you don't want me to keep Baby tomorrow?"

Baby lay in a dog bed in the corner with his massive head resting on the lamb chop toy he had reclaimed from Daisy. He lifted his head at the sound of his name, and his tail thumped against the floor.

"I got a message from one of Serafina's assistants telling me to make sure to bring him." I shrugged. "The numbers were unreal. Between Leroy's post and Serafina's video, we not only went viral, but she's trending. People love dogs and babies."

He shook his head.

"Michael, Serafina is the best wedding planner, and I want to win so she can help with a lot of the decisions. You understand that, right?"

"I understand, but you just need to trust yourself. You're better at making decisions than you think. I mean, you picked me." He grinned.

I gave him a playful swat. "Fingers crossed that all goes well tomorrow."

Michael crossed fingers on both hands and held them up for me to see. "Fingers crossed."

He kissed me, gave Baby a scratch, and left. I settled down to finish painting.

I stared at the four cakes on the counter and tried to muster up the energy to paint more flowers. Flowers were by far the most requested wedding cake decorating request. "*Boring!*"

Baby stood up and turned around so that his back was to me and then lay back down.

"My thoughts exactly. If I have to paint another flowered cake, I'm going to hurl." I picked up the brush, twirled it around in the colored icing, and then prepared to create a floral garden. Millimeters from the cake, I stopped. "Why am I doing this?"

Baby yawned.

"You're right. This is boring. Why not paint something different? Something unique." I stared at the tiers, and that's when lightning struck. I pulled out my phone and swiped until I found the picture I was looking for.

"What are you doing?"

I jumped. I was so into my phone that I hadn't noticed Leroy had come back. "You scared me."

"Sorry, but what are you doing?"

"So, there are going to be lots of other options for cakes at the bridal expo, right?"

Leroy nodded. "At least ten. Most are from River Bend, but there are bakeries from as far away as Chicago and Kalamazoo. It's going to be highly competitive. We were lucky to get a booth at all."

"Right, and most, if not all, of them are going to bring samples. They're going to have various types of beautiful floral designed, traditional wedding cakes, right?"

He shrugged. "Probably. It's what most people want."

"Right. So, what if we go for the nontraditional brides? What if we did something completely different? Instead of the traditional white wedding cake with beautiful flowers, what if we did something dark?"

"Dark? Like how dark?"

"Dark like black." I held up my phone and showed him some of the ideas that I was playing around with. His body language screamed uncomfortable. I rushed on. "It's almost Halloween. There're bound to be some goth folks who aren't into the traditional roses and ribbons. Heck, I'm not goth, but I'm ready to pull my hair and run out screaming at the thought of painting more beautiful flowers."

He took a deep breath. "Actually, that's not a bad idea. I have a friend who's getting married. They're coming to the expo but didn't think there would be anything he could afford or that he and his fiancée would like. They're not exactly the traditional type."

"Perfect. Let's do something fun. We've got photos of the other cakes we've done. People can look at that to see traditional wedding cakes. But how about we make something special? Something unique."

"Like what?"

I pulled up a couple of photos on my phone. "I'm torn between wanting to do something really dark and something more artistic. A Picasso or Klimt-inspired cake sounds fun. Or . . ." I pulled up a photo of a cake that was as dark as outer space. "What do you think it would take to get that color?"

Leroy tapped his smartwatch. "I don't think we have enough time. I have black food coloring, but usually to get a deep, rich black like what you're wanting to do with the volume we would need, we'd have to put the icing in the fridge overnight, and we don't have that kind of time."

"When you came in, I was looking at a video from Bake Angel. She has a hack that will let you create black icing quickly." I swiped on my phone until I found the video. I played it for Leroy.

"No way. There's no way it's that simple."

"You don't think it'll work?"

"I can't believe it's that simple. Play it again."

I replayed the video. When it finished, I stared at my friend and head baker. "You're the expert. If you don't think it'll work, then — "

"There's only one way to find out." He grinned and grabbed an apron.

The Bake Angel's technique involved discovering the base color of your black food coloring by applying a drop of water to a drop of the black color. The base color in our coloring was green. No surprise. The next step was to mix a batch of icing with a dark green color. Once we got a large batch of the green base colored icing, we added a few drops of the black and mixed. Soon, we had black icing.

"Wow! I can't believe how quickly that worked." Leroy stared at me. "How did you know?"

I shrugged and turned away.

Leroy moved in front of me and waited. "There's more to this story. Spill it."

"Okay, during the pandemic, I couldn't go to the hair salon and tried to dye my own hair. I followed the instructions on the box exactly, but . . . my hair turned green."

Leroy's lips curled up. "You didn't."

I nodded. "It wasn't a vibrant green like Elphaba, the witch in *Wicked*, but it was definitely green. I had to make an emergency call to my stylist. She couldn't come over, because of all of the restrictions, but she did a Zoom and had me do something similar to find out what the base color was. Then, she ordered a dye with a red base and had it overnighted."

"Red? Didn't that make you look like a Christmas tree?" Leroy asked.

I shook my head. "She said we had to counteract the green with the red. She took me step by step through the process, and when it was done, my hair was back to normal."

"Wow!"

"Yeah, well, after that, I learned my lesson and never tried to dye my own hair."

"You should have just left it green. People wear all sorts of colors these days."

"Not the daughter of a naval admiral who was engaged to marry a doctor and was heavily involved in social media and fashion. If it was deliberate, that might have been different. This was *not* deliberate and not professional."

"Too bad you didn't take pictures."

"I would have burned them if I did. Some secrets need to stay between a woman and her stylist." I laughed. "Now, get busy making that black icing, and I'll get a sketch for the Picasso-inspired cake. Also . . . what do you think about an apple-flavored cake?"

"We certainly have plenty of apples."

"I think Great-Aunt Octavia even had a couple of recipes." I pulled out my phone and scrolled through the recipes that I'd scanned from her handwritten notes. I stopped when I found what I was looking for. "Here it is." I leaned over so Leroy could look at the screen with me.

"One recipe uses sliced apples and recommends a Bundt pan," I said. "The other recipe has apples, walnuts, and raisins. The apple cider glaze would mean we shouldn't cover it in fondant."

"Agreed. I could probably adjust the apple cake so that it works in a regular pan. I'll have to play with it." Leroy studied the recipe. "Mind sending that to me?"

I didn't mind. I sent the recipe and got busy with my ideas.

Leroy and I worked shoulder to shoulder for hours. When my stomach growled, he ordered a pizza. We ate, mixed, and decorated.

It took Leroy a couple of tries before he got the apple cake to his satisfaction. Initially, he changed the flour from all-purpose to cake flour and attempted to make the cake appear more traditional. After a taste test, I could tell he wasn't happy.

I tasted it. "It tastes good, but . . ."

"Yeah, it just isn't working."

"Maybe stop trying to make it fit the traditional mold."

He narrowed his gaze. "What do you mean?"

"I mean, stop fighting the rustic-ness of the apples."

"Rustic-ness?"

"Yeah. Aren't typical apple cakes more dense and spicy?"

He nodded.

"Then, go with that. Make an apple cake that tastes and looks like an apple cake, but isn't." I shrugged. "I'm not the expert, but what if you did something that screams fall and rustic? You can cover the outside with fondant . . . or not. Maybe, combine the flavors." I thought for a moment. "What if you make the traditional, spicy apple cake and then soak the layers in bourbon? You could cover the outside with . . . pumpkins or apples or drizzle with caramel?"

Leroy's eyes lit up. "That's brilliant."

He got busy working on a new flavor combination. He also played with the apples. He used the sliced apples Great-Aunt Octavia's recipe called for, but he also chopped some apples so there were apple pieces. Then, he completely blended them so that they provided apple flavor.

We tasted the batter several times, adding more bourbon until we had it right.

He baked a small test cake, and we liked the results.

"If I had more time, I would soak the layers in bourbon, but we would need at least two days for that."

"That sounds delicious. You might even consider using brown butter. I'll bet that would add another layer of complexity to the recipe." I licked the crumbs off my fork.

"You're right." He tilted his head to the side and stared. "Who are you?"

"What?"

"Maddy Montgomery doesn't know the first thing about baking. How is it you know how to do all this?"

"I didn't bake that. You did. I didn't come up with the recipe. Great-Aunt Octavia did."

"You perfected it."

"Hardly, but I like food." I shrugged.

When he was done, he cut the layers in half, added a bit of bourbon to them, and then covered them with a skim coat of bourbon-flavored buttercream frosting. Then he drizzled a layer of caramel over the top.

"Looks great," I said.

"Yeah, but it needs something."

"What about if you topped it with a caramel apple?"

He decorated the cake with apple slices dipped in caramel and added caramel apples covered in nuts. It was fall, festive, and unique.

In the end, we had three signature designs. The first utilized the white cake that we'd already baked. I scraped off all of the traditional design and sketched one that was an interpretation of Picasso's *Girl Before a Mirror* painting. It was a favorite when I was an art history major at Stanford University.

Leroy stared at me while I painted. "I never understood modern art, but that's actually fascinating."

"I love this painting. Whenever I went to New York, I tried to get to the Museum of Modern Art just so I could see it. I've spent hours staring at this painting."

"So, it's a girl or two girls looking in a mirror?" Leroy asked.

"Actually, it's one woman, Marie-Thérèse Walter. She was Picasso's mistress as well as his muse. It's a painting of her standing in front of a mirror looking at her reflection."

"But they don't look the same."

"You can take an entire class on Picasso and still not understand the meaning of the painting." I stretched, from hours of being hunched over the cakes, and took a long look at the images. "Marie-Thérèse was only seventeen when she met Picasso. He was forty-five and married. One side of her looks young and calm, while there's another side on the right that is vibrant. One of my professors said it showed her with her makeup, and the other side was without. I've heard one side is day, and the other side is night. Maybe it's just showing that she's normal. Most people have more than one side to their personality. I've read that their relationship was wild. Her reflection in the mirror appears older and less attractive." I stared. "Honestly, I have no idea. It's complex. That's one of the reasons that I like it."

"I like it, too," Leroy said. "I don't understand it, but I like it. It's fun."

I agreed.

It was late, and we decided to skip being too elaborate by filling every millimeter with excessive decorations for the black cake. The dramatic color was enough. We agreed that less was better. The food coloring provided the perfect backdrop. We covered the three tiers with black fondant. Then, we played with texture to add interest. Leroy took some of the black buttercream and piped a few decorative elements. Then, we added three red roses. Lastly, we added a white skull to the top.

When it was done, we stood back and gazed at our masterpieces in silence. After a few moments, we fist-bumped.

Baby must have sensed that we were done because he stood, stretched, and yawned.

"What time is it?" I checked my phone. "It can't be almost five."

Leroy stretched and yawned. "Yep. We've been working all night."

"I need to get home. I still need to shower, get dressed, and freak out about meeting with Serafina tomorrow. I mean today."

"Maybe you could skip the freaking out part. You don't have time."

"Easy for you to say." I removed my apron. "Come on, Baby, we have to figure out how to destroy the competition and win that Serafina contest." I walked toward the back door.

"What's your strategy?" Leroy asked.

I stopped. "I'm going Rambo. I think my only chance of winning is to take out the competition. One competitor at a time."

CHAPTER 12

Chaos. That's the only word to describe the atmosphere inside the auditorium of the New Bison Bridal Expo. As a vendor, I was given early access to set up. Thanks to Leroy, the Baby Cakes booth was near the entrance. Personally, the location wasn't my first choice. I would have preferred to be in the heart of the action. In the middle of the room, there was a large stage. Everyone would flock to that stage at some time throughout the event. Those fortunate, and wealthy, enough bought seats near the stage. Those seats were cordoned off from the masses. The rest of the populace could stand and watch. Near the stage would be a great place to accost brides with cake samples. Leroy took a more practical approach. The booth location he chose was near a wall, so we could easily plug in our television and any other equipment we chose to bring. It was also near the door, so we didn't have far to carry the boxes of equipment we'd packed to bring along. It was also close in case Baby needed to go outside. The biggest selling feature of our location was that it was right beside an air-conditioning vent. Leroy worried that the room would be too hot once it was full. Turns out he was right on all counts. Our setup was convenient, and the air-conditioning, which was perfectly fine for most events held in the auditorium, was woefully inadequate for the hundreds of brides, their closest friends, and any family they convinced to join the circus.

I needn't have worried about foot traffic to our booth. Our Halloween-themed black cake wasn't just popular with the goth-loving brides; it was the talk of the expo. It wasn't just dark, it was elegant and sophisticated, apart from the skull on top. Between the black cake, the rustic apple, our Picasso-themed cake, and Baby, we had one of the simplest booths, but it was also the most photographed. Some people came just to take pictures with Baby. My mastiff was a celebrity. I snapped a picture posing with a heavily tattooed couple and managed to get a snap of all their tongues hanging out like Ozzy Osbourne, including Baby's.

#RockingWithBaby #BlackSabbathBlackCake #BabyLovesBridal Expo

Hannah, Leroy, and the volunteers stayed close to the booth with Baby. Candy, April, and I walked around and talked to vendors, signed up for giveaways, sampled appetizers, and sipped champagne.

There was so much to see and hear that it was overwhelming. Each vendor offered something unique and slightly different. One booth offered wedding photographs with a package that was more than my entire budget. The next booth offered photographs and videos that cost more than my new Rivian. Still another offered photographs, videos, and a drone.

"I should arrest them for highway robbery," April said. She held up a business card and read aloud, " 'Photos by Troy.' "

"Is that why you asked for their card?" I asked. "You're usually pretty cheap, uh, I mean frugal."

"I'm going to run their names through our database when I get back to the station. I'll bet that guy with the greasy hair is well-known by the bunco squad."

"Is there really a bunco squad?" I asked. "Just like on television?"

"What exactly is bunco, anyway?" Candy asked.

"Fraud. New Bison isn't big enough to have officers dedicated entirely to a bunco squad, but I'll bet Chicago does. Besides, working on that federal task force gained me access to information I didn't have before." April frowned. "If those prices aren't a crime, they certainly should be."

"I suppose we don't need a drone, but it's so incredibly cool." My gaze followed the drone Troy had brought to demonstrate their capabilities as it flew overhead.

"Did you see the dreamy look that girl Lucy was giving Troy?" Candy said. "She obviously has the hots for him."

"Lucy?" I asked.

"She's one of Serafina's assistants. The mousy girl that Serafina fired yesterday. I guess she's back on the payroll because she and Luke came in early this morning to get Serafina an iced half-caff ristretto, quad, sugar-free, cinnamon, dolce soy skinny latte."

"Wow!" I stared. "You make ristrettos? I haven't seen them on the menu."

April shook her head. "I don't even know what language you're talking."

"We're talking coffee, and I don't put ristrettos on the menu because they're too complicated to make," Candy said. "You can make a mistake with an espresso and no big deal, but you make a mistake with a ristretto and you have to start over." She huffed. "Besides, most people in New Bison have never even heard of a ristretto." Candy had mad barista skills that she learned while working as a waitress at this very casino.

"What the heck is a ristretto?" April asked.

Candy folded her arms and went into teaching mode. "Ristretto is a short, concentrated espresso shot made with the same amount of coffee, water pressure, and water temperature as a regular espresso, but with less hot water. Do you know how hard that is to make?"

I whistled. "A quad is a lot of espresso. Even I only do a double or triple shot in my red eyes."

"Right, but she wants a half-caff. So, it's like why even bother asking for a quad?"

"How did they know you could do it?"

"They called. Anyway, I figured it would be a good way to stay on Serafina's good side, especially after the stunt Daisy and Baby pulled yesterday." Candy shrugged. "Who knew she'd go viral?"

"Did you find out any intel?"

"Only that Serafina is going to have each of the contestants go on stage live. Then, she'll try to embarrass them so she can see how they'll act on camera."

Great. More public humiliation.

"That sounds mean," April said. "Are you sure you want someone like that planning your wedding?"

"Did you see all those chair options? Folding chairs, bamboo chairs, ladder-back chairs, cross-back, King Louis, Bentwood, Chiavari, Brass Chiavari— "

"Okay, I get it. There are lots of different choices and tons of decisions, but does it matter if you choose cross-back instead of ladder-back? It's your wedding. You can have whichever chair you want, and whichever one you pick is the right one."

"That would be fine if I knew what I wanted. That's why I need Serafina. She can tell me which one I want, and I don't have to worry that I should have picked the Brass Chiavari instead of the Bentwood."

April didn't understand, but then she would always make decisions based on practical considerations like budget.

We made our way through several more booths.

Candy pointed. "Look, there's Serafina."

We made our way back to the middle of the auditorium near

the stage. From our angle, we could see between a gap in the curtain. Serafina stood behind a black curtain that separated the back from the stage. Based on the expression on her face, she wasn't happy.

"Look at her face," Candy said.

"Miss Octavia would have said she was so mad you could fry an egg on her face," April said.

"Can you see who she's arguing with?" I asked.

April craned her neck. After a few moments, she shook her head. "No. Whoever it is, they're behind the curtain. But, all we need to do is check the backsides of everyone at the expo."

Candy and I turned furrowed brows to April and waited for an explanation.

"She just chewed someone's butt off. All we need to do is look to see who's missing a big chunk from their rear."

Candy snorted.

The lights flashed, and people gathered around the stage. I'd paid the extra money for three seats in the VIP section, so April, Candy, and I showed the badges we had been issued to the volunteer guarding the coveted seats. She scanned our badges and then removed the velvet ropes and allowed us to enter. We found three seats in the second row and sat. The service in the VIP section was great. As soon as our butts hit the chairs, we were swarmed by waiters who hovered nearby like bees.

We declined appetizers offered by a young man I recognized from Baby Cakes. I'd noted that his visits to the bakery were often at the same time as visits by Holly Roberts. Although he rarely did more than gaze longingly at Holly, he had an uncanny knack for being there at the same time. Coincidence? I think not. The young man had a definite crush on the girl but hadn't mustered up the courage to approach her yet. Maybe I could help him out.

We accepted glasses of champagne offered by a slightly

older man, who was undoubtedly old enough to shave but had chosen instead to allow his facial hair to grow to his collar.

"Speak of the Devil."

Since we hadn't been speaking, I turned to see who Candy was referring to. I followed her gaze, and that's when I saw her.

"Now we know why Michael couldn't get off from work to join you at the bridal expo," Candy said.

"What are you talking about?" April said. Her view was blocked by a speaker, so she couldn't see what Candy and I saw.

The music started, and that's when the object of our attention moved from behind the black velvet curtain.

"Is that who I think it is?" April asked.

Candy folded her arms across her chest and grunted.

"Dr. Alliyah Howard?" I said. "Michael's business partner and ex."

CHAPTER 13

Candy narrowed her gaze. "What's she doing at a bridal expo?"

"I thought she was going out of town," April said.

"That's what she told Michael." I sipped my champagne and tried not to glare. Michael would have hated attending this bridal expo. This just wasn't his thing. And, if I were completely honest, I didn't want him to attend. He would have cramped my style and prevented me from going all out to win Serafina's contest. Still, it was his wedding as well as mine. He'd gone into partnership with Dr. Alliyah Howard, his former girlfriend, so he would have more free time, but when he'd asked her to cover today, she said she was going to be out of town.

I might not have resented Dr. Alliyah Howard if she weren't beautiful, but she was. She was tall, dark, and slender, with light eyes and clear skin. She had long, thick hair and resembled the Bajan singer, Rihanna. Beauty was bad enough, but Alliyah Howard was also brilliant. She was a veterinarian, a canine ophthalmologist, and a human doctor. Talk about an overachiever.

"She's a runner, isn't she?" Candy asked.

"Yep. She's prepping for a marathon. I've seen her running on the beach in the morning. I'd have set Baby loose to chase her, but he loves her and would have just rolled over like a goofball and drooled all over her perfectly expensive sneakers."

"Darn it. I hate when beautiful people are smart and fit. I'd kill for calves like those."

I nodded. "You could crack walnuts on her calves."

"I don't think she's that pretty," April said. "She's not nearly as pretty as you."

"And that color isn't doing anything for her," Candy said. "She looks washed-out."

I glanced at my friends. Growing up on a naval base, surrounded by sailors, I didn't have many close female friends, but these two were perfect. I reached over and hugged them. "You both are lying through your teeth, and I appreciate it so much."

"I'm not lying," Candy said.

"Me either." April held up three fingers in the Girl Scout pledge.

We all laughed.

"That dress is by The Row," I said. "It's a Mirna midi dress. It's navy crepe and made in Italy. And it costs more than your rent for two months."

They both stared at Alliyah again.

April gaped.

Candy frowned and then shook her head. "I don't care what it costs. It just isn't doing anything for her figure."

"The big question is why is she at a bridal expo?" April asked.

"Maybe she's hiding a fiancé somewhere," Candy said.

I pondered that. Michael hadn't mentioned that Alliyah was dating anyone, but then would he? Men could be so clueless sometimes. Especially Michael.

"Earth to Maddy." April waved a hand in front of my face, and I snapped back to the present.

"Sorry, I was thinking about why she was at a bridal expo." Neither woman had an answer. I allowed my gaze to follow Alliyah as she slipped from the black curtain and disappeared into the crowd. "And, why was she arguing with Serafina?"

CHAPTER 14

I didn't have long to ponder those questions. Serafina's other assistant, Luke, tapped me on the shoulder.

"Ms. Montgomery, did you bring your dog?" He scanned the area for Baby.

I confirmed that Baby was relaxing in our booth, and he nodded and conveyed the information to someone through a headset that I hadn't noticed. He listened for a few moments and then said, "Can one of your friends bring him? You're up for your interview with Serafina in about ten minutes. She wants both of you on stage."

"I'll go," Candy said.

"Hey, can you grab me a Baby Cakes apron? I might as well get some advertising in while I can."

Candy nodded and hurried back to the Baby Cakes booth. She promised to return with Baby and an apron.

April and I followed Luke back to the area behind the black curtain to wait.

There was a loud roar from the crowd, and Serafina marched on the stage like Beyoncé in four-inch heels and wearing the Hanifa wedding dress of my dreams. *How is this possible?*

April gasped. "Isn't that . . . ?"

I nodded.

"How is that possible?"

Stunned. I shook my head.

"Maybe it's not the same."

"It's the same. It's the same dress I showed you two days ago. That's *the* dress. She's wearing my dress."

"Did you post it online?"

I shook my head, my eyes glued to Serafina as she marched around the stage like a boss.

The audience cheered and clapped.

"What do you all think of my dress?" Serafina asked.

The audience applauded louder while she posed and preened.

"I couldn't attend a bridal expo without wearing a wedding dress from one of the hottest designers, now could I?" She twirled.

I was so stunned, I missed the first few minutes of the first bride-and-groom interview.

"That was cruel."

April's comment drew me back to what was happening on stage.

There was a large monitor surrounded by about six other monitors that could be seen from around the entire expo. The bride, wearing not much more than a smile, covered every screen.

"At least they used bars to cover her . . . well, you know," April said.

From the molten red look on the bride's face, it was clear she was less than thrilled.

As shocking as the nearly nude photos of the bride were, the next photos that Serafina showed were worse. The first photo featured the groom in a lip lock with a woman who was not the blushing bride sitting next to him.

She released a high-pitched scream that threatened to shatter our champagne glasses. Then, she stood and glared at her intended. "Carla! You're still seeing her. You said it was over."

"It is over. That was months ago." The groom made the mistake of reaching a hand to his fiancée.

The hand was swatted away. Then, she hauled back and slapped the groom so hard he lost his balance and stumbled to his knees.

Before he could regain his feet, she wrenched off her engagement ring and flung it at her fiancé's head. Then, she turned and marched off the stage.

The audience was shocked silent.

The disgraced groom glared at Serafina. "You. This is all your fault. I ought to—"

Whatever he "ought to" was cut off when Serafina's assistant, Luke, and two men dressed in black with SECURITY written on the front of their shirts rushed onto the stage. Like bouncers for *The Jerry Springer Show*, they pulled the groom to his feet and off the stage.

CHAPTER 15

"What have I gotten myself into?" I asked.

"You don't have to do it," April said. "You can just walk away right now."

Candy rushed up with Baby and an apron slung over her shoulder. "What on earth just happened?"

April filled her in while I stood there. *Should I leave? Should I stay?*

Serafina was talking, and Lucy was standing by my side, tugging on my arm in an attempt to get me up on stage.

"Maddy, you don't have to do this," April pleaded. "You don't need Serafina."

I can't even decide whether I should walk away or not. How am I going to decide what kind of napkins, napkin rings, champagne, or appetizers I should have? My head spun with all of the decisions. I grabbed the apron from Candy and slipped it over my head, wrapped the ties around my waist, and tied it in the front. I stuck my hand in my pocket. "Ouch."

"I couldn't find your apron," Candy said. "That's Leroy's."

I pulled the top of the pocket and took a peek. Inside were

several sharp wooden dowels about twelve inches long with extremely sharp points that we used to secure cake tiers. I closed the pocket.

"Maddy, I think this is a bad idea," April said.

"Why? I don't have naked pictures of myself, and I seriously doubt if Serafina could find anything that could humiliate me more than the photos and videos that I've already uploaded to social media." I took a deep breath. "Besides, I'll have Baby with me. If worse comes to worst, I'll let him pee on her Bottega Veneta heels." I thought for a moment. "Okay, those shoes are fire, so maybe I won't let him pee on them, but he can definitely drool on her."

I tightened my grip on Baby's leash and marched on stage.

CHAPTER 16

"Madison Montgomery, the owner and proprietor of Baby Cakes Bakery and . . ." Serafina waved a hand in Baby's direction.

"Baby," I said.

"Yes, Baby and I met yesterday." Serafina flashed a smile that was more of a grimace.

"I'm terribly sorry about that." *She deserved an apology.*

I sat in the seat recently vacated by the screaming bride, and Baby sat by my feet.

"Now, tell us about yourself and your fiancé," Serafina said.

Hmm. That seems easy. Too easy. Was she setting me up for something? Stop overthinking. Just answer the question. I started talking. I told her about Michael. Unfortunately, when I'm nervous, I overshare. "Michael Portman is a wonderful man. He's a veterinarian. One of the best vets in the country. He's also a veteran. He served in the Army. He's in the reserves now. Of course, my dad is an admiral in the Navy. They don't always agree. The Army and the Navy that is. But then few of the branches agree all the time. Who does? Anyway, they get along in spite of that." *Darn it.* I was nervous, and not only was I over-sharing, but I was rambling. So, I quickly stopped talking.

"Wow. How is Michael's grandmother doing?"

Darn it. Had I mentioned Miss Hannah?

"She's doing great. Thank you for asking."

Serafina waited, but I bit my inner cheek to keep from talking. I sat and waited. Eventually, she got a gleam in her eyes. "This isn't your first wedding, is it?"

I felt the heat rise up my neck. "Actually, it is. I was engaged, but things didn't work out."

"I'll say that's an understatement." Serafina glanced up at the massive monitor behind her.

On the monitor was a video from my live-streamed wedding. It was a beautiful sunny day in Los Angeles. There was a video of me in my expensive, handmade gown getting out of a stretch limousine with the Admiral. The doors of the church were opened, and I walked up the steps of the church, prepared to meet my soon-to-be husband. Only there was no one waiting at the altar. Elliott hadn't bothered to show up for our wedding.

I had avoided looking at the videos from that day, but here I was watching myself at the moment of my greatest humiliation.

"What happened here?" Serafina asked.

I swallowed hard, but all of the saliva had evaporated, and my tongue stuck to the roof of my mouth.

"Madison? Are you okay?" Serafina's eyes gleamed, and she reached out a hand and squeezed my arm. "Are you able to talk about it?"

I stared at her. My mind went blank. *How did I end up here reliving my most humiliating moment?*

A scream rang through the auditorium, wrenching me back to the present.

Serafina was pale and terrified.

She was pointing at something.

I followed the direction of her arm. My hands gripped the wooden spikes as blood dripped from my hand onto the stage. I didn't remember reaching into my pocket and pulling them out. *When did I do this?*

A security guard rushed to the stage. He reached out a hand to grab me.

A low rumble rose inside Baby.

"If you lay one hand on her, it'll be the last thing you do."

I turned as Michael pushed his way to the front of the audience. He climbed up on the stage.

The hired security guards made the mistake of trying to stop him. With one quick movement, Michael twisted the guard's arm, flipped him to the ground, and put his knee to the guard's neck.

The other guard hesitated a half second too long. By the time he came to help his partner, Michael did a foot sweep that felled the other guard and had both men on the ground in less than a minute.

Someone came from behind the black curtain to assist the two helpless guards and Baby flipped a switch. Instantly, he transformed from the gentle giant by my feet into Cujo. Drool dripped like ribbons from his jowls. A growl rumbled in his belly. The hair on his back stood up, and every muscle in his body vibrated. He moved in between Michael and the man who'd rushed to help the two security guards. He bared his teeth and stared down the third guard, daring anyone to step close.

"Baby, no!" I yelled.

Baby didn't move. His gaze never wavered. Yet, his growl lowered in intensity, and his lips uncurled, exposing less of his teeth.

Michael released the guards. His stance indicated he was still ready should they want to continue the battle.

The men glared, red-faced with embarrassment.

"Stop," Serafina said with steel in her voice. She flicked her hand, indicating the guards should leave.

The security guards backed down.

Once they were offstage, Michael's shoulders relaxed a quarter of an inch, but he was still wound like a spring.

The audience applauded.

I rushed into Michael's arms.

"You okay, Squid?" he whispered

"What are you doing here?"

"I had a feeling you might need backup." Michael reached into his pocket and pulled out a handkerchief. He took a long look at my hand. Then, he wrapped it in the handkerchief.

"Would one of you get control of that beast?" Serafina said.

Michael had relaxed, but Baby was still on high alert and ready for a fight. His lips snarled, and drool flowed like a faucet as he stared at the security guards who stood in the wings of the stage.

"Baby, come," Michael said.

Baby gave a short bark and then walked over to Michael and me.

Michael gave Baby a pat. "Good boy. You always take care of Maddy, but I got this. Okay?"

Baby gave Michael's face a lick.

I took out the towel Velcro-ed to the front of Leroy's apron and wiped the drool that hung from Baby's jowls.

"Could we get back to the show?" Serafina said. She forced a smile, but her voice was strained.

I expected to see a look of disappointment or even an *I told you this was a bad idea* look on Michael's face. What I didn't expect was the look of support. He reached out and grabbed my hand. We were in this together.

Michael and I sat. He took control of Baby's leash, and the dog took up position lying on the stage at Michael's and my feet.

Lucy brought Serafina a bottle of water and then rushed off-stage.

"Dr. Michael Portman, I presume?" Serafina asked.

Michael nodded.

"I'm glad you were able to join us." Serafina took a sip of water. Those close enough noticed her hand shaking, but it was minimal. She took a deep breath. "Now, maybe one of you can tell me what's going on."

"This is my fiancé," I said.

"I gathered that. The ex-Army veterinarian. You're a bit of a Rambo, aren't you?" Serafina forced a chuckle.

"I don't take kindly to people taking advantage of someone I care about." Michael glared. Then, he flashed a smile. "Sorry about taking out your security guards. His arm will be a little sore, but he'll be fine tomorrow."

"Great," Serafina said. "Madison was just about to tell us what went wrong at her first wedding. It looks like her groom, a Dr. Elliott Lawson, was a no-show. That had to be humiliating."

Michael squeezed my hand. "Actually, we call it divine intervention."

The smile froze on Serafina's face. "What?"

"Sometimes, people stay together for all the wrong reasons. Elliott and Maddy had been together for a long time."

"Too long," I said. "We weren't in love, but neither one of us knew how to stop it."

"So you're happy that he left you standing there alone?" Serafina asked.

"Not at the time. I would have preferred to have avoided that humiliation, but we were both on a merry-go-round, and neither one of us knew how to get off. But, I can honestly say that I'm so grateful that Elliott didn't show up. If he had, I would have married the wrong man. I had no idea what real love was until I met Michael." I gazed at my fiancé and friend.

"What I felt for Elliott doesn't even come close to what I feel for Michael. Thanks to Elliott, I'm not stuck in a loveless marriage. Marrying Elliott would have been like having a knockoff Prada bag instead of the real thing. Michael is the real deal, and I'm so incredibly thankful that instead of being stuck with an imitation, I get to marry the man of my dreams and spend the rest of my life with the love of my life."

A large *aww* went up from the audience, who then erupted in applause.

"Great." Serafina's face indicated she thought it was anything but great. "Well, we need to move on to our last couple."

The crowd stood and cheered.

Michael, Baby, and I walked behind the curtain and offstage.

CHAPTER 17

The security guards Michael had humiliated earlier glared like boxers trying to intimidate each other before a fight.

"Pretty brave with Toto by your side," one guard sneered.

I was fairly confident that Baby had never seen the cairn terrier in *The Wizard of Oz*, but he must have recognized the insult when he heard it because he growled.

"I'll be right back," Michael said. He handed Baby's leash to me. "I've got some unfinished business to take care of."

Before Michael could go, Serafina stomped back behind the curtains, flinging out orders at the speed of light. She halted at the sight of the guards.

"What are you two still doing here?" She scowled. "You're fired. Both of you. What good are security guards who can be taken down like rag dolls by a veterinarian? I could never show my face again in public with the two of you by my side. I'd be the laughingstock of the criminal world." She waved a hand, flicking the guards away like mosquitos.

The guards scowled. They appeared on the verge of a protest, but Luke showed up with two uniformed and armed policemen who I recognized from the New Bison Police Department.

Between the armed cops, Michael, and Baby, who had not taken his gaze from the two guards, they must have recognized that resistance was futile. They turned and walked out.

Candy and April rushed behind the curtain.

Serafina glared. Trailed by her mousy assistant and Luke, she marched past us, steering a wide path around Baby.

Candy rushed over and hugged me so tightly I could barely breathe. "OMG! You two were fantastic."

"I can't breathe."

"Sorry." Candy released me and turned her attention to Michael. "And you took down both of those security guards single-handed like . . . like John Freakin' Wick taking out the trash. Whoop!"

Michael's lips twitched. "John Wick?"

"Heck yeah!"

A man rushed past us, followed by a woman whose mascara had run, making her look like a raccoon.

"Let me guess," I said. "The third contestants?"

April nodded.

I turned to Michael. "We need to talk."

I removed the apron and laid it on a table. Then, I clutched Baby's leash and walked out from behind the curtain.

There was an exit a few feet away, and I headed for it.

"Hey, we need you in the greenroom," Lucy, one of Serafina's assistants, said.

"We just need one minute and then we'll be right there."

"Please. She's on a rampage. Nothing's gone right, and I can't afford to get fired again today." Lucy forced a smile.

"Are you okay?" Michael asked.

"Fine." Fear flashed across her face. "Please, we need to get photos, and then you'll be free to go. Please."

We followed her to the greenroom. The other two pairs of

contestants for the "Dream Wedding" were there, but they were nothing like happy couples. Based on the storm brewing between the first couple, I would be surprised if there was a wedding. The other bride was still crying. Her eyes were puffy and red, but at least she permitted her fiancé to touch her.

"Serafina's dream wedding is turning into a nightmare," Michael whispered.

The back area was set up with vignettes. There was a buffet with a man wearing the traditional chef's whites standing next to a lopsided ice sculpture.

Another vignette was a photo booth advertising Photos by Troy. Troy was the photographer who used a drone.

There was a third vignette that included a traditional wedding cake. I recognized the name as the bakery that had tried to steal my head baker. The cake they displayed was traditional with roses, pearls, and lace.

"Nice cake," I mumbled.

"If you like that sort of thing."

I turned to look at Michael. "What? You don't like it?"

"It's fine. It's just . . ." He shrugged. "I don't know. Boring."

It took every bit of willpower I had not to throw myself in his arms. *I love this man.*

Serafina had changed into a different bridal gown. Based on the side-eye the first bride was throwing her way, I would bet this had been her dream gown.

A well-built man in a tuxedo walked up to the microphone. He was tall, dark, and handsome. He wore fashionable red glasses and had a bright dazzling smile. You could see his muscles bulging through the suit, and even though he was fully dressed, you could tell he had a six-pack.

"Ladies and gentlemen, I'm Patrick Dixon. Although, since I fell in love and married my wife, most people call me Mr. Serafina." He chuckled.

Awkward laughter from Serafina's crew.

"It's time to move to our third and final stage of the competition."

The crew clapped and cheered enthusiastically, but the contestants were too shell-shocked to join in.

"You'll notice the various vignettes around the room. These are examples of the prizes that the winners will receive. In addition to Serafina's impeccable taste, the winning couple will have their wedding meal catered by Michelin star–winning chef Yves-René Barbier."

The crowd applauded with more enthusiasm than the announcement deserved.

"Your photos will be taken by award-winning photographer Troy Lewis of Photos by Troy."

More animated applause from Serafina's crew.

"Your cake will be provided by Cakes by the Lake, a wonderful bakery in St. Joseph, Michigan."

Gasps and applause.

"The groom and all of the groomsmen will be outfitted by yours truly." He spun around and showed off his design.

"That's a nice tux," I said. "Are you sure you don't want—"

"Not on your life," Michael whispered.

Baby yawned loudly.

"See, even Baby doesn't like it," Michael said.

Patrick Dixon was a showman who knew how to milk a crowd. Sadly, this crowd was still a bit traumatized, so some of his flare fell flat. Nevertheless, he flashed a blindingly white smile and carried on. "Don't think I've forgotten about the ladies. The brides will receive a gown from the hottest wedding designer in the country, Hanifa."

The applause was much louder.

I took out my phone and snapped pictures.

#HanifaGownOfMyDreams #SerafinaMakingDreamsComeTrue #DreamWedding

"And, of course, you will have my beautiful and talented wife, Serafina, making sure that every detail of your wedding is perfect." He paused for the applause and cheers, which he egged on by cupping his hand to his ear. Satisfied that he'd milked every ounce of steam from the crowd, he continued. "Now, mingle. Ask questions. Get your photographs taken at the various vignettes. And, one of you lucky couples will win a Serafina Dream Wedding."

"Well, you can eliminate one of the couples right now."

Everyone turned to the first bride.

Arms folded and red-faced, she said, "You can eliminate us because there will be no wedding."

The groom's face was stricken. "Honey, please. I think we should—"

"You think? Maybe you should have thought before you decided to sleep with Carla."

Lucy hurried over to the bride and attempted to defuse the situation, but she had a better shot of getting Michael and Baby into one of Patrick Dixon's tuxedos than she did of convincing that bride to continue with the marriage.

Serafina marched toward her husband and took the microphone. "Marriages are messy. If you can't handle a bit of conflict now, you'll never make it." She flicked her hair. "My little game was just to see how you'd react under pressure. We may have even used AI to make the stories more interesting."

"Interesting?" The groom stopped trying to convince his bride not to cancel their wedding. "You ruined my life. I'd like to—"

He marched toward Serafina but was stopped by two of the casino's Tribal Policemen.

Serafina flashed a smile at the camera. "Never a dull moment at a Serafina wedding event."

Her husband took the microphone. "Please mingle. Take

pictures. Ask questions." Patrick Dixon turned off his microphone and forced a smile.

"Maddy, is this really what you want?" Michael frowned at all of the vignettes.

I searched the room until I found what I was looking for—an exit door that didn't have a sign indicating an alarm would go off if the door was opened. I grabbed Michael's hand. "Come with me."

Outside, I turned to face Michael. A million things went through my mind at one time. Anger for getting myself into this situation where I needed to be rescued. Frustration at not handling the humiliation better. My frustration was followed by embarrassment for being angry, frustrated, and indecisive. Just when I felt my knees buckling from the weight of negative emotions, I was hit by a wave of gratitude. Gratitude for having this wonderful man's love and support. I had a hundred things I wanted to say, but I couldn't get my brain to form the right words. Instead, I flung myself into his arms and held him as tightly as I could. "I'm sorry."

Michael held me tightly and whispered, "For what?"

"For . . . everything. If I were better at making decisions, I wouldn't have needed Serafina. But I want our wedding to be perfect, and I don't know if we should have ladder-backs or Chiavari, and there were just so many decisions." I sobbed.

Michael took my chin in his hand and lifted it so he could look into my eyes. "Maddy, I don't even know what those are."

I started to explain, but he interrupted.

"Nor do I care." He paused. "All I want is to marry you. I don't care if we go to the courthouse and get married by a justice of the peace, or if we go to Vegas and get married by Elvis. As long as the wedding is legal, and the woman that I get to spend the rest of my life with is you, then I'm good."

I kissed him hard. When I pulled away, we were both hot and bothered.

He pulled me close. "I might need you to repeat that."

"Michael, are you sure?"

"I'm sure I want you to repeat that."

I chuckled. "No, I mean are you sure you don't care if the wedding isn't perfect?"

"If you're the person I get to marry, then our wedding will be perfect."

This time I didn't resist when he pulled me close and kissed me.

"Candy said I'd find you two out here."

Michael pulled away and swore under his breath at the interruption.

"Miss Hannah, did you need us?" I asked.

"All hell's breaking loose in there. Folks screaming, trying to leave, and April trying to get everyone under control. It's a nightmare in there, and you two are out here kissing."

Michael turned to face his grandmother. "What are you talking about?"

"Someone stabbed that Serafina woman."

"Stabbed?" I asked.

"That's what I said." Miss Hannah pursed her lips. "They just found her with some of Baby Cakes' cake spikes in her neck."

The sound of sirens blared in the background.

"Dead? She can't be dead. We just saw her."

"Well, I think April would know a dead body when she sees one. She's the sheriff, after all. And she needs Michael's help."

The sirens got louder. They drowned out Miss Hannah's words, my thoughts—everything.

Michael rushed inside, followed by his grandmother.

Stunned, I paced. *She can't be dead. Serafina can't be dead.* My head couldn't seem to grasp this. *I just talked to her. She can't be dead. I just talked to her.* The thoughts raced in my head to the rhythm of the sirens. Then, in between the blaring sirens and my own thoughts, I stopped. I stopped pacing. I stopped thinking. I stopped.

Baby sat and watched me. He tilted his head to the side and listened. Then, he threw back his head and howled.

CHAPTER 18

The scene in the greenroom was strange and chaotic. A crowd stood in small clumps around the core that included Michael, Alliyah, and two EMTs. I glimpsed through the crowd, but I didn't need a medical degree to see that nothing could be done to save the body on the ground with two skewers sticking out of its neck.

The crowd included Serafina's husband. He was pacing nervously in a small circle. He dabbed at his eyes with a bright red handkerchief and paced. Even in his grief, he was immaculate. His handkerchief matched the glasses he'd worn earlier. He wasn't wearing them now.

As Baby was able to flip a switch and morph from a goofy couch potato into a vicious attack dog, April was able to transform from maid of honor into tough-as-nails law enforcement. Her shoulder-length hair, which was curly and loose earlier, had been pulled up into a ponytail. Her shield was clipped to the belt of her pants, notifying everyone that her status was no longer that of attendee but one of authority. It may have been my imagination, but she appeared taller.

"Is it true?" Leroy whispered.

I nodded.

"Who did it?" Candy asked.

I shrugged.

"Well, if it isn't Nancy Drew, Scooby-Doo, and the rest of the Baker Street misfits."

My stomach muscles clenched. I turned and stared into the steely eyes of Michigan State Trooper Robert Roberts. "Hello, Trooper Bob."

The state trooper was a big burly bear of a man. He called himself a good ole boy, but he was a cynical cop with a leather-toughened hide. He'd mastered the art of intimidation, which worked with most people—people who didn't have a Navy admiral father capable of bringing a platoon of sailors to tears. I was immune. I'd seen him wrapped around the finger of his teenage daughter, Holly, and a five-pound Chihuahua with a mastiff-sized attitude. He was one of those Keebler sugar wafers—a crust on the outside with cream in the middle. Although, I doubt if any criminals got to see that side of him.

"Trooper Bob, what brings you to the bridal expo? Don't tell me you're thinking about marrying again."

The only indication that I'd penetrated his outer shell was that the tips of his ears turned a bright red. Trooper Bob glanced over at Leroy's mom, who walked over to our group, and the color that started at his ears moved to encompass his entire face.

Fiona Danielson was in her mid-forties with dark hair and gray eyes. She was British and spoke with a delightful accent. She must have sensed the attention because she looked up and smiled. "Hello, Robbie."

"Fiona." Trooper Bob tipped his hat. Then, he did something I hadn't seen him do before. He returned her smile. He blushed and turned away. He scowled at me and looked around for a receptacle outside of the crime scene to spit his tobacco into. He turned and walked out the door that I'd just used. Spat. And returned. He didn't stop to continue our conversation but lifted the yellow crime scene tape that cordoned off the area and walked over to April and the other members of law enforcement gathered at the center of the scene.

Candy raised a brow. "Fiona?"

"Robbie?" I asked.

Fiona swatted the air. "Oh, posh. He's just a friend. Well, not really a friend, but sometimes he comes to the Carson Law Inn and has tea." She grinned. "I take my break around seven thirty and, well, occasionally, we sit down together and have tea when we're both working nights. It's perfectly innocent."

"Sure it is," Candy said.

"Uh-huh." I gave her a look that indicated I didn't believe her.

"You two are incorrigible." Fiona gave one last look over toward Trooper Bob and then directed her attention to Baby, who was sprawled on the floor by my leg.

"What's wrong with my dad?" Holly asked.

"How long have you been standing here?" I asked Holly. "And why aren't you passing out cake samples?"

"All gone."

"Seriously? We made a ton of the Chocolate Soul Cake. Not to mention the sample cakes." I looked from Leroy to Hannah.

"It was crazy. After your . . . interview, people descended on the Baby Cakes booth like—"

"Locusts," Hannah said. "They cleaned us out. We even sold the display cakes."

"What?"

"They made me an offer I couldn't refuse," Leroy said, doing a bad impersonation of Marlon Brando from *The Godfather* movie. Then he told me the amount, and I nearly choked.

"For a cake?" Candy asked.

He nodded.

"What about the other cake? Surely you didn't sell that one, too?"

"After the first couple bought the black cake, then things really got interesting." Leroy paused dramatically.

"How could things be more interesting than paying a small fortune for a cake?" I asked.

"Multiple bidders for the remaining cake."

"No way."

"Way!" Holly stepped forward and gazed lovingly at my head baker. "Leroy was amazing. He was just like one of those auctioneers."

Leroy's cheeks flushed with embarrassment.

"Seriously? Why would anyone do that? Wait. How much did you get?"

Leroy told me, and I staggered. "You're making that up."

He shook his head. "Good thing you created those QR codes. They used their phones and voilà."

"Why would anyone pay that much? I mean, we would have made them a cake just like it for half that amount of money." I frowned. "That sounds fishy. Are you sure the payment went through?"

Miss Hannah folded her arms across her chest and stared at Leroy. "That's what I said, too."

"Oh, it's a mystery," Holly said, clapping and jumping up and down.

"I don't know if I'd call it a mystery," I said, "but it's definitely a puzzle."

"Can we help you solve it? You are going to solve it, right?" Holly did a happy dance. "Pleeease let me help." She held her hands together and pleaded. "My dad thinks you're just an airhead and a busybody, but—"

Holly clamped her hand over her mouth and then searched for her father.

Aww, so that's what Trooper Bob thinks.

I watched Trooper Bob, too. I couldn't hear what was being said, but April's face was red, and she was waving her hands as she talked. That was a sure sign that she was upset.

Michael's hands were down by his sides. He pulled them into fists and then released and flexed. The vein on the side of his head pulsed, a sure sign that he was trying *not* to get upset.

In fact, the only member of that group who didn't seem upset was Trooper Bob. In fact, there was a smile on his face and a gleam in his eye. It didn't bode well that he'd managed to upset my best friend and my fiancé. *What could he be saying?*

My brain raced. Okay, so Serafina had just tried to humiliate me by playing a video from my live-streamed wedding where Elliott was a no-show. *Humiliating on so many levels.* I brought the skewers onto the stage with me. They were Baby Cakes spikes, and my fingerprints were probably all over them. *Can you get fingerprints from wood skewers? No idea, but I should probably find out.* I'd pulled the spikes out of my pocket in front of thousands of people, and Serafina had screamed. *Ugh!* Moments later, she was murdered with them. You didn't need to be clairvoyant to see that Trooper Bob undoubtedly wanted to hang this murder on me. He thought I killed her. *If I didn't find the real killer soon, I might be wearing orange to my own wedding.*

CHAPTER 19

"Earth to Maddy!" Candy waved her hands in front of my face, snapping my focus back to the present and away from an orange jumpsuit and handcuffs.

"I don't care what anyone says, orange isn't the new white," I said.

"What?" Candy asked.

"Nothing." I turned to Holly. "I have an idea. Are you still on the school newspaper?"

"Yes, but I don't see—"

"Why not tell the cake buyers that you want to do an article for your school newspaper? Make like a reporter. Take notes. Snap a few pictures with your phone."

A lightbulb flicked on, and her face lit up. "Yes. I can go undercover. I'll be like Woodward and Bernstein or Nelly Bly. Maybe I should have a disguise."

"I think it's always best to stick as close to the truth as you can. Besides, they probably saw you passing out cake earlier."

"Yeah, you're right." Holly's light flickered for a moment but was soon shining brightly.

"I don't think you should work alone. It's always best to work in pairs." I searched for the waiter I'd seen earlier and nodded in his direction. "Doesn't he go to your school?"

Holly followed my line of sight. "Carlos? Yeah, he's in my calculus class."

"Do you think he can be trusted?"

"Yeah, he's harmless."

"Great. Then, that's your assignment. I want you and Carlos to get to the bottom of the cake fraud, but don't take any chances."

Holly agreed and hurried over to Carlos. After the first moment of shock that Holly was talking to him, he smiled and nodded his agreement.

The two waved and then hurried off to find the cake buyers.

"Okay, what was that all about?" Candy asked.

Leroy and Hannah looked on.

"I'd bet my new Amina Muaddi sandals that Trooper Bob is going to try and pin Serafina's murder on me."

Leroy, Hannah, and Candy stared at Trooper Bob, who was still arguing with April.

They all shook their heads.

"No way," Leroy said.

"Sucker bet," Hannah said.

"Nope," Candy said.

"It occurred to me that I better start looking for the real killer, and I don't want Holly getting mixed up with a murderer."

"Good point," Candy said.

"So you created a mystery around the cake buyers?" Leroy asked.

"I didn't create the mystery. It's strange. Why would someone deliberately overpay for a cake? There's something weird there, but I don't think it's connected to Serafina's murder, so that should keep her safely out of the way."

Leroy reluctantly agreed. "Okay, so now what?"

"Let's find a quiet place to sit down and talk. We need to come up with a plan to find the killer. I don't think we're going to have much time."

CHAPTER 20

The exits were closed, and members of the New Bison Police, the Michigan State Police, or the Tribal Police were positioned at each door.

Good news travels quickly, but bad news travels at light speed. The news of Serafina's untimely death had cast a wet blanket over the previously festive event. The loud music that was piped in earlier was off. The conversational hum had lost its excitement and transitioned down to the whispered hum of a large funeral.

We walked and walked and walked, but there were no conference rooms where we could talk in private. After what felt like an hour, we returned to the spot where we started.

"I've had enough of this," Hannah said. "Follow me." She marched off.

After a moment, we followed after her. Hannah went to a family bathroom, pushed the door open, and went inside.

Everyone else stopped outside.

After a few moments, the door opened. Hannah stuck out her head. "Well, are y'all coming or what?"

I shrugged and walked in. After a couple of seconds, Candy and Fiona followed. We waited a few moments, and then Hannah opened the door, grabbed Leroy, pulled him inside, and closed the door.

The family bathroom was a large space, with a changing table, sink, and toilet.

"No seating?" I said.

"I found the room. Looks like somebody else could get some chairs. Do I have to do everything myself?"

"Maybe I should wait outside?" Leroy said.

There was a knock on the door.

"Just a minute," Fiona said.

"Hey, I know the perfect place," Candy said.

She opened the door and walked out, and a woman with a small girl attempted to enter but was stopped when Hannah, Fiona, Leroy, Baby, and I filed out.

The woman chuckled. "Wow, that's like a clown car at the circus. Anyone else?"

"Mom." The small girl tugged on her mother's hand until she entered and locked the door.

Candy took a moment to get her bearings, then she walked to a door labeled CATERING KITCHEN. She pushed the door open and walked through. We followed. Candy strode through the kitchen until she found an elevator. She pushed the button, and the doors opened. We all piled into the elevator. Then, she pressed the button for the fourth floor. When the doors opened, we filed out into a lounge area.

"What is this?" I asked.

The room wasn't large, but it was larger than the bathroom. There were conversation groupings of furniture. There was a leather sofa and two accent chairs on one wall. In a corner by a large window were two comfy accent chairs.

"It's one of the employee relaxation rooms. I completely

forgot about this place. There are two of these relaxation rooms on every floor for employees to come on their breaks. This one isn't big. The two on the first floor by the casino are much bigger. Those have lots more to do. There are pool tables, televisions, snacks, and video games. Most employees prefer those. The only people who use this one are the maids.

Candy's cheeks blushed, and I suspected there was more to the story than she was saying.

I threw out a guess. "This would be a quiet place for a rendezvous."

"Paul and I used to make out up here." Her blush deepened.

Paul Rivers, Candy's late husband, had been the mayor of New Bison. They separated before his murder, but Mayor Rivers had sought a reconciliation. Apparently, he'd had some limited success if he'd made it to this relaxation room.

"That's making my stomach turn," Hannah said. She sat on the sofa. "Can we get on with this meeting? Usually, Tyler takes notes, but—"

"Tyler!" Candy said. "I completely forgot." She pulled out her phone and started a Facetime. "When he heard about Serafina, he sent me a text and told me to circle him in once Maddy started investigating."

"How did he know I'd start investigating? I didn't even know myself."

Candy, Leroy, Fiona, and Hannah exchanged glances.

"What?"

"You fought with Serafina, and then she was killed with Baby Cakes skewers," Hannah said. "Stevie Wonder could have seen that Trooper Bob would try to hang this on you."

Before I could respond, my phone vibrated.

Where r u?

"Michael wants to know where we are. I'm not exactly sure how to direct him." I looked to Candy for guidance.

Leroy stood and headed for the door. "I'll get him."

Leroy OTW

In less than five minutes, the door opened, and Leroy and Michael entered.

Michael took a seat on the arm of my chair. "Trooper Bob is looking for you. He said he needs your statement."

Michael was holding back. "What else?"

"He's threatening to issue an all-points bulletin and have you arrested if you don't come voluntarily and give a statement."

I sighed. "I hoped I was wrong about him and that he didn't actually believe that I'd murdered her."

Michael squeezed my hand. "He wants to believe you did it, but I think he knows you didn't, and that's what's bothering him."

"How anyone could believe you capable of murder is beyond me," Fiona said, shaking her head. "I'm so sorry, love."

"How much time do I have?" I asked.

"It's chaos because the casino is on tribal lands," Michael said.

"What difference does that make?"

"The Pothanowi are a small band that were able to prove they were indigenous; therefore, this land is considered Native American soil. April, Trooper Bob, and the head of the Tribal Police are downstairs arguing about jurisdiction and who's taking the lead in the investigation."

"Wait, so what does that mean?"

Michael shrugged.

Tyler spoke up, and Candy held her phone so we could all see. "As the acting mayor, I was given a briefing about this."

Miss Hannah sniffed. "A briefing?"

Tyler ignored the snub. "Crimes committed on Native American soil are tricky. Technically, the Tribal Police has the authority to deal with crimes between Native Americans. The problem comes in when it's a crime by a non-tribal citizen that occurs on tribal lands. If I'm not mistaken, it's considered a federal crime and the FBI is responsible."

"That's what April told Trooper Bob," Michael said. "She called her contact from the art smuggling case. Chicago is closer, but there are agents in Detroit who could also handle it. She's still part of the special task force, so she says that gives her jurisdiction to act as a member of the federal task force representing the FBI until the agents arrive. Trooper Bob is arguing that if Maddy is the prime suspect, then April has a conflict of interest. According to him, April shouldn't be allowed to investigate."

"That sounds like he wants to hang this murder on Maddy," Leroy said.

Fiona clicked her tongue. "Robbie wouldn't do something like that."

"Robbie?" Michael mouthed to me.

I rolled my eyes. "Trooper Bob."

"Mom, maybe you would feel more comfortable downstairs?" Leroy said.

"Why?" Fiona stared at Leroy. "I want to help. Surely, if someone explains the situation, he'll have to acknowledge that there's no possible way that Maddy would hurt a fly."

"Mom, I think—"

"Mrs. Danielson, I can use all of the help I can get." I gave Leroy a hard stare.

"My thoughts exactly," Fiona said. "What can I do?"

Leroy huffed but remained quiet.

I turned to Michael. "How long before Trooper Bob tries to arrest me?"

"April said it would take about four hours before someone can drive from Detroit to New Bison. They're going to secure and process the crime scene so that no evidence is destroyed. Plus, they're going to try to keep as many people here as possible."

I glanced at my watch. "The expo is over in four hours, and they aren't going to be able to stop people from leaving."

"Then, we don't have much time," Hannah said, bringing us back to reality. "We'd better get busy."

CHAPTER 21

"This is so exciting," Fiona said. "Do we need to synchronize our watches?"

"I don't think we have to be that precise, but maybe Tyler could set up a meeting every hour for the next three hours. Then, we can all meet back here and discuss anything we find." I looked around the room at the group of people Great-Aunt Octavia called the Baker Street Irregulars.

Everyone nodded their agreement, and Tyler typed. Within moments, I heard dings as everyone started getting notifications about the next meeting.

"Now, what do we know?" Miss Hannah said, turning to Michael. "How did she die?"

"Alliyah . . . Dr. Howard and I both examined the body. We won't know for sure until the autopsy, but I'd say she was stabbed with two of those wooden cake spikes."

"Ugh," Candy shuddered. "That sounds awful."

Fiona raised a hand. "I don't want to sound sexist or anything, but, well . . . I was just wondering, would it have taken a lot of strength? Could a woman have done it?"

I smiled at her. "Women aren't necessarily the weaker sex. I met some very strong women in the Navy, but I think you have a good point."

Michael thought for a moment. "I don't think it would have taken too much strength because of the wound's location. A woman could have done it."

Candy held up her phone. "Tyler, you getting this down?"

"I have it," Tyler said.

"Are you done?" Miss Hannah asked.

Fiona nodded.

"Well, I have a question. Would it require a lot of skill? Like something only a doctor could do?"

Michael raised a brow. "Surely, you don't think I—"

Miss Hannah waved away his question. "Don't be daft. I know you didn't stab her, but I don't have the same level of confidence in that stuck-up partner of yours."

Michael frowned. "Alliyah?"

Candy snapped her fingers. "OMG, I nearly forgot. We saw her arguing with Serafina backstage before the interview."

"That's right," I said. "I had no idea she even knew Serafina." I turned to Michael. "Why was she even here? I mean, I thought she was going to be out of town."

"That's what she told me. Are you sure they were arguing?"

"We couldn't hear them, but based on their body language, I'd say, yes, they were definitely arguing."

"Plus, there's that couple who Serafina humiliated first," Candy said.

"She was always firing people," Miss Hannah said. "She fired her assistants. She fired the security guards. Maybe one of them got tired of her mouth."

"I would love to be a fly on the wall when April questions those security guards," I said.

Michael turned to me. "On no uncertain terms are you to go near those two."

"Why not? Are you afraid the Navy can't take them down as quickly as the Army?"

"Maddy, I'm serious. I had the element of surprise and years of training. You—"

"Have no intention of taking on two security guards. Stop worrying. I was joking."

Michael didn't look as though he believed me. Eventually, he shook his head. "I guess I'm going to have to stick close to you to make sure."

"They wouldn't dare bother me with Cujo nearby." I pointed to Baby, who was lying on his back with his legs in the air and getting a belly scratch from Fiona.

Michael laughed. "Some killer watchdog. All they have to do is scratch his belly or toss him a hot dog and he'd roll over in a heartbeat."

"I know he's a pussycat. And you know that, but the big bad security guards don't know that."

Michael revved up for an argument, but I held up a hand to stop him. "Fortunately, I have no intention of testing any theories with the security guards." I held up three fingers. "Scout's honor."

Michael still didn't look convinced, but his brow relaxed.

Candy bounced up and down in her seat and raised her hand. "Uh. Uh. I have something."

We turned our attention to her.

"Go ahead," Hannah said.

"When I left you and April to go get Baby for your interview, I ran into Lucy. She was crying and hanging on that guy from the photo booth. And—"

"What guy?" Hannah asked.

"What photo booth?" Tyler asked.

"We're at a bridal expo," Leroy said. "There are at least a hundred photo booths."

"Let me finish." Candy reached in her bra and pulled out a

stack of business cards and started sifting through them. When she found the one she wanted, she held it up. "Here it is, Photos by Troy."

Tyler choked and started to cough.

Leroy's ears turned red, and Michael put his head in his hands.

"Don't say one word," I warned him.

"What?" Candy asked, clueless.

"Nothing. Please continue. What did you hear?" I asked.

"Lucy, that's Serafina's assistant, was crying. Apparently, Serafina found Lucy's diary where she'd written about a rendezvous between her and Troy."

"I guess it would be embarrassing to have your boss read your diary, but—"

"Serafina didn't just read the diary. She read it on air." Candy raised a brow and gazed at each of us. "It was really steamy, too."

"That's horrible. Poor Lucy."

"That's not all." Candy leaned forward. "When Lucy found out about it, she was madder than a wet hen and said she wished Serafina would 'drop dead.'"

"We need to know where Lucy was when Serafina was murdered," Hannah said. She squinted, leaned forward, and yelled into Candy's phone. "Tyler, are you getting this?"

Tyler rubbed his ear. "Yes, ma'am."

"We need to talk to that couple Serafina humiliated first," I said. "Then, there's Lucy." I ticked off the names on my hand. "Alliyah Howard." I gave Michael a sideways look, but he didn't seem ruffled. "The security guards she fired, and me."

"I think we're crossing you off the list, unless you have something you want to tell us?" Hannah said.

I shook my head. "No confessions."

"Maddy couldn't have killed her," Michael said. "She was with me." He squeezed my hand. "I tried to tell that pigheaded Trooper Bob, but he's too stubborn to listen."

"There's one other person that might have had a reason to kill her," Leroy said.

We turned our attention to him.

"During my break, I decided to check out some of the other booths. I heard the world-famous French pâtissier, Chef Yves-René Barbier, was in Chicago for an event and would be at the bridal expo doing a demonstration. The man is a genius. Have you tasted his Kouign-amann?" Leroy kissed his fingers.

"I don't even know what that is," Hannah said. "So, I couldn't tell you if I've had one or not."

"Thank goodness I'm not the only one who's lost," Candy said.

"It's a French pastry," I said. "It's very airy, like Leroy's croissants only sweeter."

Traveling all over the world with the Admiral had given me a broad knowledge of different cultures and languages. I may not be able to make a French pastry, but I have eaten more than my fair share of them.

"Exactly," Leroy said. "Kouign-amann is very similar to croissants, but with more sugar in them and on top. Anyway, the man is a genius. When I went to the area where the demonstration was going to be, I got there a little early, and I overheard Chef Barbier and Serafina arguing."

"Serafina got around a lot this morning," Candy said.

"That woman was worse than an elephant in a henhouse," Hannah said.

"Isn't the expression a fox in a henhouse?" Michael asked.

Hannah shook her head. "Nah. A fox would be in the henhouse because he was hungry. He'd crush the eggs and eat the chickens. You'd be mad if they was your chickens, but you could understand it. Elephants don't eat meat. The only reason an elephant would be in a henhouse is to cause trouble. Just like that Serafina." Hannah sucked her teeth.

I don't know if I was more surprised that Hannah knew that

elephants were herbivores or that she had pegged Serafina so quickly. I glanced at Michael, but he just shrugged.

"Okay, so how many eggs did she crush?" Hannah asked Leroy.

"Did you hear what they were arguing about?" I asked.

"No, and they were arguing in French." Leroy pulled up his phone. "But I did manage to record it."

Leroy swiped his phone until he came across the video he wanted. Then, he put the phone on speaker and pressed play.

The video was initially of a table set up for baking. There was a curtain that blocked the audience's view. Leroy was positioned at an angle that allowed him to see both in front and behind the curtain.

The gentleman that Michael and I had seen in the greenroom earlier was the primary focus. He was an older man in chef's whites, and he was arguing with Serafina. Based on body language alone, it was clear that the two were having a vehement argument. The clincher came when Serafina, who was standing next to a huge ice sculpture in the shape of an eagle with wings spread in midflight, gave the sculpture a shove. The eagle teetered on the table. Chef Barbier attempted to steady the table and prevent the inevitable. He was too late. The ice sculpture was massive and must have weighed a ton. It toppled to the ground and shattered into thousands of pieces.

Chef Barbier's neck was beet red, and the red rose up his face to the roots of his hair. His face contorted as though he was about to explode.

In contrast, Serafina smirked in pleasure at the destruction she'd just caused.

"Wow!" I said. "Leroy, can you replay that?"

He replayed the video. This time, I translated.

"Serafina said, 'You can't just toss me aside like a pair of dirty socks.' Yves-René, 'It's over. I can't do this anymore.' Serafina, 'You can and you will. Or I will tell your precious wife everything.' Yves-René, 'She will be crushed, but she will heal. Eventually, she will forgive me. Your husband—' Serafina, 'My husband wants a divorce. Maybe I'll give it to him. Maybe I won't, but it's up to me. If you think I'm going to *go gentle into that good night*, then you've got another *think* coming. I intend to *rage*.' Serafina knocks over the ice sculpture. Yves-René swears in French, and that's it."

"What was that she said?" Candy said. "I've heard that before." She tapped her chin and gazed up at the ceiling as she tried to recall where she'd heard those words.

"That's a quote from *Independence Day*," Leroy said.

"*Independence Day?*" Fiona rolled her eyes. "Films. That's all young people know these days. Didn't they teach you anything in school? That's Dylan Thomas."

Everyone turned to look at her.

"You must be joking." She paused, and a slight flush went up her neck. "Dylan Thomas? Surely, you've heard of him."

Everyone shook their heads.

"He was a famous Welsh poet. I memorized that poem in school: 'Do not go gentle into that good night.' It goes, 'Do not go gentle into that good night; Old age should burn and rave at close of day; Rage, rage against the dying of the light.'"

I was impressed. Based on the way Leroy was looking at his mother, I'd say he was, too.

"I don't know what all that 'good night' stuff means, but Serafina certainly raged," Hannah said, quickly getting to the heart of the matter.

"True, but that chef, Yves-René, wasn't the one who got himself murdered," Candy said.

"No, but maybe Serafina's 'rage' made him feel there was no other way," I said. "Maybe he knew that the only way to be free of her was to kill her? That would certainly give Yves-René Barbier a good motive for murder."

CHAPTER 22

"Let's count our suspects," Hannah said. She turned to the phone and started yelling at Tyler, "Name off who you have."

Tyler rubbed his ear again. Then, he read off his list. "Serafina's assistant Lucy, who Serafina humiliated by reading her diary publicly. Dr. Alliyah Howard. Why was she arguing with Serafina? The couple Serafina humiliated on tape before Maddy." Tyler stopped and blushed. "Sorry, Maddy."

"No worries," I reassured him.

He took a moment to find his place in his notes before continuing. "The security guards she fired. And Chef Yves-René Barbier, who was having an affair with Serafina."

Leroy wiped his brow. "Whew! That's a long list."

"We have to divide and conquer. Leroy, can you talk to Chef Barbier?" I asked.

"I'd love to . . . I mean, I'll talk to him."

It took effort, but I fought the urge to laugh at Leroy fanboying about a pastry chef. I forced my lips to remain neutral. "Great." Then, I turned to Michael. "Do you want me to tackle the security guards or—"

"I've got them." He cracked his knuckles.

"Do you think you could manage to do it without fighting?"

"I won't start anything, but the Army is always ready."

"That's the Coast Guard."

He waved away my correction.

"Candy, do you think you could talk to Lucy? Maybe she would be willing to open up if you talk to her . . . you know, woman to woman."

"Absolutely." Candy bounced in her seat with excitement.

"What about us?" Hannah said, pointing from her to Fiona.

"I have a couple of special assignments for you two. If you feel up to it."

"Oh, yes, I want to help," Fiona said. She stopped scratching Baby's tummy, and he responded with a moan before using his paw to direct her hand back into position.

"Fiona, you seem to have a relationship with Trooper Bob. I was hoping that you could . . . run interference."

She frowned. "I don't think I understand."

"I need you to see what you can find out from Trooper Bob. Keep him from interfering and trying to arrest me. And, perhaps, drop a few hints that maybe he might want to investigate some other suspects. But, if it gets to the point where you think he's going to arrest me, then can you give me a warning?"

"I'd be happy to, love."

"Miss Hannah, I think that bride who learned her fiancé was cheating on her could use a motherly shoulder to cry on. Maybe you could tell her that if she does get married, Baby Cakes will provide her wedding cake, free of charge."

"I don't see how that's going to help figure out who murdered Serafina," Hannah said.

"Well, as she's meeting with you to discuss what type of cake she wants, maybe you could discreetly ask a few questions about Carla and . . . well, find out if she or her fiancé murdered Serafina."

Hannah nodded. "Got it."

Tyler waved. "What about me? Just because I'm not there in person doesn't mean I don't want to help."

"I need you to do some research. See what you can find out about all of the people on the list, but especially focus on Serafina. Jessica Barlow might have some information."

Tyler nodded. "Got it."

"What are you going to do?" Michael asked.

"I'm going to talk to your partner. Why was she here, and why was she fighting with Serafina?"

"Are you sure you don't want me to—"

I was shaking my head from the moment he started to speak. "She didn't even tell you she was coming to a bridal expo. It's time that I talk to her, woman to woman. There's more to Dr. Alliyah Howard than meets the eye, and I intend to find out what that involves."

CHAPTER 23

Michael squinted. "That sounds like you're gearing up for a fight. Should I be concerned?"

"Why? Surely, you're not concerned about the Navy's ability to handle themselves in a battle?" I cracked my knuckles as he had done moments earlier.

Leroy made a point of scooting farther away from Michael.

Tyler pulled out a white handkerchief and waved it. "Stand down. Don't fall for it. It's a trap."

"I have nothing but the highest regard for the Navy. I was just wondering if I'm going to have to go looking for another partner for my vet practice." He grinned.

"Good answer, soldier." I leaned across and kissed him.

"All right, we all have work to do and not a lot of time to do it," Hannah said. "We better get busy."

Fiona stood up. "This is so exciting. "

"Let's meet back here in an hour," I said.

Everyone nodded their agreement and filed out of the room, leaving Baby and me alone.

I walked over to Baby, who was stretching as though he had

just worked a twenty-four-hour shift. "Come on, boy. We have work to do."

Suddenly, Baby's ears perked up. His body was tense. He was wound as tight as a spring about to pounce.

"*Woof.*" Baby gave one bark and then trotted over to the door.

I stared at the door and wondered if the killer had tracked us to this room. Now, I was trapped. I scanned the room for a weapon, but the casino decorator must not have thought violent weapons would be needed in a room designed for relaxation. Soft lighting, comfortable chairs, and a super comfy sofa made up the majority of the décor. I grabbed a lamp from an end table and moved behind the door. I lifted it over my head, prepared to bash whoever entered.

The door opened, and Baby lunged forward. He pounced on the intruder.

I expected to hear screams as Baby ripped the flesh from the bones of the killer. Instead, I saw Baby's tail wag, and I heard the annoyed voice of Dr. Alliyah Howard. "Baby, off."

I replaced the lamp on the end table and hurried from behind the door. "Baby, come."

"Oh, good. You are here." Dr. Howard stepped into the room. She was wiping drool from her hands with a small tissue.

I handed her a larger towel. I always kept one nearby for drool cleanup.

"Thanks."

Baby sat and stared. His tail swiped the floor with each wag.

My dog was a good judge of character, and he liked Dr. Alliyah Howard. I wasn't a fan, but my feelings were related to my own insecurities. No matter how much I tried not to compare myself to her, it was hard to avoid. Especially since she had been my fiancé's ex. She was not only a veterinarian, but she was also a human doctor. I, on the other hand, was not a doctor. Sure, I graduated from one of the best colleges in the country, but I certainly hadn't spent over a decade in medical school. Brains and beauty were a powerful combination, and Dr. Alliyah Howard had both.

"If you're looking for Michael, he just left. I'm sure if you—"

"I wasn't."

"Oh." My brain tried to process that, but it wasn't working. I should have been able to put things together quicker, but words were hard. "Were you looking for me?"

"Yes."

I moved into the room, away from the door, and sat. "You're in luck. You found me." I was disoriented. Had Alliyah Howard heard me boasting moments earlier about the Navy's ability to fight? Was she here to show me that she could handle herself with a Navy brat? Surely not. I was the one who was supposed to be questioning her. I was supposed to be the one pumping her for information to find out if she'd actually killed Serafina. *Holy cow. I could be in a room with a killer. As a medical doctor, she would know exactly how to use those skewers to kill. She would know where to insert them to cause the most damage. And my big, massive dog would be no help because he liked her.* I wracked my brain for something to say, but my mind went blank. I simply stared. "How can I help you?"

"I know you saw Serafina and me arguing. It's only a matter of time before the police find out. They're going to think I did it. They're going to think I killed Serafina. And they're going to arrest me."

"What do you want me to do?"

"I want you to help me prove that I'm innocent."

"How do you expect me to do that?"

"By finding Serafina's killer."

CHAPTER 24

It took a moment to recover from the shock. *Find Serafina's killer? Are you kidding? I think you'd make a great suspect. Much better than me.* "Whoa. Why come to me? You should be telling your story to the police."

Alliyah paced. "Because you're friends with the sheriff. You can tell her that I didn't do it."

"Just because April and I are friends doesn't mean she'd listen to me when it comes to her job. Besides, there's no guarantee that April will even be investigating this crime. I understand there's a question of jurisdiction. Trooper Bob could get permission since he represents the state and not just the county, and he doesn't like me at all. Although, I believe the federal government is ultimately responsible, and I don't know anyone who works for them." I shouldn't have told her all of that. *Geez! I needed to stop oversharing.*

"Trooper Bob is a Neanderthal."

"He isn't as ancient as he comes across. I think deep down inside, he's probably a nice guy,"

"It must be buried way deep down inside because I have yet to see it." Alliyah paced.

"Look, why do you believe Trooper Bob will arrest you for Serafina's murder? Just because the two of you argued doesn't make you a suspect. I mean, a lot of people argued with her. She angered a lot of people."

Alliyah stopped pacing. She turned and faced me. "Because none of those other people were having an affair with her husband, and I was."

CHAPTER 25

I didn't see that coming. I sat for several moments before I realized my mouth was hanging open. I closed it and tried to find something to say, but again words failed.

"Don't be so shocked. It's the twenty-first century. It happens."

"I'm not shocked." I lied. "You and . . . Serafina's husband were . . . um, an item. So, maybe you should tell me about it. Is that why you came today? To confront Serafina?"

Dr. Howard flopped down on the chair. "That was stupid, right?"

"Um . . . yeah." I waffled between wanting to comfort her and wanting to make her squirm. "Sorry, but it was."

"I didn't start out as an adulterer." She leaned her head back on the seat. "God, I sound like one of those pathetic people on those talk shows who want to rationalize their bad decisions." She leaned forward and placed her arms on her knees.

Baby came up and sat in front of her. He gave her a lick.

She smiled and scratched his ear.

"I didn't plan to get involved with Patrick."

"Patrick?"

"Patrick Dixon, Serafina's husband. He was just so . . . exciting. He was kind, gentle, funny, and he appreciated the finer things in life. He liked to travel in style. He liked nice clothes, going to the opera, the symphony, and the ballet. He was cultured."

Hmm. Until that last part, I thought Patrick Dixon sounded a lot like Michael. But Michael wasn't into those things. That was one of the reasons they had broken up.

"How did you meet?"

Alliyah thought for a few moments. Then she grinned like a schoolgirl. "We met in Chicago. I had been attending a conference at Northwestern medical school."

"Is he a doctor?"

"No. He wasn't attending the conference. After the conference, I decided to stay for a few days. You know, rest, shop, go to the theatre. Anyway, I was staying at the Ritz-Carlton at Water Tower Place on Michigan Avenue, and so was he. The Ritz has a fantastic spa. Well, we were both sitting in the spa waiting, and they thought we were together. So, they brought us back to have a couples massage. We explained that we weren't together, and they apologized, but Patrick said he didn't mind if I didn't mind. Well, I didn't mind, so we did."

"Did what?"

"Got massaged." She smiled, but then quickly added, "It was all perfectly aboveboard. I was covered, and he was covered. We were both on tables side by side. That's the only thing."

I held up a hand for her to stop. I didn't need the explanation. "What happened next?"

"Afterward, we both got dressed, and then we ran into each other again in the dining room. I was sitting alone, and he was sitting alone. He asked if I would mind company. I didn't mind. And he sat down. We talked and talked. Before we knew it, the restaurant was closed, and we had been talking for hours.

Well, we arranged to meet the next day. We went shopping and ate and then we went down to Navy Pier and took one of those architectural boat cruises down the Chicago River. Then, we had a romantic dinner, and it was so perfect. We had the most amazing weekend ever."

"And he never mentioned the fact that he was married?"

Alliyah's smile slid off her face. "No. Not then."

I forced my facial muscles to remain neutral, although I wanted to roll my eyes and my neck and give her a look that said, *Girlfriend, what are you doing with this louse?*

"Later, much later he told me. He said he never felt anything like this before, and he was scared. He and Serafina had drifted apart. They were separated, and he was sure she was having an affair. He had been working up the courage to ask for a divorce. Their marriage was over. Serafina was flying back and forth between their townhouse in Manhattan and their house in Bel Air. He was living in their condo in Florida. They weren't even living in the same state, let alone the same house."

"But he didn't tell you any of that before . . . before things got serious."

"Don't you see? He was afraid if he said something that I would leave. In the meantime, he had consulted his attorney and was working out the details for a divorce settlement."

"What type of settlement?"

A flush rose up her neck, and she dropped her gaze. "What do you mean?"

"I mean, what does Patrick do?"

"He's a naturopathic consultant."

"What's that?"

"Naturopathy is a form of alternative medicine. They take a holistic approach to healing. By focusing on the mind, the body, and the spirit, they use nature and the body's ability to heal itself to get to the root cause of a problem and to heal."

"Is that a doctor?"

"No. Not exactly. He's not a medical doctor."

"Oh."

She squinted. "Don't tell me you're as snobbish as everyone else around here. People have been using natural remedies and alternative medical techniques for centuries. Everything from chiropractic medicine to acupuncture, herbs, and—"

"Whoa." I held up both hands as a sign of surrender. "I have nothing against holistic medicine. I spent a few years in Okinawa and learned a lot about herbal teas and alternative medicine. I'm just trying to understand."

She took a deep breath. "Sorry. It's just been an uphill struggle for him to build a solid client base in the United States because people don't respect you unless you're an MD. But what he really wants to do is design men's formal wear. He's super talented. One day, he's going to be the male equivalent to Vera Wang."

"Okay, but right now he's a naturopathic consultant. I don't understand why he can't just divorce Serafina—"

Alliyah's eyes flashed. "You're judging him because he isn't a doctor or a veterinarian or an admiral in the Navy. He isn't wealthy, but—"

"Hold your horses. I'm not judging him at all. I spent years as a social media influencer. I'm the last person to look down on anyone else's career pursuits. If working as a naturopathic consultant makes him happy, then more power to him. I would never pooh-pooh anyone's dreams."

She took a deep breath. "Sorry."

"But the divorce settlement he was talking to his lawyer about, that wasn't to determine what he'd have to pay to leave Serafina, was it?"

"No. Serafina had all of the money. If he was going to be free to set up his own business independent of her, then he needed money. So, the settlement would determine how much he could get if he were to divorce her. He was sure she was having an affair. If he could prove it, then it would make all of the difference, but she was careful."

I wanted to say, *Serafina wasn't the only one having an affair*, but that wouldn't be conducive to getting Dr. Howard to talk. "He signed a prenuptial agreement?"

She sighed and eventually nodded. "If he left, then he got nothing. But, courts have started awarding money to spouses even if they had signed a prenup. His lawyer said if he could prove that the reason the marriage dissolved was because of *her* affair, that would help. Also, if he could prove that *he* helped Serafina's career substantially, then there was a chance he might get something for all of his hard work and years of suffering. And he had. When they met, she was overweight and out of shape. She had awful migraines. That's how they met. She'd tried everything and nothing worked. Patrick helped her. He really did. He helped her with diet and exercise. Her diet was garbage before she met him. She was one Big Mac away from a heart attack. And the migraines were so bad that she could barely function. Thanks to Patrick and massage, diet, acupuncture, and increased physical activity, she did a complete one-eighty. She hired him as her personal trainer."

I began to see things a lot more clearly. "So, he helped her lose weight and get in shape and reduce the migraines."

She nodded. "She was doing wedding planning in Chicago on a small scale, but then the pandemic hit and she got on social media. That's when her career skyrocketed. She moved to California and New York. She was traveling around the world, and that wouldn't have happened if Patrick hadn't helped her."

"So, Patrick asked for a divorce, and Serafina said . . . ?"

She stood up and started pacing again. "He didn't get a chance. He kept saying we had to wait. Just a little longer. Well, I got tired of waiting. When I found out she was coming to New Bison, well . . . I said that was it. Either he tell her about us or I would."

Ouch. This isn't looking good. "So you told her that you were having an affair with her husband?"

"No."

I waited.

"She already knew. As soon as she saw me, she said 'Oh, you're the little . . .' Well, you can imagine the names she called me."

I could indeed.

"You're the one keeping Patrick entertained."

Double ouch.

"She said she knew all about me. She said if I wanted him, then I could have him, but she wasn't paying one thin dime. In fact, she said if he tried to make things difficult, then she would take it out on me. She threatened to ruin me. She said she would make sure that everyone knew about the little tramp. She even threatened to take me in front of the medical ethics board and have my license revoked."

"Could she do that?"

"No, but it wouldn't matter. The scandal would have sunk my career. Even in New Bison, no one would want a doctor or even a veterinarian who was a home-wrecker. And who would want to hire a naturopath who cheated on his wife? She was powerful, and she would make sure he would never be able to live his dream of designing men's formal wear."

Yikes!

"So, what happened then?" I asked.

She didn't answer for so long that I thought she wouldn't. Eventually, she said, "That's when I lost my temper. I told her that if she tried to ruin me, I would make sure it was the last thing she ever did."

CHAPTER 26

"You threatened her?" I gaped.

"I was just so angry. I mean, she was threatening me and—"

"Stop." I waved my hands to silence her. "You threatened her and then she was murdered less than one hour later."

Her silence filled the room. She flopped back down into her chair and put her head in her hands. "I didn't kill her."

"Did anyone hear you threaten her?"

She sobbed. "I don't know."

"Where were you when she was murdered?" She lifted her shoulders, but I wasn't sure if it was a shrug or a sob. "Look, if someone can verify that you were upstairs getting a pedicure in the spa at the exact time that Serafina was murdered, then you have nothing to worry about."

She lifted her tear-streaked face. "That's just it. I don't have an alibi. I wandered around the auditorium . . . alone."

"Dr. Howard, I'm not sure what I—"

"Stop with the Dr. Howard. I work with your fiancé, and I think given everything I've just shared with you about my personal life . . . things I've never told anyone, that we've moved to a first-name basis. Don't you?"

"Fine. Alliyah, I'm not sure what you think I can do."

"I know you've solved several murders in the past. Based on the way Michael brags, I expected—"

"Wait. Michael brags about me?" A ball of warmth filled my chest.

She rolled her eyes. "All the time. 'Maddy figured this out.' 'Maddy is a genius.' 'Maddy is so smart.' 'Maddy, Maddy, Maddy.'" She squinted at me. "He's head over heels in love with you. You know that, right?"

Did I know that? I knew that. Of course, I knew that. But it was nice to hear. My lips had a mind of their own and refused anything except an upward curl. Finally, I stopped fighting it and let them curl as much as they wanted. I grinned like a giddy schoolgirl.

"If you two weren't so sickeningly in love, it would be cute."

"Hey, don't be a hater."

We both laughed.

The door opened, and Michael and April entered.

Michael stood in the door looking from me to Alliyah. "What's so funny?"

That just made us laugh more.

"I wish someone would share the joke," April said. "I could use a good joke right about now." She pushed past Michael and came into the room.

Alliyah stopped abruptly as if someone had tossed a bucket of cold water on her. She stared at April like a scared puppy. "Are you here to arrest me?"

April raised a brow. "Why? Did you murder Serafina?"

From the angle where I was sitting, I could see Trooper Bob in the hall, but Alliyah couldn't see him.

"No. No. I didn't do it. I was just telling Maddy that I threatened her, but I didn't murder her. I just—"

"Stop!" I yelled.

Alliyah clamped her mouth shut.

I thought I overshared when I was nervous. Holy cow. She was about to talk herself into the electric chair.

"Alliyah, I suggest you talk to a lawyer before you make any statements to the police. My lawyer . . . former lawyer always said that."

Michael and April stared at me.

"Seriously, you're quoting Chris Russell?" April asked.

"After everything he did to you?" Michael asked.

"He may not have been a very nice person, but that didn't mean it wasn't good advice. As Miss Hannah says, 'Even a broke clock is right twice every day.'" I raised my voice. "Wouldn't you agree, Trooper Bob?"

Upon hearing his name, Trooper Bob stopped hiding behind the door and walked into the room. Steam poured from his ears, and his face was as red as a volcano. "It is your right to have an attorney present, but you are certainly free to talk without one."

"I recommend an attorney," I said.

Trooper Bob scowled, then forced his face into neutral as he turned to Alliyah. "It's my opinion that innocent people don't need an attorney."

Hannah marched into the room. "Ha. That's what you cops always say. Don't you believe it. There are as many innocent people in jail as there are guilty people wandering the streets."

Trooper Bob's nostrils flared as though he could spit fire.

"You need to watch your blood pressure," Hannah said to Trooper Bob as she walked into the room and took the same seat she'd occupied earlier.

"I don't know an attorney," Alliyah said. "Do you?"

I shook my head.

"What about Tyler?" Hannah said.

"Tyler who?" I asked.

"Tyler Lawrence." Hannah frowned at me as though she was questioning my sanity.

"Our Tyler?" I said. "The Tyler Lawrence who knits and owns a yarn shop?"

"That's the only Tyler Lawrence I know," Hannah said.

"Miss Hannah, are you feeling okay? Would you like to lay down and rest?"

"I'm feeling fine, and I do not need to rest." Miss Hannah turned to Michael. "Maybe you should take her home. She's not making sense."

"Wait. Are you seriously telling me that Tyler Lawrence is an attorney?" I looked from Hannah to Michael to April.

"He used to be. He passed the bar, but he hated it so much, he quit to do what he loved. I thought you knew that?" Miss Hannah tilted her head to the side and stared at me.

"Did everyone know that except me?" I asked.

Michael shrugged.

April shook her head.

"I did." Candy waltzed into the room and sat down. "He hates being a lawyer, but he promised his mother he would keep his license. He paid a fortune for law school, too."

Tyler has had a mammoth-sized crush on Candy for as long as I've known him. I didn't know if he and Candy were dating now that she was a widow, but they were friends. If anyone knew his past, it was probably her.

"What are you all doing here?" I asked.

"Now, I know there must be something wrong with her." Miss Hannah walked over to me and took my temperature by putting the back of her hand on my forehead. I resisted the urge to swat her hand away and endured the humiliation. When she was satisfied that I didn't have a fever, she walked back to her seat.

"She doesn't have a fever, but that don't mean she ain't sick," Miss Hannah said to Michael. "You probably need to take her home."

"Don't you dare laugh at me." I glared at Michael, who had raised his hands in protest, but he was shaking from laughter.

He wasn't able to hold the laughter in and snorted.

Candy gave me one of those looks that parents give small children when they're trying to explain something complicated. "We agreed to"—she gave a sideways look at Trooper Bob and then started to talk very slowly—"eet-may ack-bay ere-hay every-ay our-hay."

"What?" I frowned.

Candy huffed. "For someone who speaks multiple languages, how is it you don't know pig Latin?"

Because that's not a real language. I blinked and shook my head like Baby.

"Don't tell me the Scooby gang is investigating Serafina's murder?" Trooper Bob said. No one answered, and he fumed. "You meddling busybodies need to leave the investigating to the professionals." He pointed a finger at me. "If I find that you are interfering in a police investigation, I'll—"

"The police are investigating?" I asked innocently. "Which police?" I looked from April to Trooper Bob. "State police? New Bison Police? County? Tribal Police? Or did I miss hearing that the federal authorities had arrived?"

The red molten lava that had started at his neck had now made its way upward and encompassed his entire face. He was ready to explode. He took a step forward.

Michael and April were up and in between Trooper Bob and me almost instantly.

"Candy, you get your phone out and get this on video in case we have to sue the state," Miss Hannah said.

Candy swiped her phone and then held it up to indicate she was filming.

Trooper Bob glared. Then, he snorted in disgust and stepped back.

"You need to watch your temper," Hannah said. "You're going to give yourself a stroke."

Trooper Bob squinted but kept silent.

Leroy walked in. The tension was so high that he must have felt it. "What's going on?"

"Trooper Bob was just leaving," Hannah said.

"Was I?" He glanced around. "This room looks cozy. I might just want to sit down and relax. Been on my feet all day."

"I thought you were planning to question Dr. Howard, but I guess I misunderstood," I said and stood up. "Do you want my seat?"

Trooper Bob folded his arms across his chest and grinned. "Ms. Howard lawyered up."

"I don't know what that means," Alliyah said.

"It means you won't talk to the police without your lawyer present," April said.

"But, I don't have a lawyer yet."

Leroy strolled to the sofa and sat. "You should call Tyler. He's a lawyer. Well, he used to be."

Darn it. Leroy knew that Tyler was a lawyer and I didn't.

Candy shook her cell phone. "Want me to call him?"

Alliyah looked from April to me to Michael. For someone who made a bazillion decisions every day, she appeared as confused as me when I was trying to decide what shoes to wear.

I pretended not to hear the huge sigh that Trooper Bob did not attempt to hide.

"Alliyah, I really do think it would be a good idea to talk to a lawyer," I said. "Even though you didn't murder Serafina and have nothing to hide."

"Good point," April said. "Would you like a lawyer present?"

Alliyah nodded.

Candy stopped the video and dialed. She gave Tyler a quick rundown on the situation and then handed the phone to Alliyah.

Alliyah took the phone and stepped out of the room.

CHAPTER 27

There was an awkward silence as we all stared at each other.

Trooper Bob scowled at me. "Now that you've ruined our opportunity to interview Dr. Howard before she talks to her shyster, maybe I should use this time to interview you."

"Me? I'm just here to look at things for my wedding."

"Your wedding?"

"You had to know we got engaged. I mean, it's been all over social media." I held up my left hand and wiggled my fingers so he could see the engagement ring Michael had given me.

Trooper Bob's frown intensified. Then, he turned to Michael. "And you? What's a vet doing at a bridal expo?"

"It's my wedding, too." Michael reached over and squeezed my hand.

"Everyone here is part of our wedding party," I said. "The bridal expo is huge, and there was no way I could visit all of the booths alone."

Trooper Bob narrowed his gaze, but he didn't say anything.

There was a tap on the door.

Candy was the closest, so she jumped up and opened it.

I expected to see Alliyah but was surprised to see Carson Law enter the room.

"This place is massive," she said. "I thought we were going to need to call for help."

"Mrs. Law, I didn't know you were here." I jumped up and ran over and hugged her.

Carson Law was a petite woman with red hair and impeccable taste. She was the only child of New Bison's wealthiest and most notable resident. She was also a world-renowned milliner and entrepreneur who had turned her family mansion into the Carson Law Inn.

When I released her, I saw that Mrs. Law wasn't alone. Standing a few feet behind her was her assistant, Jessica Barlow.

Carson Law loved vintage apparel, and her hats reflected that aesthetic. Today, she looked fresh and delicate. She wore a floral A-line dress with orange, yellow, and white flowers against a lemony yellow background. The dress had a bateau neckline, short sleeves, and a layered skirt with a slight apron at the hips. Her yellow pumps matched her dress perfectly. She wore a yellow pillbox hat and white gloves. In contrast to that vision of the 1950s, Jessica Barlow, who towered over Mrs. Law like a dominatrix, wore black tights, a long white ruffled blouse, a black leather corset, and thigh-high black leather boots. All she needed was a riding crop to complete her ensemble, but she must have thankfully decided to leave that at home. If she had one.

As soon as I released Mrs. Law from the hug, she made a beeline for Baby, who was wagging his tail so much he was in danger of knocking over a lamp.

Under normal circumstances, I would have restrained my big drooly mastiff. However, Mrs. Law loved Baby. She had had a mastiff when she was young and had an affection for the giant, messy breed.

The two greeted each other as if they hadn't just seen each other a few days earlier when Baby and I had joined Mrs. Law for tea at the Carson Law Inn.

Jessica gave a severe eye roll before she slipped off her black leather backpack. Then, she reached in and pulled out a box of wet wipes and a dry towel. She handed them to her boss.

Carson Law stood up and extended her hand.

Jessica reached back into the bag and pulled out a Ziploc bag with a giant ham bone. She handed it to Mrs. Law.

Mrs. Law looked to me for permission. When I nodded, she opened the bag and gave Baby his treat.

Drool hung from the sides of his jowls like strings of spaghetti, but he didn't care. He carried his prize to a corner, leaving a trail of drool in his wake. Then, he turned around three times before he lay down and got busy gnawing on his treat.

Michael rose and politely offered his seat to Mrs. Law.

"Thank you." She sat, cleaned off the excess drool, and then gazed lovingly at Baby.

"What brings you two here?" I asked.

"Serafina," Carson Law said. "What else?"

A silence filled the room.

"You heard she was murdered, right?" I asked.

"Oh, yes. We heard." Carson Law waved her hand as though she were flicking away a pesky mosquito. "Bound to happen sooner or later."

Trooper Bob snapped to attention. "What?"

"Why, the woman was a terror." Carson Law sat prim and proper with her ankles crossed. "She was brutal to her staff and not much better to the people she worked with. I'm just surprised it didn't happen sooner. In fact, I was just about ready to kill her myself."

CHAPTER 28

That got Trooper Bob's attention. "What do you mean?"

The idea of warning Carson Law that she might want to speak to an attorney flashed across my brain for a moment, but I could not see this petite, proper lady stabbing Serafina with a cake skewer. Besides, I felt confident that Trooper Bob would have arrested me for interfering with his investigation if I'd caused another one of his potential suspects to *lawyer up*.

"We weren't supposed to be here," Carson Law said, "but somehow that woman found out that Maddy and I were friends." She smiled at me. "Probably one of the staff."

"Or, she checked Maddy's social media feed," Jessica said.

"I suppose you're right." Carson Law sighed. "Anyway, Serafina demanded that I come."

"Why?" I asked.

Trooper Bob scowled. "I'm asking the questions."

"She said she wanted me to design a hat for the winner of her contest. I knew Maddy was one of the finalists, so I assumed she wanted me to design something for her." She reached over and patted my hand. "Well, of course, I'd make a veil for Maddy."

"That is so nice. I would love a Carson Law bridal veil." I reached over and hugged her. "But, you've already been so generous, allowing us to have the wedding at the Carson Law Inn. I can't let you do that unless you allow me to pay for it."

Michael reached over and hugged her, too. "Yes, thank you."

"I'd do anything for you two. And I absolutely won't hear of taking any money. Such a sweet couple. The Admiral and I were talking just the other night and—"

"Yeah, yeah, can we get back to Serafina and the murder?" Trooper Bob said.

Carson Law frowned. "She implied that if I didn't come, she had information that she would make public."

"What kind of information?" I asked.

Trooper Bob grunted. "Miss Montgomery, I'm not going to tell you again. Now—"

Carson Law ignored Trooper Bob as though he weren't present. "That's just it. I have no idea what information she had. I mean, she'd already learned about you and Elliott."

Michael raised a brow. "Anything else you want to tell me? Any other ex-fiancés I need to know about? Arrests?"

I shook my head. "That's the most embarrassing thing in my past. What about you?"

He shook his head. "Nothing."

Carson Law flushed, and something in her body language told me that she knew more than she was saying. However, it was clear she had no intention of sharing anything with Trooper Bob here.

"Anyway, I thought I'd better come and see what she was up to. Plus, it would give me an opportunity to see you and Baby again."

Before I could pump Mrs. Law further, the door opened and Alliyah Howard returned.

"Okay, I'm ready to give my statement." She handed Candy back her phone. "Tyler said we can do it via Zoom. He can meet us at the police station. Or, if you want to give him permission to come here, then we can do it here. He said it's up to you."

The lines on Trooper Bob's forehead were going to be permanent if he didn't stop scowling. I could almost see the gears turning in his head as he went over the options. He wanted to talk to Alliyah, but thanks to me, she wouldn't talk to him without an attorney. If he left the scene to go to the police station, then he was giving up territory to April, the Tribal Police, and the federal authorities. There was only one option, and he knew it.

"I'll leave word for Tyler Lawrence to be admitted," Trooper Bob huffed.

"He thought that was the option you'd choose," Alliyah Howard said. "He's on his way."

Trooper Bob, April, and Alliyah Howard walked out to meet Tyler and find a quiet place to talk.

The room felt large and open without law enforcement.

"I never liked that girl, but she didn't kill that woman," Hannah said.

I was fairly sure she hadn't killed her, too. Murder was messy. Too messy for someone like her. Between her clothes, shoes, nails, hair, and overall demeanor, killing someone would have been beneath her. Alliyah Howard wouldn't have killed Serafina. At least, I didn't think she would.

CHAPTER 29

"Are we meeting?" Hannah brought us back on task.

Everyone nodded.

"Should I leave?" Mrs. Law asked.

"No, you're welcome to stay," I reassured her.

"Goodie." She clapped. "I didn't get to help much last time there was a murder. I hope I can help this time."

"It may be a short investigation if Trooper Bob arrests Alliyah Howard," I said.

"Why? What's her motive? You have to always have a motive. At least, that's what those detectives on television always say," Carson Law said.

I shared what I'd learned with the group.

"So, Dr. Howard was having an affair with Serafina's husband, and Serafina knew about it?" Jessica asked.

I nodded.

"She did it," Jessica said.

"What? Where did that come from?" I asked.

"Serafina tried to kill her, but your doctor friend was too smart for her."

"She did not kill Serafina," I said.

Jessica folded her arms. "I would have killed her if I were Serafina and found out she was having an affair with my spouse."

"It takes two to tango. I would have killed my spouse." I glared at Michael so he understood what I would do should he ever consider cheating on me. "After all, he's the one that pledged his fidelity."

Michael shook his head. "Considering we know that Serafina was having an affair with that French chef, Yves-René Barbier, it sounds like neither one of them took their marriage vows very seriously."

"Haitian," Leroy said.

"What?" Michael asked.

"Chef Yves-René Barbier is from Haiti. He's a French-trained chef, but he's not French." Leroy was distracted. After a few moments, he took a deep breath. "I talked to Chef Barbier. Did you know he was a lawyer, too?"

"None of us know anything whatsoever about him." I looked around for confirmation. Everyone shook their heads. So, I turned back to Leroy. "Why don't you tell us about him."

"Like Tyler, he hated being an attorney. He loved baking, and at first, he just did it on the side. He practiced law by day, and at night, he baked. He was married and had a family to support. Then, his wife got cancer."

"That's horrible. Poor woman."

Leroy took a deep breath. "He claims the affair with Serafina was just a lapse in judgment. One he regrets." He paused. "Anyway, he tried to break it off, but . . ."

"But Serafina refused to *go gentle into that good night?*"

"Yeah."

"So he killed her?" Jessica asked.

Leroy shrugged. "He claims he didn't. He claims he was busy. Serafina damaged his ice sculpture, so then he had to use one that he'd started earlier but didn't finish because it had a flaw."

"It was lopsided," I said.

"He said he was ashamed to present that sculpture, but Serafina insisted."

"But you don't believe him?" Candy asked.

"I don't know what to believe. I tried to talk to some of his assistants, but they were crazy busy. I'll try again when I go back down. Don't worry." Leroy gave me a look that spoke volumes more than his words.

"Well, I talked to that couple that Serafina humiliated before you," Hannah said.

"And?"

"And, I don't think you'll have to worry about a free cake for their wedding."

"The wedding's off?" I asked.

Hannah nodded. "Unless he can convince *Carla* to marry him, that man ain't getting married."

"She might still have killed—"

Hannah was shaking her head before I finished speaking. "She's starting to realize she dodged a bullet. She's swinging between tears and relief, but she's almost to the point where she's thankful for Serafina's revelation. Almost." She looked down her nose.

"What about the groom?" Michael asked.

Hannah shrugged. "I couldn't find him, but I'll try again. He's bound to be here someplace."

"Did you find out their names?" I asked.

"Kelsey Morgan and Roger Livingston."

"Any idea what they do for a living?"

"Kelsey's a . . ." Hannah tapped the side of her head and squeezed her eyes closed in an effort to remember. "I don't know what she called it, but she's one of those people that take your blood."

"A vampire?" Candy giggled.

"A phlebotomist?" Michael asked.

"Yeah, that's it." She scowled at Candy for a few seconds,

then continued her conversation. "Roger Livingston is a dentist."

"Both of them would know exactly where to stick those skewers to do the most damage," Michael said.

"Who's next?" Hannah asked.

"The security guards were talking to Serafina's manager and trying to get their final paychecks from the time she fired them to the time she was found dead," Michael said. "Serafina may have had quite a bit of money, but she wasn't good about paying her people."

Jessica Barlow stepped forward. "I heard the same thing."

"Sit down and tell Maddy everything you know, dear," Carson Law said, smiling at her assistant.

"When the crew was at the inn, I overheard them and several of the other contractors complaining. That's all."

Fiona slipped into the room and sat down near Hannah.

"I talked to Troy, the photographer, and Lucy, Serafina's assistant," Candy said. "According to them, Serafina was a talented wedding planner with a bad reputation. She treated the contractors she worked with abominably. She yelled, threatened, tricked, and cajoled to get her way. She owed money to almost all of the florists, photographers, caterers, and rental companies she worked with."

Carson Law gasped. "That's horrible. Why did they continue working with her? They should have reported her to the Better Business Bureau."

"Fear," Jessica said, her cheeks red.

Candy nodded. "That's what I heard, too. They were all afraid to report her because they didn't want to get blacklisted."

"Blacklisted?" Hannah asked. "How?"

"Serafina was flying high in wedding circles," Jessica said. "They were afraid one bad word from her would mean they would never get another job."

"But that's awful," Carson Law said.

"Unfortunately, it's how things work."

I exchanged a glance with Jessica. She knew a lot about the pettiness of influential people. Before working for Carson Law, she had been the personal assistant to Brandi Denton. Brandi wasn't just a social media influencer; she was *the* influencer who had stolen my fiancé. She was also a world-class mean girl. *Petty* should have been her middle name. Even though Jessica was a talented artist, Brandi treated her like an indentured servant.

Carson Law shook her head. "Shameful."

"She may not have paid them for their hard work, but her weddings got tons of publicity, which led to other opportunities," I said.

"But to use threats and manipulation to control people is just . . . inhumane," Carson Law said. "I feel horrible for those poor people. They're just human beings trying to make a living. They deserve to be able to get paid for their work."

"It's a wonder she wasn't killed sooner," Hannah said.

"And her assistants would be the first ones in line," Fiona said.

CHAPTER 30

All eyes were on Fiona.

"Robbie went to take Dr. Howard's statement, and I couldn't go in the room with them. So, I tried to find my way back here, but I got lost."

Leroy shook his head every time his mother called Trooper Bob *Robbie*. Otherwise, he remained quiet.

"I found myself downstairs near the kitchen," Fiona said. "That's when I overheard Serafina's assistants talking."

"Luke and Lucy?" I asked.

Fiona nodded. "Luke Overton, Serafina's assistant, was worried. He has a criminal record. He's afraid that the police will find out and will automatically assume that he murdered Serafina to keep her quiet."

"What kind of record? What did he do?"

"Robbery. He was seventeen and desperate. It was a stupid thing to do."

"Seventeen?" Carson Law said. "He was just a kid."

Leroy frowned. "Don't tell me they tried him as an adult."

Fiona sighed. "No. They wanted to, but couldn't. He took a deal and spent nine months in a low-security facility. Apparently, he robbed a bank, but there were some kind of special circumstances, and he got off relatively light. There was a special class offered by a world-renowned cinematographer. Luke took classes and learned about film, cameras, and movies. When he got out, he worked hard to get his current job." She shrugged. "Serafina found out about his record even though they were supposed to be sealed. She's been using that knowledge to keep Luke under her thumb."

Jessica frowned. "I heard about this, too."

"You knew?" I asked. "How?"

"One night at the inn, I couldn't sleep. I went downstairs for a snack. I overheard Luke and Serafina arguing. He wanted to leave. He had an opportunity to work on a documentary in L.A., but Serafina wouldn't let him go. She barely paid him more than minimum wage. He had to work two side jobs to keep a roof over his head."

"What did they say?" Michael asked Jessica.

"He begged her to let him go. She laughed. She said if anyone found out he'd been arrested for robbing a bank, he'd never work again. She said she would crush his dream of working in production like a cockroach if he tried to work for anyone else."

"Ouch."

"That would certainly make me want to kill her," Hannah said.

"Do we know where Luke was when she was murdered?" I asked.

"He claimed he was talking to Lucy at the time Serafina was murdered," Candy said.

Something in her demeanor told me that she didn't believe it. Before I could ask, Hannah said, "He's a liar."

We turned to Hannah.

"How do you know he's lying?" I asked.

"He couldn't have been talking to Lucy when Serafina was murdered because I was talking to her," Hannah said.

CHAPTER 31

"You were talking to her?" I said. "When? How come you never said anything?"

"Hold your horses and stop slinging questions at me," Hannah said. She sat up straight and tall and gave us "the look."

I never knew my mom, but I'd seen my friends' moms, teachers, and drill sergeants implement *the look* with great success.

We stopped talking and waited.

After a few moments, Hannah continued. "When the videos of Maddy getting stood up at the wedding to that no good, low-account, rat—"

"Tell us how you really feel?" Leroy joked.

"That's what I was doing."

"The dirty blighter," Fiona added.

"I don't know what that is, but if it means a dirty rat, then I agree," Hannah said.

Fiona nodded.

"Anyway, that video was playing all over the auditorium, and I got mad. I marched right over to that platform, and I was going to give that Serafina woman a piece of my mind." Hannah pursed her lips and scowled. "How dare she think she's going to waltz in here and embarrass my soon-to-be granddaughter-in-law?" She turned to me. "You're family. You were Octavia's family, and you're mine, too. And nobody messes with my family."

I thought my heart would burst with joy at the love I felt for this woman. I rushed over and threw my arms around her and hugged her.

She endured the hug for several moments. Then, she pulled out a handkerchief and dabbed at her eyes. "I should have known Michael had it all under control. He broke those two wannabe security guards like a bad habit."

He chuckled.

I gave Hannah a final squeeze and then returned to my seat.

"Anyway, by the time I got through the crowd, Michael had taken care of those rent-a-cops and taken Miss Serafina down a peg or two." Hannah chuckled. "Even Baby was ready to take a piece out of her hide."

At hearing his name, Baby tore his attention from his bone. He focused on me, but then he quickly returned to his treat.

"Anyway, I saw that girl, Lucy. She'd been working her heinie off behind the scenes. Running. Toting. Fetching this and that for that woman. 'Get my sweater.' 'Bring me a Voss.' 'This one isn't cold enough. Bring another.' One order after another. Not one please or thank-you. Just command after command. And that poor child was 'bout run off her feet. It was criminal."

"Well, I suppose that was the job, and Lucy was probably used to it," Jessica said.

"Although Serafina didn't have to be mean, and she certainly should have been more polite," Carson Law said. "There's just no excuse for bad manners."

"But bad manners aren't a crime," I said.

158 / *Valerie Burns*

Hannah stared at me as though I'd suddenly grown another head. "Bad manners are mean and show a lack of home training, but that's not what I think was a crime."

"Oh, sorry." I waited for Hannah to elaborate.

"The crime was for Serafina to work a pregnant woman like some type of slave."

CHAPTER 32

We sat in shocked silence for an eternity of moments while Hannah's words seeped through our skin. Once her words finally sunk in, we all started talking at once.

"What?"

"She was pregnant?"

"How far along is she?"

"Who's the father?"

Hannah frowned. "Now, I told y'all not to shoot questions at me like a machine gun."

"Sorry," we mumbled.

Candy raised a hand. "Miss Hannah, may I ask a question?"

Hannah nodded.

"How did you know she was pregnant?"

"I could tell by looking at her."

"Was she showing?" I mouthed to Candy.

She shrugged.

"Was she showing?" Jessica asked out loud.

"She's got a little bit of a pooch. But I could tell by her face."

"That's not exactly scientific," Michael said.

"Doctors. Y'all are all the same. Y'all think you gotta pee on a stick to determine if a woman is pregnant or not. Well, we didn't have that back in my day. I could tell by the way her face filled out. Her bra was about two sizes too small. Plus, she has a little melon in the oven, and she kept patting her stomach. She's pregnant all right." Hannah folded her arms across her chest.

Michael held up his hands in surrender. "I believe you."

"You do?" I asked.

"I can usually look at a dog or cat and tell when they're pregnant."

"So, she confirmed it?" Jessica said.

"She did." Hannah nodded. "After Serafina got finished yelling at her, I went over and told her she needed to eat something so she didn't get sick. And she needed to rest. I got some cake samples and gave them to her along with a bottle of water."

"Good for you," Carson Law said.

"She wanted to know how I knew, and I told her pretty much what I told y'all. Plus, she seemed emotional. She was crying one minute, and I felt sure her hormones were in overdrive."

"Did she mention who the father was?" I asked.

"Not in so many words, but based on the way she kept looking at that photographer, Troy, my money's on him."

"What does Serafina's assistant being pregnant have to do with her murder?" Jessica asked. "Don't tell me you think her hormones went into overdrive and that's why she killed her." She smirked.

"Lucy hadn't told Serafina. She felt sure that as soon as she did, she'd lose her job."

"Serafina had Lucy's diary, too," Candy said. "She probably read it in there."

"Good point," Michael said.

Candy beamed.

"She said it was just a matter of time until Serafina got to that entry in her diary. And when she did . . ." Hannah whistled.

"How did she know Serafina hadn't gotten to it yet?" I asked.

"Because Serafina would have blown her top. She was afraid Serafina would throw her weight around and blacklist the baby's father, and then both of them would be out of work."

"Yikes!"

"Are you sure there's no way Lucy could have killed her?" Candy said. "A mother protecting her baby will go to extreme lengths."

"Including murder," Jessica said.

CHAPTER 33

There were no other revelations, and time was running out.

"What now?" Hannah asked.

"We don't have much time," Candy said.

"Do we need to keep this up?" Michael said.

I turned to him. "What do you mean?"

"I don't believe Alliyah murdered anyone, but . . . if Trooper Bob and April have enough evidence, then it takes the focus off Maddy, and that's all I really care about."

I reached over and squeezed his hand. "But she didn't do it."

"How can you be so sure? You barely know her. And, up until an hour ago, you didn't like her. How can you be sure she didn't murder Serafina? I'm not."

His attitude surprised me. Michael wasn't in love with Alliyah, but he did respect her skill as a veterinarian and a doctor. There's no way he would have allowed her to join his practice if he thought she was capable of murder. There was something else going on.

"I never did like Little-Miss-Booshie-Pants-Howard," Hannah said.

"That's Little-*Doctor*-Booshie-Pants-Howard," Leroy joked.

"Well, excuse me." Hannah allowed herself a brief smile but then quickly returned to the subject. "I may not like her, but I have to agree with Madison. She would be too afraid she'd break a nail or, heaven forbid, get blood on her expensive dress."

"We've ruled out the security guards and Alliyah," I said. "That leaves Chef Barbier, Luke, Lucy, and Troy the photographer. We need—"

"Maddy, I'm serious," Michael said. "We need to stand down and let the police handle it. Alliyah may or may not have killed Serafina, but as long as Trooper Bob isn't planning to arrest you, then I think we should leave it to them to figure out. It's what they get paid to do. Let the professionals do the jobs they get paid to do, and we can get back to ours."

The silence that followed rolled in like a dense fog over the ocean.

I stood up. "Could you excuse us for a few minutes?" I walked out of the room and into the hallway. After a few moments, Michael followed.

My brain raced as I tried to figure out what to say.

"Maddy, I'm sorry, but—"

I reached up and kissed him.

His initial shock wore off quickly. He responded passionately and with intensity.

I heard a door open. We reluctantly separated.

Leroy stuck his head out of the room like a turtle. "It's okay. They're kissing," he yelled to the others. Then, he put his head back in the room and closed the door.

Michael swore under his breath. His shoulders relaxed. "Okay, Squid, what was that for?"

"What? Can't a girl kiss her fiancé without having a reason?" I asked as innocently as I could.

"You are free to kiss me whenever you want, but I know you. There was something behind that kiss."

"I don't know what you're talking about."

He folded his arms across his chest, leaned against the wall, and stared at me. "The first time you kissed me like that was when I got shot and you were afraid I was going to pass out from shock."

"It worked. You didn't pass out." I smiled at the memory.

He grinned. "Were you afraid that I was in shock a minute ago and about to pass out? Not that I'm complaining about your technique. It works for me."

"Michael, do you trust me?"

"With my life."

"Then, what's the problem? Don't you think I'm smart enough to figure out who murdered Serafina?"

"Maddy, you're incredibly smart. You're determined, creative, resourceful, funny, beautiful, kind, and smart. If you put your mind to it, there's nothing you can't accomplish, but—"

"Then, why—"

"Why don't I want the woman that I love getting close to a murderer? Maddy, this is dangerous. The last time you got involved in a murder, you got shot. Remember?"

"Of course, but I'm fine." I grinned. "I have an excellent doctor . . . um, veterinarian."

"You shouldn't have needed a doctor. And what if the next time you go up against a killer, he has better aim? Or what if Baby, the Admiral, or I am not around? What if something happens to you?" He lifted my chin and gazed into my eyes. "I love you, Madison Renee Montgomery, and I don't want to risk losing you. There's no need to take risks and place yourself in danger. Not for Serafina. Not for Alliyah."

I reached up and kissed him softly. "I love you, too. But, I can't stand back and let an innocent woman get arrested for a murder she didn't commit." I could feel him revving up for a response and cut him off. "Michael, why did you join the Army?"

"To serve my country."

"Even though you knew there was a chance that you might be killed?"

"This isn't the same thing. When I was a soldier, that was my job. It was risky, and I knew that going in. I accepted those risks, but this isn't your job. You don't have to put yourself in danger."

"I never wanted to join the military, even though I think the Admiral would have liked me to have enlisted. I'm not brave. I'm afraid of spiders, rodents, reptiles, and anything that resembles a rodent or a reptile, but I also wouldn't be able to live with myself if I went home and didn't at least try to help. You didn't see her eyes when she asked me to help her."

He gazed into my soul. "You really think Alliyah's innocent?"

"Yes. Even Miss Hannah thinks she's innocent. You dated her for over a year. You know her better than any of us. The big question is, why don't you think she's innocent?"

He shook his head. "The more I hear, the more I realize that I didn't know her at all. I never believed she would have an affair with a married man. I mean, marriage vows are sacred. At least, they are to me."

"They better be." I grinned. "They are to me, too. But it sounds like she didn't know he was married until . . . well, until it was too late. I didn't get the impression that she deliberately went after him knowing he was married. Plus, we don't know what he's told her."

He rubbed his neck. "What do you mean?"

"I had a friend who got involved with a Navy lieutenant she *thought* was in the process of getting a divorce. He and his wife weren't living in the same house. It was just a matter of time before the divorce became final, etc., etc., etc. In all honesty, I think he meant it. Anyway, his wife and her attorney wouldn't agree to anything. If he said the sky was blue, they would argue that the sky was magenta and ask for a delay. It went on for years."

"What happened?"

"He died in a training exercise. My friend was devastated, but technically there wasn't anything she could do. Legally, he was still married. My friend couldn't even attend the funeral. I'm not condoning what Alliyah did, but maybe she was . . . misled."

His jaw relaxed, and while his eyes were still full of skepticism, they were the slightest bit softer. "Maybe. I guess I'm just old-fashioned. Adultery is wrong."

"Adultery is a sin, but it isn't a crime."

He wrapped his arms around me. "Okay, so if I were to have an affair, you'd be understanding?"

"If you had an affair, I'd rip out your heart and toss your body over the bluffs into Lake Michigan." I grinned.

"Whew! And I thought you weren't a violent person."

"No. I said I wasn't brave. I never said I wasn't capable of violence. Two different things." I kissed him. "Now, are you going to help me find Serafina's killer?"

CHAPTER 34

Michael and I reentered the room hand in hand.

"I can tell by the smile on your faces that y'all worked out the problem, so maybe now we can get down to business and get this murder solved," Miss Hannah said. "I have a bushel of apples soaking in the sink, and I need to make a couple of apple walnut cakes and some cider."

Michael pointed to me.

I cleared my throat. "Leroy, can you talk to some of Chef Barbier's assistants? Find out where he was when Serafina was murdered."

Leroy nodded.

"Candy, I need you to talk to Luke."

Candy gave a thumbs-up.

"Miss Hannah, since you already have a relationship with Lucy, maybe you could—"

"I wish we hadn't gave away all the cake. She's probably in need of a snack."

"We can order something from the kitchen," Candy said. "I still have some friends who work in the kitchen. I'll get them to make her a sandwich."

Hannah nodded.

"Michael, I'd like you to talk to Troy."

"The photographer?"

I nodded and turned to Fiona. "Mrs. Danielson, if Trooper Bob is still busy, would you mind helping Miss Hannah with Lucy?"

"I'd love to." Fiona smiled.

"What about us?" Carson Law asked. "We want to help."

"I have a special assignment for you two."

Carson Law glowed with excitement.

Jessica rolled her eyes, but the eye roll didn't have the same disdain as her normal eye rolls.

"Serafina's husband, Patrick Dixon, wants to design men's formal attire. I think he would love to meet a designer with your name and clout."

"How exciting." Carson Law clapped. "What do you want to know?"

"Where he was when his wife was murdered will be a good start."

"We'll do it. Won't we?"

"Whatever you say, Mrs. Law," Jessica said. She turned to me and asked, "What will you be doing while we're interviewing potential killers?"

"First, I'm going to take Baby outside so he can take care of his business. Then, I'm hoping to get a look at the crime scene. I'm curious why no one saw the murder. Maybe I can get one of the staff to tell me what they know."

"That's actually a great idea," Fiona said. "People ignore the hired help. They treat us as if we weren't even there. I've heard some of the most embarrassing conversations. It's like we're invisible."

We agreed to meet back in an hour, and then split up.

Baby was reluctant to give up his treat. When he clamped his jaws around it, I learned not to try to wrestle it away from him. Instead, I told him to drop it. He thought about it for a few seconds, but he eventually opened his mouth and let the saliva-soaked bone drop to the ground.

I picked it up, put it back in the plastic bag, and reassured him that he would get it back later.

I'm not sure if he believed me, but he complied.

It took a few minutes for Baby and me to find our way to the elevator, but once we did, I followed the exit signs and made my way outside.

Baby sniffed around for just the right corner and then hiked his leg.

I waited to see if that was it. When he sat and stared up at me, I knew he was done.

I casually wandered around the outside of the building until I found the door that Michael and I had used earlier. As I suspected, this exit wasn't guarded. I twisted the knob and was happy to see that the door wasn't locked. I took a deep breath, opened the door, and entered.

Inside, I found myself behind the stage where we'd been earlier, but behind the black velvet curtain. Guards and police stood at the entrance that led out to the main auditorium, preventing entrance. Fortunately, Serafina's body had been removed. Although, there was a tape outline marking the place where her body had been and numbered cones all over the floor.

I closed my eyes and removed the image of Serafina's body that tried to pop up in my memory. Instead, I forced myself to picture the scene before she was murdered. The cake booth. Troy's photography. The contestants. With my eyes closed, I turned to orient myself. *Michael and I were there. Chef Barbier was near the back wall. Serafina and her husband, Patrick, at the front of the room.*

"Hey, you're not supposed to be here."

I jumped and turned around to face my accuser. I opened my eyes and stared into the bright blue eyes of Officer Jerrod Thomas and breathed a sigh of relief.

"Madison, what are you doing? How did you get in here?"

"You scared me." I patted my chest.

Officer Jerrod Thomas was a member of the New Bison police force. He had fire-engine red hair and bad acne that made him look twelve. For nearly a year, he had been attempting to grow a beard. The red stubble coming from his chin made him look like a wirehaired terrier.

"You're not supposed to be here." He glanced over his shoulder. "If Trooper Bob sees you—"

"What are you and that mangy dog doing contaminating my crime scene?"

"Speak of the Devil," I mumbled.

Officer Thomas and I had been engaged in our conversation and hadn't seen Trooper Bob enter the room.

He marched over to us and scowled.

"Trooper Bob, what a coincidence."

"How'd you get in here?" He glared at Officer Thomas. "If you let her and that mutt in here, I'll see to it that you'll be lucky to get a job as a crossing guard at New Bison Elementary School."

Officer Thomas gulped, and the tips of his ears flamed.

"Hey, stop that. Officer Thomas did not let me in. I was out walking Baby, and I must have come in the wrong door."

"Then let me see you out." He grabbed my arm, but Baby didn't like it.

Baby growled and bared his teeth.

Trooper Bob froze. He released the grip he had on my arm and slowly moved a hand toward the revolver strapped to his side without taking his gaze from Baby.

"That dog is a menace."

Baby kept his gaze focused on Trooper Bob, and drool dripped from his mouth.

"Baby doesn't like it when people manhandle me," I said.

"I wasn't manhandling you. I was escorting you away from an active crime scene that you weren't supposed to be in in the first place."

"I think Baby would disagree. However, I think if you were to move your hand away from your gun, it would do wonders to de-escalate the situation."

Trooper Bob's frown deepened. I could see the gears turning as he weighed his options. By the time he removed the snaps securing his weapon, Baby would have him on the ground and incapacitated.

"That beast is going to hurt someone." He slowly moved his hand away from his gun.

Baby's growl moved from audible to a tummy rumble, but his gaze never left Trooper Bob.

"Good boy." I patted Baby. After a long pause, he cut his gaze away and turned to me.

Both Trooper Bob and Officer Thomas released breaths.

"Sir, I'm sorry. I—"

Trooper Bob held up a hand to stop the apology.

"Dad." Holly Roberts came through a door and made a bee-line toward us.

"Is this a crime scene or a tourist stop?" Trooper Bob turned to glare at his daughter.

Holly, followed by her friend Carlos, rushed over. Right before she reached her dad, Holly dropped to her knees and hugged Baby.

Baby dropped to the ground, rolled on his back, and let Holly rub his tummy.

"Some menace to society," I mumbled.

Trooper Bob heaved a heavy sigh. "Is there a reason you're here contaminating a crime scene?"

Holly stood up and gave her father a peck on the cheek. "Hi, Dad."

"Well?" Trooper Bob folded his arms across his chest. "And who is this?"

"That's my friend Carlos. We've been doing some sleuthing for Maddy . . . um, I mean Miss Montgomery, and we—"

"Sleuthing?" Molten lava rolled up Trooper Bob's neck and

into his face. He was about to explode like Mount Vesuvius any minute.

"Chill, Dad."

"Trooper Bob, it isn't what you think," I said.

"Not what I think? How do you know what I think? You . . ." Trooper Bob clutched his chest.

"Dad."

He staggered backward and then slumped down to the ground.

CHAPTER 35

Emergencies were not my thing, but I wasn't about to use the same techniques on Trooper Bob that I'd used on Michael. No way was I kissing him. Instead, I pulled out my phone and made a call.

"Hey, I was just—"

"Trooper Bob just fell to the ground. I think he's having a heart attack."

"Where are you?"

"The greenroom."

"On my way. Did you call nine-one-one?"

I turned to Officer Thomas, who was frozen in place with his mouth open. "Call nine-one-one."

Holly leaned over her dad.

I heard a commotion and glanced over as Michael was arguing with a policeman trying to block his access. "Let him through. He's a doctor."

Officer Thomas nodded his consent.

Michael ran over. He dropped to the ground and checked Trooper Bob's pulse. He lifted his eyelid. Then, he rattled off a series of questions.

Holly answered what she could.

Michael ripped open Trooper Bob's shirt and started chest compressions.

Carlos pulled Holly out of the way.

Baby watched the activity. He moved over to Michael and sat by Trooper Bob's head. He reached down and sniffed him and then licked his face.

"Baby, move," Michael said between compressions.

Baby didn't budge.

Sirens from the ambulance blared, and Officer Thomas hurried to open the door.

An EMT rushed over. Michael spouted off some medical terms, and they worked like a well-choreographed dance team.

Within seconds, they had Trooper Bob hooked up to machines.

I held Holly close and tried to distract her, but it was no use. Her gaze never left her father, and I could feel her shivering.

After a few moments, Michael injected something in Trooper Bob's arm, and then they waited.

The equipment beeped.

Trooper Bob opened his eyes and stared up into Baby's face.

Baby gave his nose a lick.

Trooper Bob's eyes widened as he stared at the mastiff. Then, something passed between the two of them. And Trooper Bob's lips curled upward.

Holly whimpered.

Trooper Bob's gaze wandered from Baby to Michael and then to his daughter.

Michael helped the EMTs get Trooper Bob onto a stretcher.

"Can I go with him?" Holly asked.

Michael nodded.

Holly followed the EMTs out as they wheeled her father to the waiting ambulance.

"How is he?"

I hadn't heard April's approach until she spoke.

I shrugged.

Dr. Howard rushed past us. She and Michael talked, and then she climbed into the back of the ambulance with Holly.

Michael hurried over to me. "You okay?"

"No. Not okay. I'm pretty sure I'm going to have a nervous breakdown. Is this a good time?"

"Sure. Go ahead. I got you." Michael pulled me into his arms and held me tightly.

I'm not sure how long I stood there bawling, but Michael's shirt was soaked and covered in makeup, and I was exhausted.

I pushed away. "I must look horrible."

"You couldn't look horrible if you tried." He leaned in and kissed me. "Hmm. Salty."

"I need to wash my face."

"Hold up." April walked over. "Before you leave, can someone fill me in?"

"Um, excuse me." Carlos had been standing anxiously nearby. "Is Holly coming back? Should I maybe go to the hospital? She left her sweater." He held it up.

"I'm sorry, I completely forgot you were there," I said. "Do you drive?"

Carlos nodded.

"I think Holly would appreciate a friend."

"Her dad is going to be fine," Michael said, "but he's going to have to stay in the hospital for a few days. They'll want to run tests."

"Maybe you could go to the hospital," I said. "She'll want some of her things while she's there. She'll need food and possibly a ride home."

Carlos nodded.

"Mostly, she's going to need a friend." I smiled.

"Yeah. Um. Okay. I can do that." He cleared his throat. "Miss Maddy?"

"Yes."

"I know Holly was excited to share what we found out. Is this a good time?" I must have looked even more puzzled than I felt, but he quickly explained. "You know, about the Great Cake Caper."

"The Great Cake Caper?" April said.

Carlos blushed. "That's what we called it."

"Oh, yes," I said. "What did you find?"

"Holly figured out what was up. I was just . . . you know, following directions, but she learned that the people who won the cakes were from a company called . . ." He paused and tapped the side of his head trying to remember. Then, he must have remembered something because he pulled out his phone. After a few swipes, he stopped. "Here it is. The Bandy Corporation."

"The Bandy Corporation? Why does that sound familiar?"

"Because it's huge," April said. "They launched some of the biggest food trends in the country. I've read about them, but they like to keep a low profile."

The lightbulb came on. "Aren't they the company that launched Yummy Gummy Mummys?"

April nodded. "That's them."

"I love those things."

"Aren't they just like all the other gummies?" Michael asked. "Gummy worms. Gummy bears. Gummy fruit."

"Dude, no," Carlos said, shaking his head. "Yummy Gummy Mummy candy is like a unique taste experience."

Michael raised a skeptical brow.

"It's like they figured out how to take the concept behind a mood ring from the 1970s and turn it into something that you can eat."

"A mood ring?" Michael asked.

"The candy interacts with each person's unique saliva, and the taste experience is different for each person. Dude, you've got to try them."

"He's not wrong," April said. "At least, that's what the advertisement says. You and I could try the exact same candy, and to me it may taste like oranges, and you might taste mangos or peaches or whatever. It's crazy."

"How did I miss these?" Michael said.

"Why would the Bandy Corporation pay a fortune for our cakes?"

April smacked my arm. "OMG! You don't think . . ."

"It can't be . . ." I jumped up and down.

"Will one of you tell me what the big deal is?" Michael asked.

We stopped jumping. I took a couple of deep breaths to steady my nerves. "I saw something on social media that the Bandy Corporation was looking for their next great find. Word around social media circles is that the company was going to do their version of *America's Got Talent*, only for food."

Michael repeated the action his grandmother performed earlier by placing the back of his hand on my forehead to check my temperature. I endured the accusation from Miss Hannah that I must be running a fever, but I didn't have to put up with it from my fiancé, so I swatted away his hand.

"I do not have a fever."

"But you aren't making sense," Michael said.

"Actually, she is," April said. "It makes total sense. Can't you see?"

"Maybe I'm the one who's sick." Michael put his hand to his own forehead.

"The Bandy Corporation is doing their own food search," I said. "They've always been very private. So, it would make sense that if they were considering buying a small, little-known recipe, they might try to get a taste in secret. Then, if they like it, they can approach the owner with an offer."

"How do you know they won't take the food to their chemist and figure out how to make it themselves? Then they could sell it as their own and circumvent you."

I paused for a moment. Was he right? Maybe I was being naïve. Should I be more concerned? The anxiety rose in a lump from my stomach to my chest. The lump stuck in my throat. I closed my eyes and swallowed hard and forced it back to my stomach. "Everything I've seen on social media about the Bandy Company is positive. They're one of the top companies to work for. They're known for their integrity and commitment to the environment." I pulled out my phone and swiped.

"Maddy, when it comes to social media, you know your stuff. If you say the Bandy Company is trustworthy, then I believe you. But . . ."

"But what?"

"Is that what you want?"

I paused. I hadn't thought about it. It would mean that Great-Aunt Octavia's Chocolate Soul Cake could be in every grocery store in the country. It could even go international. I'd be rich. I could buy all of the Hanifa dresses I wanted. But, was that what I wanted? "I don't know."

"What are you, crazy?" Officer Thomas colored. "Sorry. I didn't mean to . . . I'm sorry."

April forced her lips to remain neutral. "Officer Thomas, maybe you could give us a moment."

Officer Thomas nearly ran to the entrance and as far away from us as he could get.

"You sure scared him," I said.

April gave in to a chuckle. When she was done, she said, "What are you doing in here, by the way?"

"I was just looking at the crime scene. That's what Columbo always did."

"Columbo? That cop with the curly hair and the rumpled raincoat who used to say, *Just one more thing?*"

"Yeah. Although, I have no idea what Columbo saw at those crime scenes. This one just looks like a big empty room to me." I looked around the room. I didn't see anything that would solve the murder and prove that Alliyah Howard didn't murder Serafina. I was about to admit defeat when Baby screamed.

All eyes turned to stare.

Baby stood on three legs. He held his right front paw in the air, and blood dripped from his pad.

CHAPTER 36

"He's okay. It's just a cut. He's going to be just fine." Michael repeated this over and over in his soft, soothing, I've-got-everything-under-control-just-breathe voice while he examined Baby's paw.

It took me several minutes to realize that the reassuring words and soft tone were for my benefit rather than my dog's. "What happened to him?"

Michael poked, squeezed, and prodded Baby's paw. For the most part, Baby took it like a champ, but one poke too many caused a major yelp and an attempt to remove his paw from Michael's grasp.

"It's okay, boy. Sorry about that."

I sat on the floor with Baby's massive head in my lap.

"It's just a cut," Michael said.

"But there's so much blood. There's too much blood. You need to do something. You have to help him."

"Maddy, he's going to be fine, but I need my bag. It's in my truck." Michael reached in his pocket to hand me his key fob.

I shook my head. "I'm not leaving. He needs me."

"In order for me to help him, I need my bag. I have supplies in my car, but I need you to bring my bag." Michael extended the fob.

I shook my head.

"Maddy, he's going to be fine. I promise you, but—"

"Nope. I'm not leaving." I stroked Baby's head. "In that movie with Tom Hanks, that vet told him to keep his hand nearby so Hooch could smell him."

"*Turner and Hooch*?" Michael asked.

"Baby needs to smell me. I'm not leaving."

April extended her hand to Michael for the fob. "I'll bring it. Where did you park?"

Michael explained where he'd parked, and April hurried out to get what he needed. She rushed toward the exit, but before she left, she stopped and spoke to Officer Thomas, who got on his radio and then hurried into the main auditorium.

April rushed outside.

Michael turned to me. "He's going to be okay. You know that, right?"

"Hooch wasn't all right."

"Ignoring the fact that we're talking about a movie, which isn't real, Hooch was shot in the chest. Baby has a small piece of glass embedded in the pad of his foot. It looks a lot worse than it is, but he's going to be fine. I promise."

I sniffed. A tear fell onto Baby's nose. I hadn't even realized that I'd been crying. "How did it happen?"

"He must have stepped on it." Michael glanced around.

Officer Thomas returned with a first-aid kit and a member of the casino staff.

Michael checked the first-aid kit and removed a gauze bandage. He ripped the bandage from its package and used the pad to control the bleeding.

A few moments later, April rushed in carrying a large medical bag that I knew Michael kept in the back of his truck.

He pulled out a small vial and a syringe.

"What's that?" I asked.

Michael filled the syringe. "It's just a mild tranquilizer for the pain and to help keep him calm." He tapped the syringe and then inserted it in Baby's arm.

Baby's head popped up at the prick of the needle, but after a few moments, he returned it to my lap.

Michael put on a pair of plastic gloves. He took a bottle with clear liquid and cleaned Baby's paw. Then, he took a sharp pair of tweezers and cleaned them. He reached in the bag for a muzzle.

"What do you think you're doing with that?"

"This isn't my clinic where I can put him completely out. He could feel this, and he might bite you or me. This is just a precaution."

"Nope. Baby would never bite me."

Michael started to argue, but he must have sensed that I meant business. Instead, he returned the muzzle to his bag. He picked up his tweezers and worked to remove the glass from Baby's paw.

Michael worked quickly. Only once did Baby protest. He lifted his head and yelped. I tightened my grip on him, and he returned his head to my lap.

"Got it." Michael held up the tweezers, showing a long shard of glass. Then, he took a small magnifying glass and inspected Baby's foot. Satisfied that he had it all, he flushed the pad with a sterile saline and then wrapped the paw with gauze.

"Will he need stitches?" I asked.

"I think it will be best to just bandage his foot and let it heal together on its own." Michael finished wrapping Baby's paw.

When he finished, he looked in Baby's eyes. "You're going to be okay, but you need to take it easy for about a week. Okay?"

Baby gave his nose a lick.

"Glad to see there's no hard feelings." Michael petted Baby.

"Is that it?" I asked.

"That's it." Michael removed his gloves.

"Can I see that?" April asked.

Michael handed her the tweezers with the shard of glass.

April stared at the glass shard. "Baby, you were about to walk out of here with evidence from my crime scene. We can't have that."

CHAPTER 37

Baby was groggy, but at close to an eighth of a ton, carrying him was out of the question. Fortunately, April moved Michael's car close to the exit, so with a bit of help, Michael, Officer Thomas, and the casino manager who had brought the first-aid kit managed to get him into the back of Michael's truck.

I wanted to go with him, but Michael and April convinced me that would be a mistake. Michael assured me that Baby was fine and just needed to rest. He was going back to the clinic and would get some antibiotics and anti-inflammatory meds, but then he would drop him off at my house to sleep.

April reminded me that even though Trooper Bob was in the hospital, I still needed to talk to the Feds when they arrived in a couple of hours. Without actually saying the words, she reminded me that I might still be considered a suspect in Serafina's murder and needed to hang around a bit longer.

My heart knew that Michael was right and that Baby would be fine, but in the short time that I'd lived with that dog, I'd grown to love him more than I thought possible. He wasn't just a dog. He was my friend.

"I promise Baby will be just fine," Michael said. "He just needs to rest." He kissed me and then left to get Baby home.

"We'd better get busy if we're going to solve this murder so I can get home to Baby. Where did that glass come from?" I sniffed and wiped away my tears.

"That's what I want to know, too." April held up the plastic bag containing the glass shard. "I suppose someone could have dropped a glass, and it got missed when they cleaned, but we won't know until we get it to the lab."

"Does New Bison have a crime lab?"

"New Bison doesn't, but there's a lab in St. Joe that covers all of Berrien County." April handed the bag to Officer Thomas. "It might not mean anything."

"Why?" I asked.

"The crime scene's been compromised. Between you, Baby, Michael, the EMTs, the casino staff . . ." She shrugged. "Everyone and their brother have trampled through here. That glass could have happened long after Serafina was already dead."

"I'm sorry. If I hadn't come in here to see the crime scene, then none of this—"

"Maddy, it's not your fault. This glass could have gotten here before Serafina was murdered. Or, it could have happened after she was murdered but before the police cordoned off the area." She shrugged. "The forensic people from the Tribal Police went over the scene. It just happened."

A disturbance near the door captured my attention. I looked around and caught a glimpse of Chef Barbier arguing with one of the Tribal Policemen guarding the door.

April walked over, and I followed her.

"What's the problem?" April asked.

"He wants to remove his equipment," the Tribal Policeman said.

"It's ruined," Chef Barbier said, his hands flailing. "The ice sculpture is ruined. My equipment. I need my equipment to work. It wasn't used to kill Serafina. I need to work. I need to stay busy."

I stayed back and took a good look at Chef Yves-René Barbier.

He was about five feet ten, light-skinned with gray-green eyes. He looked to be in his mid to late fifties, with salt-and-pepper hair that was more salt than pepper. He was an attractive man who reminded me of Harry Belafonte.

"Mr. Barbier, I understand your concern, but we can't allow you or anyone to remove anything, yet. If you need me to explain to the casino management, I'll be more than happy to—"

"Explain? They don't understand. How can you explain? *Use other equipment*, they say. *Go out and buy another tool, and we'll reimburse you.*" He snorted. "Would someone say to Picasso, *Go buy another paintbrush*? Or tell Michelangelo to use a different chisel or a different mallet while he was sculpting *David*?" He closed his eyes. "This, you do not understand. You cannot explain. The tools that I use are like old friends. Hours of scraping at a block of ice year after year, and it fits my hand and only my hand. It is an extension of my hand. It is a part of me." He leaned his head back and took a deep breath.

I stepped forward. "I kind of understand what you mean. It's like when I'm working on social media. I take photos and videos all the time. I upload them to social media. My dad bought me a lot of fancy equipment that's supposed to make it easier. I've got expensive cameras and high-tech sound equipment, but honestly, I prefer to just use my phone. The equipment's nice, but it just isn't the same. I'm used to my phone. It may not take the best quality photos, and the sound isn't the greatest, but that's what I prefer to use."

Chef Barbier stared at me for several seconds. Then, he smiled. "Yes. You understand. You are an artist?"

"No. I'm just a . . . I own a bakery, and I'm a content creator."

Chef Barbier nodded, although something in his eyes told me he had no idea what a content creator was.

"I know that you and Serafina were . . . close," I said. "Please accept my condolences."

His eyes filled with tears. "You knew?"

I nodded.

April looked from me to Chef Barbier. We hadn't had time to fill her in on what we'd learned, so she was puzzled, but she hid it well.

I placed a comforting arm around Chef Barbier and attempted to guide him toward the door. "Perhaps we can go someplace quiet and talk?"

He hesitated and looked as though he would resist. At least, he did until my stomach growled.

The one thing no cook can resist is the sound of hunger.

"Ah, but you are hungry. You must eat. I will cook for you." At the thought of food, Chef Barbier became even more animated. "Yes. You must eat. You are too thin. You will collapse from hunger."

Thin wasn't one of the adjectives people used to describe me. Curvy, yes. Thin, no. But, he was like Leroy and Hannah, who used cooking and food to show their love, deal with stress, provide comfort, and work through problems. Cooking would keep him talking, and I was more than willing to eat, so it worked perfectly.

Chef Barbier took me by the arm and propelled me out of the room.

April hesitated a split second but quickly realized that following us would be her best opportunity to question Chef Barbier.

The chef led us through the auditorium to a door marked KITCHEN. Once inside, the room was buzzing with activity. White-coated men and women mixed, marinated, diced, and plated food. Noting our entrance, several of them snapped to attention. "Chef."

Chef Barbier waved them to continue and walked past. "How about an omelet?"

I nodded. "That sounds great."

April and I stood by and watched as he took out eggs, milk, and a host of other items.

"You want to help? You can crack those eggs." Chef Barbier slid the bowl and the eggs closer to me.

Not eggs. Anything but eggs. Eggs were my Waterloo. A knot formed in my stomach. "Perhaps I should just watch."

"No. No. We cook together. We talk." Chef Barbier handed me an apron.

"Great." I pulled the apron over my head. *If I'm careful, I can do this*, I told myself.

I picked up an egg and tapped it against the side of the metal bowl. Nothing happened. I tapped again. Still, nothing. *What are these shells made of, cement?* I tapped harder. Still nothing. *Fourth time's a charm.* I tapped the egg against the bowl. This time, I crushed it. Literally. The egg, shell, yolk, and all of the egg drool dripped from my hand onto the counter.

Chef Barbier stopped chopping and stared at me.

I felt heat rushing up my neck as I glanced around and noticed that the bustling activity in the kitchen was frozen as everyone stopped and stared at my pulverized egg mishap.

April was the first to snap out of the trance and handed me a towel.

Chef Barbier glanced at the staff and let out a bellow that shook the workers back to their jobs. "What are you all staring at? Back to work."

Without a word, Chef Barbier came over and singlehandedly cracked a half dozen eggs. Then, he handed me a whisk. "You're a strong woman. Ha! Not so much muscle this time. You beat, yes?"

I nodded, grateful for the opportunity to give these eggs a beat-down.

In record time, Chef Barbier chopped, diced, and sliced. He relieved me of whisking duty and beat those eggs into submission in record time. He'd created an omelet bar, and April and I identified our preferences. In less than fifteen minutes, we had two fluffy omelets with fruit and golden triangles of toast. The food was perfectly plated, hot, and delicious.

We took our plates and glasses of freshly squeezed orange juice to a small employee dining area. We found a quiet seat, and April and I dug into the food with gusto.

"This is delicious," April said. "I didn't realize how hungry I was."

"Aren't you going to eat anything?" I asked the chef.

Chef Barbier shook his head. "It is enough for me to watch you eat. Please, eat. Enjoy."

April took a sip of her orange juice and wiped her mouth. "Chef Barbier, I need to ask you some questions. Would you mind if I recorded this?"

The smile faded from his face, but he waved his hand for her to continue.

April pulled out her phone. She got Chef Barbier's consent to record on camera, then announced the date, time, and people present. "Tell me about you and Serafina."

Chef Barbier took a deep breath. "Serafina was . . . a vibrant, intelligent, strong woman. She was driven. Success. Power. She was the complete opposite of my wife, Marion." He paused. "Marion is petite, shy, and meek. Don't get me wrong. I love my wife, but she was . . . isn't very strong. Serafina was like the wind rushing over the ocean before a storm." He shook his head.

"So, you had an affair with Serafina?" I said.

"An affair. That hardly seems the right word. An affair seems so . . . casual, so mild, like the flame from a candle flickering in the wind. What we had wasn't mild." He chuckled. "It was like a raging inferno." He grinned for a few moments, then the grin disappeared. "But our flame burned too hot. Too fast."

"What happened?" I extended my hand and gave his hand a squeeze.

"I came to my senses." Chef Barbier took a deep breath. "Being with Serafina was like being brainwashed. I was drugged. But my wife had a tumor near her heart. It was cancerous, but because of the location, no one was willing to operate to remove the tumor. They tried to shrink it, but it didn't work. The tumor didn't grow, but it also didn't shrink. It was still there. And the treatment. The chemo was killing her. We heard about a specialist in Switzerland. He was the only one willing to operate, to remove the tumor. We went to Switzerland. Just the two of us. We were there for over six months. I didn't see Serafina at all. I barely talked to her." He glanced up, and his eyes were filled with tears. "It worked. My wife was healed. He cut out the cancer, and she was healed. Going through something like that, it changes you. We had a second chance. A second chance at life and a second chance to make our marriage work."

"And Serafina?" I said. "Based on the argument you two had earlier, it didn't sound as though she was taking this well."

"Ah, Serafina. No, she did not take it well." He spread his hands wide. "But the healing wasn't just for my wife. It was for me, too. I went through a detox program. Six months without seeing Serafina. Six months without touching her. Six months without . . . well, you know." He chuckled. "I cleansed her from my system. For the first time, I was able to see clearly. I could see her for what she was. She was beautiful and strong and intelligent, but she was also vicious, ruthless, and cruel. And I didn't want that in my life. Not anymore."

"So, you came here and told her that it was over, and she didn't take it well," April said. "Then what?"

Chef Barbier shrugged. "Then, we argue. We scream. We make threats. But . . ."

"Did you stab her?" April asked.

"No. No. No. I did not kill Serafina." He paused. "I will admit, I wanted to kill her. I wanted to . . ." Chef Barbier picked up a dishcloth and wrung it. Then, he stopped and closed his eyes. "I wanted to kill her. Perhaps I might have killed her if someone had not beaten me to it." He shrugged. "I don't know."

"Where were you when Serafina was murdered?"

"After the announcement of the prizes, I was still angry. I was furious. I needed to pull myself together. I couldn't stand there and smile. Take pictures. Ack! I was disgusted. She was there with her husband. I was there watching them and thinking of the damage we caused. Just like my ice sculpture she pushed over. Lives were shattered. Her husband. My wife. It was too much. I left. I don't know where I went. This place is massive. I walked around for a long time. When I came back, she was dead."

"Did anyone see you?" April asked. "Can anyone confirm your story? Prove that you didn't come back, meet Serafina and kill her?"

"I was full of rage. Disgust. Shame." Chef Barbier shook his head. "I saw no one."

I wanted to tell Chef Barbier that he should consider getting a lawyer before continuing, but I remembered that he was a lawyer. If anyone knew better than to talk to the police without a lawyer, it should have been him.

My phone dinged, indicating I had a text. I glanced at my phone and saw the message was from Tyler.

Chef Barbier finances r a hot mess

R U Sure?

Yes

How hot of a mess?

Chef and Serafina partners. Business in toilet.

Yikes

One step from bankruptcy

April frowned at my rudeness in texting instead of concentrating on the people in front of me. I casually slid my phone so that she could read the message.

"I'm sorry," I said.

Chef Barbier was deep in regret and memories. He sat with his chin down to his chest.

"Chef Barbier, were you a partner in Serafina's business?" April asked.

"What? Oh, that." He waved his hand. "I cosigned a loan."

My phone continued to ding, but April kept it in front of her, so I couldn't read anything else that Tyler sent.

"Well, that loan is in default, and as the cosigner, you're now responsible."

Chef Barbier's head shot up. "What? Surely not. Her husband—"

"Her husband didn't cosign the loan. You did."

"But . . . now that she's dead . . . surely, the loan will . . . her estate will have to . . . I mean, the insurance will cover that. I can't be held responsible. My wife's cancer treatment took all of our savings. We even mortgaged our home to help cover the expenses. Six months in Switzerland, plus all of the doctors, nurses, medical staff . . . it cost a fortune. I can't possibly pay for Serafina's debts."

"Is that why you took out an insurance policy on Serafina?" April asked.

"How did you know?"

"Just answer the question, please."

"It was . . . business. It's common in business partnerships. Serafina was the head and the heart of her brand. Without her, there is no business. The insurance policy is to protect the surviving partners to make sure that we are not liable in the event of her death."

I'd never seen April interrogate anyone before. She was deceptively calm and nonthreatening. Once Chef Barbier was at ease, she went for the jugular.

"Now that she's dead, your financial troubles are over. Aren't they?"

"You can't possibly think I killed Serafina?"

"Chef Barbier, that will be for the FBI to determine. I'm just trying to confirm where everyone was at the time of the murder. But I would suggest that you don't try to leave until you've given an official statement."

Chef Barbier hung his head. "It is what I deserve. You can't play with fire and expect to walk away unscathed."

CHAPTER 38

"You don't honestly believe he killed Serafina, do you?" I asked as April and I walked down the aisle of the auditorium.

"I don't know. I think he seems like a nice man. He's a great cook. That had to be the best omelet I've ever had, but that doesn't mean he didn't kill her. The insurance policy gave him a solid motive. Plus, Serafina was threatening to cause trouble and *'not go gentle into that good night.'* Whatever that means."

"But he loved her. I don't think he would have killed her."

"He could have easily taken those skewers from your apron. And he does have an alibi. Motive, opportunity, and means. He's got them all."

We pushed our way through the throng of people, but this time, I barely noticed the booths displaying flowers, party favors, food, and wedding dress preservation companies. Instead, I sifted through the information I'd learned so far. None of it made any sense.

"Maddy, watch out."

April's warning came too late as I was nearly run over by the overhead drone from Troy's photography. Before the drone was able to take me out, I was shoved aside.

"Are you okay?" The man I recognized as Troy Lewis looked me over.

The woman who had been operating the drone giggled. A nudge in the ribs forced a half-hearted apology. "Sorry."

Clearly not sorry, she went back to playing with the drone controller.

"You sure you're okay?" Troy asked.

"Yeah, I'm fine," I reassured him.

April scowled. "The FAA doesn't recommend indoor use of drones."

Troy nodded. "I know, but it isn't against the law. However, I think we can take a break for public safety." He walked over to the woman who had been operating the drone and removed the controller. "We're shutting down, but please don't forget to drop your contact information in the jar for a chance to win a free drone for your wedding with Photos by Troy."

The woman wasn't thrilled. In fact, she stormed away without entering the giveaway, but I suspect Troy knew she had no intention of paying for his services.

The crowd around the booth dispersed, and Troy returned to us.

"Sorry about that, Sheriff," Troy said.

"We were hoping to talk to you anyway," April said. "Is there some place we can go, away from all of this?"

Troy swallowed hard but nodded.

We followed him out of one of the doors near his booth. We found ourselves outside. There was an RV with PHOTOS BY TROY painted on the side. Troy opened the door and held it while we entered.

"You're back, I was—"

Lucy, Serafina's assistant, came from the back of the RV and stood frozen in the middle of the aisle as she stared at April and me. "Oh, I didn't realize you weren't alone."

"I don't think we were ever formally introduced." I extended my hand. "I'm Maddy Montgomery, and this is—"

"I know who you are." Lucy passed a frightened-deer-in-headlights glance from me to April before her gaze landed on Troy.

"We needed a quiet place to talk," Troy said. He sidled past April and me to stand near Lucy. "Did you get some rest?"

"Yes. I feel tons better now." She looked at me. "That woman, Miss Hannah, she works for you?"

I nodded.

"She brought me a sandwich and made me lie down. I feel a lot better now. Please thank her for me."

"I will." I looked at Troy. "Can we sit?"

"Yes, sorry about my manners." Troy indicated that April and I could sit on the built-in sofa.

Based on the décor, the Winnebago wasn't new. It wasn't large, either. Standing in the middle of the RV, we could see a bed at the back. There was also a door, which I suspected led to a bathroom. I'd seen shows on television about tiny houses that had less space than this, and I always wondered where people kept their clothes. However, I suppose if you lived in a small space, then you probably had fewer clothes and shoes. The middle was a kitchen, living room, and dining room. The table was full of cameras and equipment. Troy pushed everything aside, and he and Lucy sat at the table.

"You wanted to talk to me?" Troy said.

April pulled out her phone. "May I record this?"

Troy and Lucy both nodded.

After getting everyone's consent to record on camera, she repeated the process of announcing the date, time, and people present. "I wanted to ask where you were when Serafina was murdered." April glanced from Troy to Lucy. "Since you're here, perhaps you could tell us your whereabouts, too."

"We were together," Lucy said.

Neither Lucy nor Troy were great liars. She blushed, and

Troy looked dazed. After a few moments, he adjusted his puzzled expression and replaced it with one of nervous acceptance. He squeezed Lucy's hand.

"I guess we should have talked about that first, so we would have been better prepared." He gave a nervous laugh.

"No, Troy, I—"

"It's okay, we need to tell the truth. Neither of us killed Serafina. We don't have to lie." Troy squeezed her hand and smiled. He looked April in the eyes. "Let's see . . . Serafina announced that the winner of her contest would get a photography package, including drone photographs, from Photos by Troy. But she'd managed to tick off all of the contestants. Plus, Serafina wasn't planning to pay me for the photographs or the use of my drone."

"It wasn't fair," Lucy said. "Serafina was going to make millions from the network for the reality television deal, but Troy was going to get one thousand dollars. That's it. She wasn't planning to cover his travel expenses, the batteries for the drone, nothing. Not to mention the hours he spends editing the footage. Troy's an artist, and he produces a quality product. He deserved to get paid."

Troy patted her hand.

"If that's the case, why did you agree to the one thousand dollars?" April asked.

Troy rubbed the back of his neck.

"He did it for me," Lucy said. "Serafina threatened to fire me unless he agreed to her terms."

"From what I've heard, working for Serafina was barely one step above indentured servitude," I said. "Surely, you could have done better working for someone else."

"Ha! You got that right. I would have been better off working a pole than working for Serafina." She patted her tummy. "But, I couldn't do that in my current condition."

"When is the baby due?"

"April. If it's a girl, that's what we're going to name her, too." Lucy grinned.

"Right, so you're expecting and didn't want to lose your job," April said. "So, what were you doing when she was killed?"

"I was probably bawling my eyes out in the ladies' room." Lucy squirmed.

April turned her attention to Troy. "How did you plan to get the money you felt Serafina owed you?"

Troy hesitated a beat. "I was on the phone with my lawyer, praying he could find a loophole, some way for us to get out of that contract. I don't care about Lucy not working. In fact, I'd rather she did just about anything rather than work for Serafina." He squeezed Lucy's hand and took a breath.

"But?" April prompted.

"But he said there was no way. So, I went to confront Serafina. I know it was stupid, but I thought if I confronted her and told her what I really thought of her, maybe she wouldn't want to work with me." April opened her mouth, but Troy hurried on. "I know, it was dumb."

"I thought you both didn't want to be unemployed with a baby on the way," I said.

"We didn't," Lucy said. "Not at first, but then we realized that no amount of money was worth our peace of mind."

"I already quit my soul-sucking day job and sold everything I had to buy this RV, a drone, and all of the camera equipment, computers, and technology to follow my dream and start my photography business. It'll be tight in here with all of my equipment and a baby, but we'll make it work."

April frowned. "Living on love is fine for two adults, but what about the baby? How were you planning to make that work?"

"Babies don't need much," Lucy whispered.

April frowned. "Just diapers, formula, bottles, clothes, a car seat, crib—"

"Enough." Troy banged his hand on the table. "We'll figure it out."

"I'll need the name of your lawyer so I can verify that you were on the phone with him at the time Serafina was murdered." April stopped her recording. Then, she reached into her pocket and pulled out a notepad. She handed it and a pen to Troy.

Troy pulled out his cell and jotted down a number in the book and then passed the book and the pen back to April. "Now, if you don't mind." He rose to get up.

April took out a business card and scribbled something on the back. She handed the card to Troy as she stood. "If either of you think of anything else that will help us figure out who murdered Serafina, call me."

"Yeah, sure." Troy held open the RV door.

"And the number on the back is an organization in New Bison that helps with all the things that I mentioned a baby needs. Plus, they provide free medical help for pregnant mothers. Tell them Sheriff Johnson sent you, and they'll throw in a free car seat and bassinet." She walked past Troy and out of the RV.

CHAPTER 39

April had long legs, and when she was determined, she knew how to use them. I had to run to catch up to her. "Hey, wait."

She stopped.

"That was nice. How did you know about that organization?"

"I'm the sheriff. I see people like them all the time." She sighed and walked in a circle. "Young people who find themselves over their heads. I shouldn't have been rude. They're good kids. They want to work. They want to take care of themselves and their baby. They just need a helping hand. That's what that organization does. They give people a hand when they need it. I should know. When I first came to New Bison, I needed a hand. I was young. I barely graduated from high school. I was running away from my husband." She stopped pacing and gazed into the past. After a few moments, her lips curled up into a smile. She turned to me. "That's where I met Miss Octavia."

"Wait, what?"

"I came into the bakery looking for a job. She took one look at me and told me to sit down. I thought she was going to have me fill out an application. Instead, she gave me a plate of thumbprint cookies and a slice of pie, and then she went into the kitchen and came back with a peanut butter sandwich and a glass of milk. She said she didn't want to hear one more word from me until I finished eating." April smiled. "I couldn't remember the last meal I had. I'd been surviving on pride and the money I got picking up aluminum cans."

"I had no idea."

"No reason you should. After I ate, she said she couldn't hire anyone unless she knew their family. She wanted to know who 'my people' were. She asked me a million questions. I didn't plan to tell her about CJ, but I did. I ended up telling her everything. She listened. Then she told me to go upstairs to take a shower and get a good night's sleep. Baby Cakes opened early. I needed to be ready to bake at five in the morning, and I better not be late." April chuckled. "I worked in the bakery for six months, living upstairs in that tiny apartment. Miss Octavia took me to Helping Hands after work. They helped me with everything from my résumé to interview clothes."

"Helping Hands . . . that's the organization the church sponsors, isn't it?'

April nodded. "I found out later that Miss Octavia, Miss Hannah, and Sister Sylvia saw a need in the community and went to the pastor with a plan, but they didn't want it run by the church because, according to Miss Octavia, 'They may have to do things to help people that didn't align with the church's doctrine.' So, the church is one of the sponsors, but they don't run it."

"I had no idea."

"Anyway, I learned that their goal is to give a hand to folks who need it. Not a handout. Not charity. Not a government or church program. But, a hand. They gave me one when I needed it. Hopefully, Troy and Lucy will take advantage of it and get a hand to help with their little one."

I reached over and pulled April into a hug. When we separated, we both needed a tissue.

"I sure hope neither of them murdered Serafina," I said. "I don't suppose Helping Hands would cover legal fees for a murder trial."

"I'm sure they would find a lawyer if they needed to, but I don't think they'll need it."

"You don't think either one of them killed Serafina?"

"I could be wrong, but I don't think so." She looked at me. "Do you?"

"No. I don't. At least, I hope not."

April's cell rang just as we were reentering the auditorium. She stepped aside to take the call.

I glanced around and caught a glimpse of Serafina's husband, Patrick Dixon. I hurried over to him. "Mr. Dixon, my name's Maddy Montgomery, I—"

Patrick's cell rang, and he held up a finger and answered it.

"Pilar, yes. You heard?" He paused and listened. Patrick Dixon turned to me. "I have to take this call."

I nodded my understanding. "I'll wait."

Based on the look on his face, that was not the reply he expected or wanted. He frowned and turned so his back was to me.

"*Sí, es verdad. Ella esta muerta. Por favor cuéntame las buenas noticias. Yo heredo, ¿verdad? Esto resuelve todos mis problemas financieros, ¿verdad?*" He paused to listen. Then he glanced over his shoulder to confirm I was still there.

I smiled.

"*Tengo que irme. Te llamaré después. Adiós mi amor.*"

Mi amor? My love? Really?

He disconnected, put his phone in his pocket, and then turned around to me. "Now, how may I help you?"

"My name is—"

"I don't need your name. What do you want?"

"I wanted to give you my condolences on the death of your wife. I only met Serafina face-to-face yesterday, but I have followed and admired her work for quite some time. She was a trailblazer and extremely creative."

"Thank you. Serafina would have appreciated hearing that. We worked hard to develop her business and to make her way... yeah, thanks." He turned to go.

I scrambled to figure out what to say next, but my brain went blank. Fortunately, I didn't have to.

"Patrick Dixon?" April walked up and flashed her shield. "Can I have a word with you?"

He froze.

Something flashed across his face so quickly I couldn't identify it. *Was that fear?*

Whatever emotion it was, it was gone so quickly I couldn't be sure. "Actually, Detective, I was just about to—"

"Sheriff. Not detective. Sheriff Johnson. This will only take a few minutes." April held out her arm. When Patrick Dixon hesitated, she added, "We can find a quiet place to talk here or we can talk down at the station. Whichever is more convenient."

Patrick Dixon's nostrils flared. But he simply nodded and then followed April down the hall to a door that was labeled OFFICE.

The room held a desk, an office chair, and two guest chairs. There wasn't room for anything else.

"The casino had this room cleared out for us to use for questioning." April took the position of authority behind the desk and sat, leaving the two guest chairs for Patrick Dixon and me.

Patrick sat and then narrowed his gaze as he looked at me. "Excuse me, but why are you here?"

Before I could come up with a reply, April chimed in. "Whenever we have to interview someone, we prefer to have a witness. Given the size of this facility, we're a bit short-staffed. However, if you would prefer an official witness, I can pull one of the NBPD or Tribal Police from their other duties. It may take a few minutes." April rose as though she were ready to leave.

"No. That's fine. I just wondered. That's all. This is fine."

"Are you sure?" April waited a beat. When Dixon nodded, she returned to her seat and pulled out her phone and a notebook. "Do you mind if I record this?"

Patrick Dixon grunted his approval.

April turned her phone on and started the video. She announced her name and then scanned the room and gave my name and that of Patrick Dixon. "Mr. Dixon, do you consent to having this statement recorded?" She pointed the camera at him.

"Yes."

April propped the phone on the desk so that the camera pointed toward Patrick Dixon and me. Then, she gave the date and time. "Now, Mr. Dixon, can you please tell me where you were when your wife was murdered."

"Where was I? Well, I don't know exactly, but after I talked to the contestants and told them what their prizes would be, I got stopped by the security guards Serafina fired. They wanted to get paid. Then, I talked to the lighting guy from the last wedding Serafina planned. He claimed he never got paid, and he threatened to sue if he didn't get paid within the next three business days. Oh, and then I got a call from my lawyer. I was doing what I always do."

"And what was that?" April asked.

"Cleaning up the messes that Serafina left." He closed his eyes for several moments and took in some deep breaths. Then he opened his eyes. "Look, I'm sorry, Sheriff, but Serafina was a brilliant and talented wedding planner. She was *not* a businessperson. She made promises and entered into contracts with no idea how business really worked."

"But you do?"

He pulled his shirt cuffs down, which drew attention to his appearance. Something about Patrick Dixon was different from when I'd seen him earlier, but I couldn't place my finger on it.

"I knew more than my wife did about business. In fact, it's only because of me that she was able to be the success that she became. She was the face that everyone saw in front of the camera, but I worked behind the scenes, making sure that everything ran smoothly and all the *i*'s were dotted and the *t*'s crossed."

"But they weren't."

"What?"

"The *i*'s weren't dotted, and the *t*'s weren't crossed. Isn't that why Serafina's business dealings were in such a mess? Isn't that why people weren't paid?"

I was sitting next to Patrick Dixon, so I saw the vein on the side of his face vibrate. He gripped the arms of his chair. He reminded me of Clark Kent, who was the dapper reporter one minute and Superman the next when he removed the suit and his glasses and—

I snapped my fingers. "That's it."

Patrick Dixon stared at me. "What's it?"

"I've been trying to remember what's different about you. It just dawned on me. Earlier today, you were wearing glasses. Red glasses."

"So?"

"Where are your glasses?"

"I decided to wear my contacts instead."

"Why?"

He glared at me and then turned to April. "Do I have to put up with this?"

"No, you do not. Like I said, you're more than welcome to

come down to the police station with me and answer questions there. Or, if you would prefer to have a lawyer present, you can certainly call one. If you are unable to afford an attorney, the court will appoint one for you. Again, we would have to go down to the station for that."

He rose. "I want an attorney."

"Certainly. I'm expecting the FBI shortly. I'll notify them of your decision and have them meet us at the NBPD so we can continue getting your statement as soon as your lawyer and the FBI arrive." April picked up her phone.

"The FBI? Why on earth?"

"It's the location. This casino is on Native American soil. We're still getting clarification of jurisdiction."

Patrick Dixon returned to his seat. "Okay, maybe I over-reacted. I'd rather just give my statement to you and be done with this. I don't have anything to hide."

April stopped texting and returned her phone to the desk. "It's completely up to you."

I was impressed at how cool, calm, and collected April was.

"I believe the question was why you switched from your glasses to your contact lenses," April said.

"It's no big deal. I dropped my glasses and broke them. That's all."

"When and where did you break them?"

"I don't remember exactly. It must have been while I was running around trying to put out Serafina's fires. Does it matter?"

April glanced at me, but I shrugged. It probably wasn't important. Not as important as the fact that Patrick Dixon was cheating on the woman he had been cheating on his wife with.

"Mr. Dixon, are you sure you don't want to call your lawyer?" I asked.

"I don't think that will be necessary. As I mentioned, I just overreacted."

"It's just when I was talking to Dr. Alliyah Howard earlier,

I recommended that she contact a lawyer before talking to law enforcement. Dr. Howard didn't know an attorney, but it turns out one of our friends, Tyler Lawrence, is an attorney. I had no idea." I was rambling, but I couldn't stop myself.

Patrick Dixon looked at me as though he thought I'd just stepped off a spaceship from another planet. He smirked and then turned his attention to April. "Is there anything else?"

Before April could respond, I jumped in. "Amazing that I've known Tyler all this time and had no idea he was an attorney. Seems like there are several attorneys around. Sheriff Johnson and I were talking to Chef Barbier, and we learned that he was also an attorney." I took a breath.

Patrick Dixon must have caught on to what I was doing because he leaned back in his seat and crossed his leg over his knee. "Aw, Chef Barbier. Now I see where you're going with this." He chuckled. "You want to know if I knew that my wife was having an affair with Chef Yves-René Barbier. Well, the answer is yes. I knew all about it. In fact, that's the main reason that I contacted a lawyer." He sat up and replaced his casual façade with a serious, deeply concerned one. "I found out about Serafina and Chef Barbier, and I realized that our marriage was over."

"Did you confront her with this knowledge?" April asked.

"I did. She told me it was over, and I believed her. At first." He pinched the bridge of his nose.

"When was that?"

"About six months ago. Maybe longer. I don't know exactly."

"And you were okay with your wife having an affair with another man?"

"Of course not. I was furious." He must have realized how that came across, so he backpedaled. "Not furious enough to murder her. I was angry. I was hurt. And . . . I admit that I was petty."

"Petty how?" I asked.

"I wanted to get back at Serafina. Give her a taste of her own medicine. That's when I had a brief affair with another woman. It wasn't serious. Just a fling. A one-night stand. At least, that's what I planned. But, the lady took it a bit more seriously."

"Who was she?" April asked.

"I'd rather not say unless it's absolutely necessary."

"It is necessary."

"Dr. Alliyah Howard."

CHAPTER 40

Patrick Dixon maintained that his relationship with Alliyah Howard was purely superficial and temporary. At least, from his standpoint. He claimed that she knew from day one that he was married, but that Alliyah took things more seriously. She refused to accept that he wasn't in love with her and pursued him like Glenn Close in *Fatal Attraction*.

I was too stunned to ask questions and sat listening to him toss Alliyah Howard under the proverbial bus in stunned silence with my mouth open. I only snapped out of my stupor when he got up to leave and headed for the door.

"If there's anything else, we'll be in touch," April said.

Patrick Dixon grasped the doorknob and pulled it open.

"Fue un placer hablar con usted y darle el más sentido pésame por la muerte de su esposa. No dude en comunicarse con nosotros si hay algo que pueda hacer para ayudarlo en su momento de duelo."

The only signs that he understood me came from the fact that he paled, which isn't easy for a Black man. And the vein on the side of his head beat a lot faster. He opened the door and walked out.

CHAPTER 41

"What was that all about?" April stopped the recording.

"Nothing. I expressed my condolences and suggested he reach out if he needed anything."

April raised a brow. "That's it?"

"That's it."

"Then why do it in Spanish?" She leaned back in her chair and watched me.

I told her about the conversation I'd overheard him make earlier, and when he thought he was safe, he started talking to his lawyer, Pilar, in Spanish. "Weird, that people think no one else speaks another language."

"Most people may know how to count in another language," April said. "Or they learn a few phrases to help them order in restaurants or get a taxi if they're visiting another country. Sadly, few Americans can speak anything other than English fluently. The number drops exponentially when you count the people who are fluent in seven other languages."

"Not on a military base. There are people of all colors and speaking lots of different languages."

April tapped her fingers on the desk. "So, Patrick Dixon believes his financial problems will be solved now that Serafina is dead and he inherits?"

"That's what he said to Pilar. Do you think that's true? I mean, if Chef Barbier took out an insurance policy on her, what happens to her money?"

"Good question." April picked up her phone and swiped until she came to the number she was looking for.

She asked for information on Serafina's financial state and her will. "Who gets her money?"

Whoever she was talking to must have responded because she took notes. "Um, okay. What does that mean?" She listened. "Anything else?" When she was done, she thanked someone named Roger and ended the call.

I waited.

"The Feds have all the best databases," she said, scribbling. "Serafina wasn't as dumb or naïve about financial matters as her husband would have us believe. According to my sources, she set up a trust. All of her assets were placed in an irrevocable trust. Her will leaves her spouse the clothes on his back and five hundred thousand dollars, provided at the time of her death he has paid back the money she invested in his schooling for naturopathic medicine, fashion design school, acupuncture, and physical training. Otherwise, he gets nothing."

"Wow. That's harsh, but does she even have anything to give? I mean, it sounds like her finances were in horrible shape."

April scanned her notes. "My source tells me that the trust is in good shape."

"If she didn't leave her money to her husband, then who gets it? Who benefits?"

"Luke Overton."

It took me a couple of minutes to put two and two together. "Luke? Her assistant?"

"Yep."

"But why? According to Jessica Barlow, Luke was trying to get away from Serafina. She barely paid him a fraction of what he was worth. He's been working three jobs to make ends meet, and he was trying to get away from Serafina to make documentaries, but she wouldn't let him go. This doesn't make any sense. Why would she leave her money to Luke? And how much are we talking about?"

"Once her debts are paid, he'll probably get somewhere around two million, but that was a rough guess."

"But I thought she was facing bankruptcy?" I said.

"Some people use bankruptcy as a way to avoid paying creditors." April frowned. "My late husband was like that. CJ used every loophole his highly paid lawyers and financial advisors could find to avoid paying taxes, gain a financial advantage, or manipulate the system. Serafina was close to filing bankruptcy, but she was far from destitute. Just like CJ, she had layers of security, including a trust that I'd guess her husband had no idea existed."

It took a few beats for me to realize my mouth was open. I closed it. Then opened it again. "But she was blackmailing Luke. You don't blackmail people you like. You don't underpay people and treat them like scum and then turn around and leave them two million dollars."

"Serafina did. And because it was in trust, Luke doesn't even have to pay taxes. Sweet deal."

"But why? I don't believe she had a change of heart and suddenly realized that she was acting like Ebenezer Scrooge and did a complete one-eighty." I paced. "Did Luke know that he was going to inherit?"

"I don't know if he knew, but I intend to find out." April rose. "Let's go talk to Mr. Overton. Maybe he can make it make sense."

CHAPTER 42

I doubted that anyone could make this make sense. My brain felt like it was stuck in mud, and I was trying to pull it out.

April started out of the room but stopped so suddenly, I bumped into her back. "This auditorium is huge." She turned around and returned to her seat, pulled out her cell, and dialed.

"Hi, Sheriff." Even without the phone being on speaker, the room was so small that I couldn't help but hear both sides of the conversation.

"Al, can you find Luke Overton and bring him to the room at the back of the greenroom, please?"

"Yes, ma'am. He's right here. We'll be there in two minutes."

Officer Al Norris was a round, pudgy member of the New Bison police who reminded me of the Pillsbury Doughboy.

A few minutes later, he knocked on the open door. "You wanted to see Luke Overton?"

"Yes, thank you," April said.

Luke Overton's curly head popped around the door and came inside.

Officer Norris turned to leave but stopped when April said,

"Al, can you check on the glass that I gave Officer Thomas to have analyzed, please?"

Al Norris nodded and then stepped out of the small office, closing the door behind him.

Luke Overton stood behind the guest chair. "You wanted to see me?"

April extended her arm for him to sit. "Yes, I need to get your statement, and I have a few questions."

She went through her spiel to gain permission for the recording and then set up her phone. "Now, can you tell me where you were when Serafina was murdered?"

Listening to Luke Overton's statement, I felt like I was watching the *Titanic* head straight for the iceberg. I bit the inside of my cheek to keep myself from yelling out, *Iceberg. Iceberg. Danger. Are you crazy? Don't you know better than to lie to law enforcement? What are you thinking? Don't you see that iceberg ahead?*

"Talking to Lucy. We were out in the main auditorium. Maybe if we had been there with Serafina we might have been able to save her." Luke hung his head.

Not!

"Did you like your job?"

"Yes, of course. I was working with one of the hottest wedding planners in the country. What's not to like? Serafina was tough, but lots of geniuses are."

Liar!

"Can you think of anyone who would want to kill Serafina?" April tapped her pen on the desk.

"No. Everyone loved her."

Ugh!

"So, you weren't planning to leave?"

"No."

Watching someone dig a hole for themselves was painful. April paused for several moments, then she tossed Luke a life preserver.

"Mr. Overton, we have a witness who overheard you and Serafina arguing. You were overheard saying that you wanted to leave to go and make a documentary."

Catch it. This is your chance to tell the truth.

He chuckled. "We weren't arguing. We were talking. We were both passionate about our art, and sometimes that passion could sound like we didn't get along and that we were angry with each other, when in actuality, nothing could be further from the truth."

Iceberg!

"Mr. Overton, are you familiar with Serafina's will?"

Cue the music from Jaws, *right before the shark attacked.*

"Her will?" Luke asked with genuine surprise. "Why would I know anything about her will?"

"So, you had no idea that Serafina named you as her beneficiary?" April watched Luke.

Bingo!

"Me? You must have me confused with someone else. There's no way Serafina made me her beneficiary." Luke stood and rubbed his neck. "You're pulling my leg, right?"

"No, I'm not." April adjusted the phone so that it would catch Luke while he paced in the small office.

"That can't be. There's no way. Why? Why would she do that?"

"I was hoping you could tell me the answer to that."

"Me? I don't know. That's crazy. It must be some kind of mistake. There's no way Serafina would leave me her money. I mean, why? We weren't even close. We weren't—"

April waited for him to finish, but his eyes darted from one side of the room to the other. He looked like a rabbit caught in a trap. I almost felt sorry for him.

"Luke, why don't you tell us the truth," I suggested.

"It'll be easier if you come clean now," April said.

Luke was speechless.

"We know you hated working for Serafina. She paid you a

pittance. You wanted to leave to make your film. It was a great opportunity for you. But she wouldn't let you go. In fact, she blackmailed you into staying."

Any color left in Luke's face drained, and he flopped down into the chair.

April wasn't finished. She circled him like Jaws and went in for the kill. "Serafina threatened to tell everyone about your criminal past. You were afraid it would get you blackballed and end any chance you had of pursuing your dream. You found out about her will. With Serafina gone, you got money, and you got your freedom. So, you saw your chance. You took the skewers from Maddy's apron and you—"

"No. No. No." Luke banged his fist on the desk.

April rose and had her gun in her hand. "Mr. Overton, I suggest you calm down and sit."

Stunned, I stared from April to Luke Overton.

He deflated like a balloon. "I'm sorry. I didn't mean. Oh God. This can't be happening. I just wanted to be free."

"Would you like to confess?" April returned her gun to its holster and sat.

Luke sat up. "Confess?"

"If you're going to confess to killing Serafina, I need to advise you of your rights," April said. "You have the right to remain silent. You have the right to an attorney. If you can't afford one, an attorney will be appointed for you. Anything you say can and will be used against you in a court of law. Do you understand these rights?"

Dazed, Luke Overton stared at April with his mouth open. "I didn't kill Serafina."

"Mr. Overton, do you understand your rights?"

He nodded.

"I need you to say *yes* or *no*," April said.

"Yes. I understand my rights. But *no*. I did not kill Serafina."

CHAPTER 43

"Luke, tell us the truth. What happened?" I said.

Luke swallowed hard. "Can I get some water?"

The casino management had left several small bottles of water on the side of the desk. April handed Luke one of the bottles and waited.

He twisted the cap off. His hands were shaking so badly, he spilled water down the front of his shirt and on the top of the desk. "Sorry." He used his sleeve to wipe the water from the desk.

"No worries," April said. "Take your time and tell us what happened."

Luke took several breaths, and his right leg jiggled. "Serafina was horrible. She was a monster, and I hated working for her. She was a bully, and she took credit for other people's ideas."

"Serafina didn't plan the weddings she did?" I asked.

April rolled her eyes but didn't interrupt.

"Ha. Most of her ideas came from Lucy. Lucy was brilliant. She's the one who came up with all of the elaborate plans that everyone loved. But Lucy was just a mouse. She let Serafina take the credit for her designs. Then, she went and got herself knocked up." He shrugged. "Anyway, Serafina found out that I did time. She didn't say one word until I wanted to leave. Then, she threatened to ruin me if I tried to leave. We had a huge argument at the Carson Law Inn." He closed his eyes. "I guess someone must have heard us."

Neither April nor I confirmed or denied it.

After a few moments, he continued. "Serafina wanted that reality television spot so badly, there was nothing she wouldn't do." He turned to me. "She's the one that had me get the photos of your wedding dress from your phone that day at the bakery."

The lightbulb went on. "That's what you did when you asked to use my phone. You downloaded my photos."

"Serafina was fine with using my criminal skills as long as it was benefiting her." Luke took a sip of water, and his hands weren't shaking as much this time. "Criminal skills? I'm not even a good criminal."

"What did you do?" I asked.

"I robbed a bank. I didn't even have a gun. I just stuck my finger in my pocket and pointed. Then, I dropped the money running from the police. I never even got the money that cost me my freedom and dignity. Serafina was more of a criminal than me. She was definitely tougher." He sipped his water. "She wanted to embarrass you and the other brides. She wanted to be like the Howard Stern of wedding planning. No studios would give her a show if she was just a nice person. She wanted the shock value." He snorted. "It might have worked, too. If she had lived." He bowed his head.

"What happened?" April asked.

"Nothing. I don't know where I was when Serafina was murdered, but I know where I wasn't. I wasn't the one sticking those wood things in her neck." He shuddered. "I was probably running interference between Serafina and the million people that she had ticked off today. God, was it just today? It feels like a million years have passed."

"Why did Serafina make you her beneficiary?"

"I have no idea. If she had a conscience, I would have said it was because she felt bad for being such a witch, but she didn't."

April asked a lot of questions, but she got the same answer no matter how she came at it. Luke didn't kill Serafina. He didn't have any idea who did. And he had no idea why Serafina made him her beneficiary.

After what felt like hours, April turned off her recording.

"Luke, you shouldn't have lied to the police. That isn't going to look good."

Luke hung his head.

"I may have additional questions. You'll need to make yourself available to answer them. And I suggest you talk to a lawyer." She rose.

Luke stared up at April, stunned. "You're not arresting me?"

"No. Not right now, but if you try to leave town, I will arrest you."

Luke stood. "So I can go?"

"Yes, but don't leave New Bison."

Hope flashed across his face. He rushed to the door and wrenched it open.

"Luke."

He turned.

"Stay out of trouble."

"You don't need to worry about me. I'm not even going to jaywalk." Luke grinned.

"Do you believe him?" I asked April after he was gone.

She sat. "Yeah, I do. If he killed her, he would have made sure to have a better alibi. Plus, he's got to be one of the worst liars I've heard in a while."

"I believe him, too. I don't think he killed her. Although, I still don't know why she left him everything."

My phone rang. Michael's face popped up on the screen. "We meeting?"

I looked at the time. "Absolutely. I'm with April. We'll be right there."

CHAPTER 44

April was better at directions than me, so she navigated us to the relaxation room. My brain rolled around all of the details like a cement mixer. *Why did Serafina make Luke her beneficiary? Was Patrick Dixon cheating on the woman he had cheated on his wife with? Geez! Did Lucy get tired of taking a back seat to Serafina? Had she or Troy killed Serafina? If so, were they in it together?*

Outside the room, April got a call.

"I need to take this." April stepped away from the door so I could enter.

Inside, the relaxation room was crowded. Hannah, Leroy, Fiona, Candy, Tyler, Carson Law, Jessica Barlow, and Michael crowded into the room. Taking up more than his fair share of space was Baby.

"Baby." I rushed to him and dropped to my knees.

He lifted his head and gave my face a lick. Then, he placed his head in my lap.

That's when I noticed the scratches on his muzzle. I glanced up at Michael. "Is he okay? What's wrong with him? I thought you were taking him home to rest? What happened?"

He held up his hands. "Hang on. I did take him home. But he went crazy. He beat his head against the bedroom door and tried to eat his way through."

I glanced down at Baby. "He's only behaved that way when he knew I was in danger and needed to get to me."

"I was afraid he would injure himself if I left him." Michael squatted down and scratched Baby's ear.

"Couldn't you have drugged him?" Candy asked.

"He is drugged," Michael said. "He's a big boy, and I gave him a large dose, but he's fighting it. Whenever he started to drift off, he would bite at his feet." Michael held up one of Baby's legs for me to see. Baby had gnawed on his leg and there was an area that he called a hot spot.

"Yikes."

"I could give him a larger dose. In fact, I brought it with me just in case." He patted his pocket. "I wanted to discuss it with you first."

"Is it dangerous?"

"No, but given the amount he's already had, I worry that he may have difficulty performing." Michael smiled.

"What do you mean?"

"He's got a date tomorrow with Grand Champion Windstone's Chyna, Ninth Wonder of the World."

I smacked my head. "OMG. I completely forgot about that."

"Chyna's in heat, and I didn't want Baby to miss his time with the lovely mastiff. Plus, I know you wanted the stud fees. I thought it might be better to just let him stay here."

"Poor Baby." I rubbed his head. "I don't want him upset. Thank you." I kissed Michael.

"All right, round one to you, boy." He gave Baby a scratch but also took the opportunity to look in his eyes. "But, at some point we're going to need to talk because she's my girl. You know that, right?"

Baby gave a short snort.

"All right, enough fawning over Baby," Miss Hannah said. "Let's get this show on the road so he can rest and I can get home to my apples."

I took out my phone and snapped a quick picture of Baby and uploaded it to social media.

#MyBabyLovesMe #BabyOnTheMend #BestVetEver #Ready 4Love

I put away my phone. I had a lot to share with the group, so I asked if anyone minded if I went first.

No one did.

I started with our conversation with Chef Barbier and went in order. When I got to the part about Trooper Bob, Fiona gasped.

"Poor Robbie. Do you know how he's doing?"

April walked in just as Fiona asked the question. "I just got off the phone with Dr. Howard. Trooper Bob suffered a mild heart attack. Thankfully, he got good medical care." She glanced at Michael. "All indications are that he's going to be fine."

There was a sigh of relief.

"That man gets under my skin, but I sure don't wish sickness on him," Miss Hannah said.

"They're going keep him overnight for observation. He should be home tomorrow," April said.

"He should take it easy," Michael said. "With diet, exercise, and reduced stress, he should be as good as new in no time."

I forgot that everyone wasn't aware of what happened to Baby. I shared how he cut his pad on a shard of glass found at the crime scene. I elaborated on how Michael not only saved Trooper Bob, but thanks to him, Baby is on the mend. I explained that I sat in on April's interviews with Chef Barbier, Lucy, Troy, and Patrick.

"Wow, that's a lot," Tyler said, typing frantically. "I can barely keep up. Maybe I should start recording these meetings like April does."

Leroy raised his hand. "I talked to some of Chef Barbier's assistants. They said he was in the kitchen spewing out orders and throwing a tantrum because Serafina ruined his ice sculpture. No one remembers him leaving the kitchen."

"We fed Lucy and made her go lie down in that camper," Fiona said. "I'm afraid we didn't get much more out of her than you did."

"I'm going to make some vegetable soup when I get home," Miss Hannah said. "Michael, you can bring it to her. A woman in her condition needs to eat more fruits and vegetables."

"Yes, ma'am."

I was surprised that he agreed so quickly. No eye rolls. No snarky comments or side looks. I turned to give him a full frontal stare.

When the heat got too much, he caved. "What? I was supposed to talk to Troy, but I got distracted with Trooper Bob and Baby. Thankfully, you and April talked to him. Taking soup to Lucy is the least I can do."

I squeezed his hand.

Carson Law raised her hand. "I know you already talked to Patrick Dixon, but Jessica and I also talked to him."

We turned our attention to Carson Law and Jessica Barlow.

"He's a low-life rat," Jessica Barlow said.

"I have to admit that I didn't like him very much either." Carson Law pursed her lips and adjusted her hat. "He's what my papa would have called a snake-oil salesman."

"That bad?" Miss Hannah tsked.

"My grandmother would have called him a mountebank," Fiona said.

"Sounds fancy," Candy said. "What is it?"

"A charlatan," Tyler said. "Fraud. Scammer."

"Mountebank," Candy said, rolling the term around on her tongue. "I think that sounds nicer than a scammer."

"When Mrs. Law introduced herself, he fell over himself trying to impress her," Jessica Barlow said.

"Now, Jessica, he wasn't that bad." Carson patted Jessica's hand.

"What about his designs?" I asked.

Carson Law took a deep breath and then searched for the right words. "He's not bad, and in my opinion, men's formal wear is hard. You don't have a lot of options. There are pants, shirts, and jackets. Some of the more avant-garde designers on the cutting edge are taking chances, which is what it takes to really stand out. But he isn't."

"So, he's not talented?" Candy asked.

"It's not that. It's just that his designs aren't different enough. They don't stand out from everything else that's in the market. As a new designer, he needs something unique. I tried to tell him that, in a nice way. I don't think he heard me."

"He was too busy fawning over you," Jessica said. "He drooled more than Baby."

"He was a bit over-the-top. He kissed my hand."

"And held on to it so long, I was two seconds away from smacking him. His wife isn't even cold yet, and he was flirting with Mrs. Law."

"Did he actually flirt with her?" I asked.

Jessica Barlow leaned forward. "He offered to show her his sketches. And, he was not talking about clothes."

Carson Law nodded. "It did seem in poor taste."

"Geez!" Candy said. "He was cheating on his wife with Dr. Howard. Cheating on Dr. Howard with his lawyer, Pilar. And trying to cheat on Pilar with Mrs. Law. How in the world does he keep it all straight?"

"Keep what straight?"

We were so engrossed in the conversation that we never noticed when Dr. Howard entered.

CHAPTER 45

Silence fell like a wet blanket over the top of us.

Dr. Howard had aged twenty years from the last time I saw her.

Michael, Leroy, and Tyler all rose and offered her their seats. She chose Michael's, which was closest.

Michael hovered nearby. "Are you okay? You look exhausted."

"I'm fine. What were you—"

"How's Trooper Bob?" I hoped to distract Dr. Howard from the previous conversation.

"He's going to be okay. If he takes care of himself, he'll be fine. The heart attack wasn't bad, but it should be a wake-up call. What's going on?"

"I was just about to share what April and I learned from talking to Luke Overton." I glanced at April, who nodded her approval. I shared everything we'd learned from our conversation.

Tyler whistled. "Things don't look good for that young

man. He's got motive, opportunity, and means. I can't imagine the police will delay in bringing him in for questioning."

All eyes moved to April.

"The district attorney says we have enough to pick him up and hold him for Serafina's murder," she said.

"Then why am I still here instead of home making soup and washing apples?" Miss Hannah looked at April. "And why do you look like you're about to get a root canal?"

"It sounds like a solid case," Tyler said. "Men have been convicted on a lot less."

"I don't think he did it," April said. "I don't believe Luke Overton killed Serafina. And unless we come up with someone else before the FBI arrives, then I'm going to be forced to arrest him. He'll be tried for Serafina's murder and probably convicted."

CHAPTER 46

The silence lasted for two seconds before it exploded. The chaos that followed was overwhelming.

April held up her hands to stop the barrage of questions, opinions, and outrage. "Listen, I'm not saying that an innocent person is going to jail. For all I know, Luke Overton's hands aren't squeaky clean. But there is enough evidence to arrest him. He argued with Serafina. He wanted to leave, and she was preventing him from pursuing his dream. She wasn't paying him. Maybe he felt like he had no other choice. Maybe he knew about the trust. With Serafina's death, he went from working three jobs to make ends meet to never having to work a day in his life." She paused. "I'm not saying he killed her. I'm not saying he didn't. That's not for me to determine. My job is to follow the law. It's up to the court to try the case."

"But you don't believe he's the killer," I said.

She paused. "I don't, but that's not enough. We need proof."

"Then let's find it," Miss Hannah said.

April's phone pinged as she got a text message. "The lab analyzed the shard of glass that Baby cut his foot on. It was prescription glass that's used in eyeglasses."

"Patrick Dixon mentioned that he broke his glasses," Michael said. "This proves he was telling the truth. At least about this." He shot a sideways glance in Alliyah's direction, but she was dazed.

April got a text and glanced at the phone. "The FBI's here. I have to go." She stood and walked toward the door. "I suggest you work fast."

After April left, we talked for a few minutes. Candy decided to talk to the people with booths closest to the main stage in the hopes that someone saw something that would help.

Miss Hannah looked tired. She'd done a lot of work, and I was worried about her.

"Miss Hannah, I hate to bring this up, but I'm starving. Would you and Fiona mind picking up some food for everyone? I was thinking an order of fried chicken from Love's Soul Food Kitchen with all of the fixings would help us to keep our energy up. I can place an order if you two wouldn't mind . . ."

Miss Hannah looked momentarily as though she would balk at the idea of skipping out on the investigation. However, food was her way of showing how much she cared.

"I don't suppose that would be a problem," Miss Hannah said reluctantly. "I'm a little hungry myself, and the prices of the food in the casino is a crime. Do you know they charged ten dollars for a grilled cheese sandwich? No sides. Just bread and cheese."

I breathed a sigh of relief and pulled out my phone.

"I can just take a look and see what Dru Ann has fresh," Miss Hannah said. She looked down her nose and stared at me. "That is if you trust me to choose."

"Of course I trust you. Don't be silly." I put my phone in my pocket.

"See if she has any of that red velvet cake," Michael said.

"I love her cobbler," Leroy said.

"Well, Maddy don't like cobbler, so I'm not getting that. Although, the cobbler is delicious."

"Please, get whatever you want." I started to look for my credit card, but Michael was quicker than me and handed his card to his grandmother. "With any luck, we'll be done by the time you get the food."

"Then, we'll just go to Maddy's house," Miss Hannah said.

Miss Hannah and Fiona got up and headed for the door. They stopped long enough to pet Baby and then hurried out.

"Do you really think we'll be done soon?" Leroy asked.

"Yep. Trooper Bob is in the hospital. The expo ends in less than one hour. Now that the FBI is here, things will move quickly. So, I think we'll be leaving soon. Can you start taking down our booth?"

Leroy saluted. "Absolutely."

I turned to Tyler. "Could you maybe talk to Luke?"

"I can't represent him if I'm representing Alliyah, but I can advise him to keep his mouth shut until he can get a lawyer, and I can recommend a good lawyer who can help him pro bono."

"Thank you."

"What do you want us to do?" Jessica Barlow asked.

"I don't think the first couple that Serafina humiliated will be marching down the aisle anytime soon. However, the last couple might. Could you see if they might be interested in a Carson Law original veil?" I held up my hands as though in prayer. "I'll pay for it."

"Pish posh." Carson Law waved away the idea of money. "I have a ton of lovely hats that I would be pleased to modify free of charge. I love a wedding." She smiled broadly. "Weddings always make me feel hopeful for the future."

Jessica Barlow rolled her eyes, but she helped Mrs. Law up and accompanied her out of the room.

Alliyah sat in a chair with her head down.

"Alliyah?" I said.

"What aren't you telling me?" she asked.

I looked to Michael, who gave a brief nod.

"It looks like Patrick Dixon may have been having an affair with a woman named Pi—"

"Pilar Torres."

"You knew?"

"I suspected there was something more going on between the two of them, but Patrick denied it." She put her head in her hands. "I can't believe I was so stupid."

I reached over and hugged her. It was the most contact that I'd had with my fiancé's ex-girlfriend, and it was awkward. At first. After a few moments, I felt her shoulders relax. Then she shook as she sobbed on my shoulder.

Michael quietly left.

After a while, the tears slowed. Eventually, what started as a flood, transitioned into a trickle.

That's when Baby went to work. He scootched over and placed his head in her lap.

Alliyah turned her head to look at him. She extended a hand and scratched his ear.

Baby licked her hand while she scratched.

A few moments later, she sat up.

Baby stood on his back legs and placed his paws around her neck.

"What a good boy. You knew I needed a hug, didn't you."

Baby licked her face.

I handed her several tissues from a box on the coffee table and took several for myself. I didn't even realize I'd been crying, too. "I must look like a hot mess. This is the second time I've cried today."

Alliyah glanced at me. "You always look beautiful, even when you cry."

"Liar, but thank you."

"Baby is such a good boy. I should have known Patrick wasn't a nice man when I found out he didn't have any pets."

I chuckled. "Dogs are a good judge of character, at least

Baby is, but not everyone can have a pet. I didn't have one until I moved here."

"Really? You're so good with him. I assumed you always had dogs."

"Never. It was hard with my dad in the Navy. We traveled abroad a lot, and some countries have tons of restrictions. Until recently, dogs had to be quarantined when traveling to the U.K."

"I never traveled abroad."

"Why not?"

Allyah squirmed for a few moments. "I never had the money."

"Oh, I assumed . . ."

"I grew up on the South Side of Chicago in Altgeld Gardens. Right in the projects."

"I had no idea."

"I've worked hard to make sure that nobody would know. I was smart, and I worked my butt off to get away, to make something of myself. I took out loans and got scholarships to pay for college. Then, I went to veterinary school and medical school. Any kind of school, I was all about learning as much as I could." She chuckled. "Plus, when you're in school, you don't have to pay back your school loans."

"Is that why you're a veterinarian, a canine ophthalmologist, and a medical doctor?"

Alliyah nodded.

"And here I just thought you were an overachiever."

She glanced at me and then chuckled.

Michael must have been standing outside, because when he heard us laughing, he poked his head in the room.

"It's safe to enter. Maddy told me what a fool I've made of myself."

"I'm sorry, Alliyah," Michael said.

"It's fine. I should never have trusted that fashion designer, naturopath, acupuncture specialist, and jazz singer." Alliyah stood. "I'm going to go home and take a long soak." She walked to the door. "Thank you, Maddy."

"You're welcome."

She walked out, leaving Michael, Baby, and me alone. "Well, Squid?"

"I'm exhausted."

"Are we done?"

"Almost. There's just one more thing. I'm sure the Tribal Police are already on top of this, but I was hoping you could buddy up to one of them, you know, man to man, and see if they would share any footage they have from the cameras."

"Man to man?" Michael grinned.

"Yeah. You're the one who took down two security guards single-handedly. Tell them you want to see the video. Maybe they'll show it to you. I don't know, but it's worth a try."

"Okay, but what am I looking for?"

"Anything that will help prove who killed Serafina."

"If the killer was on video, the police would already have them in handcuffs. The Tribal Police may not be staffed to the same level as the FBI, but I can assure you that the officers are well trained, and checking film footage would have been one of the first things that they did."

"I know, but you won't be looking for the same thing." A thought flitted through my head.

"What exactly am I looking for?" Michael asked.

"They're looking for suspects. You'd be looking for glass shards."

CHAPTER 47

"What?" Michael asked.

"When did Patrick Dixon break his glasses?" I asked.

Michael shrugged. "I don't know, but what difference does it make?"

"He made a big point that he wasn't in the same place where the murder happened. He couldn't have killed Serafina. But when we saw him he was wearing those red glasses, remember?"

Michael nodded.

"But, after the murder, when we went back in the room and were talking to the police after Serafina's body was found, he wasn't wearing his glasses. The glass shard that cut Baby's paw was prescription glass. What are the chances that two people broke their glasses in the exact same spot where Serafina's body was found?"

"So, you want me to look for glass?"

"Can you look to see when is the first time that you noticed the broken glass or when is the last time that you saw Patrick Dixon without his glasses?"

"Okay. I can't promise that they'll just let me check out the videos, but I'll give it a try. What are you going to do?"

"I'm going to take Baby downstairs and put him in my truck to rest. Then, I'm going to help Leroy pack up our booth."

Michael narrowed his gaze and stared. "Are you okay?"

"Yeah, I'm fine. It's just been a really long day. First, there was all of the excitement of the expo and the contest. I was really looking forward to having Serafina help with the wedding details. Even if I didn't win the contest, although I fully intended to win, I hoped I could pick her brain for help."

"Maddy, you don't have to worry about the details. We don't have to impress anyone. It's our wedding. Yours and mine. As long as we're happy, that's all that matters." He hugged me. "Now, what's really bothering you?"

I snuggled against his chest and enjoyed the safety I felt with his arms wrapped around me. "I feel like I've lived a lifetime in a few hours. I started the day so excited about our wedding and the possibilities of winning the contest. Then, Serafina was so awful. She had Luke steal my phone, and wore my dream dress because she knew it would annoy me. Then . . ."

"Then what?"

"It feels like marriage doesn't mean anything. Serafina and Chef Barbier were having an affair. Alliyah and Patrick Dixon were having an affair. Patrick and Pilar Torres were having an affair. Even Roger Livingston was cheating on Kelsey Morgan."

"Who?"

"Roger and Kelsey, the first couple in the competition."

"Got it."

"Well, it made me wonder if anyone values their marriage vows."

"Hey, Squid, listen to me. When I say *I do*, I intend to keep those vows." Michael cupped my chin in his hand. He gazed in my eyes, and I knew that he would.

"I do, too."

He kissed me.

"You better."

CHAPTER 48

Michael left Baby and me alone as he went to talk to the Tribal Police.

"It's just you and me now, boy." I scratched Baby's ear. "Let's go downstairs and go home. I'll bet you a liver treat Miss Hannah will have a surprise waiting for you along with our fried chicken."

Baby yawned and stretched.

The door to the relaxation room opened.

Patrick Dixon entered.

"What are you doing here?" I asked. "If you're looking for Alliyah, she just left."

"I found who I was looking for."

Something in his voice sent a shiver up my spine.

"Well, we were just going downstairs so we can pack up. It's been an exhausting day." I grabbed Baby's leash.

Patrick Dixon blocked the door, but I heard the click as he turned the lock.

Baby growled.

"You couldn't leave well enough alone. You had to go poking your nose where it didn't belong."

"I have no idea what you mean."

"Don't play dumb. I heard you."

"I don't know what you think you heard, but you're mistaken."

"I followed you up here. Did you know there's a closet next door to this room?" Patrick Dixon took a step forward.

"No." I gulped.

"A utility closet. It's just big enough for one person. Me." He took a step forward.

I took a step backward. "Interesting."

Baby yawned, but he shook his head to shake off the sleep that was trying to overtake him.

Patrick pulled a gun from his pocket, and he pointed it at me. Baby growled.

Patrick pointed the gun at Baby. "Get rid of that mutt. Put him outside, now, or I'll shoot him right here."

I pulled on Baby's leash, but he wouldn't budge. He dug his heels in. "Baby, come."

Rarely had my well-trained mastiff ever disobeyed a direct order. Until today. He stared down Patrick Dixon while drool dripped from his lips.

"Baby, no. Please." I pushed my body in between Patrick Dixon and Baby and used my knee and every bit of strength I had to push him closer to the door.

If he hadn't been drugged, I probably wouldn't have been able to move him an inch. However, I managed to slide him to the door. I unlocked the door and used my knee to get Baby into the hall.

He lunged, but I managed to get him out, and the door closed. *Crap. What did I just do?*

"Good job." Patrick Dixon grinned.

I was too exhausted from wrestling with Baby to stress about myself. I turned and stared into the eyes of a killer.

CHAPTER 49

Outside the room, Baby barked and lunged at the door. However, after a few moments, I heard heavy steps trotting away from the door.

Good. Run. Be safe.

"That's better," Patrick said.

"What are you going to do with me?" I asked.

"I'm going to shoot you." Patrick lifted his gun.

"Someone will hear the gunshot. You'll never get out of here."

Patrick grabbed a throw pillow from the sofa. "Silencer."

"They'll find me. My friends know where I am."

"Good point. They know about this room, but I doubt if they know about the utility closet. Thanks." He smirked.

What am I doing? I shouldn't be helping him kill me.

"Now, we're going to walk out of here quietly and just go next door." He pointed the gun toward me.

"Why didn't you just leave? Why try to kill me?"

"You're smart. You would have convinced them that I was guilty. I heard you tell Alliyah about Pilar and me."

"That's your fault. You shouldn't assume that people don't know other languages."

"You should mind your own business and not interfere in conversations that have nothing to do with you." Patrick stepped forward.

I tried to step backward but was backed up to the sofa.

"Although I suppose you did me a favor. I was done with Alliyah Howard anyway. Now that Serafina's dead and I can finally get my hands on her money, I don't need her."

"If you heard me, then you have to know that you won't be able to get your hands on Serafina's money. She made Luke her beneficiary."

"It pays to be in bed with a lawyer." Patrick laughed. "If Luke Overton goes to prison for killing Serafina, then he can't benefit from the trust. And it looks like Luke will be going to prison for a long time."

"You knew about the trust?"

"Of course I knew. I'm dating a lawyer. There's no way I was going to walk away from that marriage with nothing."

He used the gun to indicate I should move toward the door, but my feet were cement blocks. *I need to keep him talking.*

"Why Luke?"

"Because he was the start of everything. I figured since this entire mess started with Luke, then it would be fitting to have it end with him."

"What are you talking about?"

"Nancy Drew didn't figure that out yet?" He laughed. "Luke provided the money that Serafina used to launch her career. Luke was her secret benefactor."

CHAPTER 50

Tilt. Tilt. Tilt. "What? How?"

"Luke's one and only claim to fame and notoriety came when he decided to rob the Parkway Gardens Savings & Loan."

"Robbing a bank is serious. He went to jail."

"That fool didn't even have a real gun. He just stuck his hand in his pocket. They put the money from the drawer in a pillowcase, and he ran away and dropped the pillowcase."

"Okay, but they caught him."

"You're missing the point." He waited, but I wasn't connecting the dots. "He lost the pillowcase with the money. He robbed a bank and didn't even get the money."

"That's a good thing. The bank got their money back so he—"

He shook his head. "No, they didn't. He tossed the pillowcase with the money into an alley and hoofed it. Before the police searched the area, Serafina found the pillowcase."

"Serafina took the stolen money?"

Patrick nodded. "Now a goody-two-shoes like you probably would have turned that money over to the authorities, right?"

I felt heat rising up my neck.

Patrick Dixon laughed. "I thought so. Well, Serafina didn't. She kept it."

"Luke and Serafina were working together?"

"Naw. He never saw her and had no idea she was the one who took the money. But she knew. She knew he went to prison and she didn't do anything. She just took the money and started living her best life. Following her dream of fame and fortune."

"So, that's why she hired him to work for her when he got out of prison?"

"Now you're catching on." He smiled. "Serafina was a wicked witch. She probably thought she would live for fifty or sixty more years, and when she was old and kicked the bucket, then she would let Luke benefit from the money she invested and grew."

"But it wasn't her money," I said.

"It wasn't Luke's either. She must have thought she was being so clever by setting up that trust and making Luke the beneficiary, but she just played into my hands. Luke will go to jail for murder, and you can't benefit from a crime. Pilar is a smart lawyer. She'll work it out so that I get the money."

"Are you in love with her?"

"Love? I can't afford love. Maybe when I'm rich I can. For now, she's convenient." He reached for the door but stopped and turned to me. "All right, I have one question for you, Nancy Drew. What gave me away?"

"Your glasses. You were wearing glasses earlier, but not after Serafina was murdered. Then, my dog cut his foot on a shard of glass from your glasses. When April had it analyzed, we found out it was from prescription glasses."

"So? That doesn't make me a killer. If I hadn't broken my glasses, and missed a shard of the lens, you never would have figured it out." He reached toward the knob, so I kept talking.

"Also, I had forgotten that you were a naturopathic doctor, but Alliyah reminded me that you were an acupuncturist. You stole the skewers from my apron and knew precisely where to put those skewers to stab Serafina."

"Ah . . . I might have to make sure that Dr. Alliyah Howard has an unfortunate accident soon, too." He glanced at his watch. "Right now, Nancy Drew, I need you to stop stalling and move." He grabbed the doorknob and wrenched the door open.

I hate being called Nancy Drew. Anger is probably one of the few things that could have gotten my feet unstuck.

Patrick Dixon pushed me out the door.

I stumbled and fell to the ground, but instead of getting up, I curled up like a ball.

"What are you doing? Get up."

The ground vibrated.

CHAPTER 51

I looked up in time to see Baby galloping toward Patrick Dixon with spaghetti-sized strings of drool hanging from each corner of his mouth.

Patrick caught sight of Baby. He lifted his arm and pointed his gun.

"Oh no you don't." I lifted my head and grabbed ahold of Patrick Dixon's arm. Then, I clamped down with my teeth and bit as hard as I could.

Patrick screamed and tried to shake me off, but Baby was on top of him.

Baby pushed him to the ground.

"Baby, stop," Michael yelled.

I released my grip on Patrick's arm.

Michael stepped on the wrist with the gun and then kicked it from his hand, and the gun flew across the floor.

Patrick screamed from the ground, "Help! Get this beast off me!"

With teeth bared and drool dripping from his jowls, Baby stood firmly with over two hundred pounds on Patrick Dixon's chest.

"If you move a fraction of an inch, I'm going to let him rip your throat out," Michael said.

April rushed down the hall. Her gun was out and pointed at Patrick.

A rainbow of law enforcement swarmed the hall. Officers Thomas and Norris, in their blue NBPD uniforms, stood shoulder to shoulder next to brown-shirted state police, tan-shirted Tribal Police, and agents wearing navy nylon jackets with a bright yellow FBI prominently displayed.

Michael helped me to my feet. "You okay?"

Those were the last words I remember.

CHAPTER 52

"Maddy. Are you okay? Maddy, say something." Michael lifted my eyelid as he hurled questions at me.

"Where's Baby?" I asked.

Michael let out a breath. "I should be jealous that your first thought is for your dog instead of your fiancé, but I'm so thankful that you're okay." He completed a cursory exam that was all medical. "Are you hurt? Did he hurt you?"

"I'm fine."

I tried to sit up, but Michael pushed me back onto the sofa. "You need to rest."

"I need Baby. Is he okay?"

Baby squeezed his massive head through two officers' legs and rested it on my chest.

I hugged my mastiff. "You were such a good boy. I should have known you would bring help."

Michael sat on the sofa. "I'll say."

"What happened?" I looked from Michael to April. "How did you all get here?"

"Baby came running through the auditorium barking and

flinging drool like Cujo," Leroy said. "Folks were screaming and running like crazy. He didn't stop until he found Michael."

"I was talking to Officer Thunderhawk when Baby came barking toward me." Michael reached down and scratched Baby's head. "I knew something was wrong."

"I almost shot him." Officer Thunderhawk laughed. "I thought he was rabid."

"Baby started tugging on my pants trying to get me to follow him," Michael said.

"You haven't seen anything until you've seen a giant dog acting like Lassie and trying to tell you that Timmy fell down the well," Tyler said.

"Once I figured out he wanted me to follow him, that's what I did," Michael said.

"That's what we all did," Leroy said. "So, now you've got April and a dozen law enforcement officers following a giant, foaming-at-the-mouth mastiff as he rushes through a crowded auditorium with people diving for cover."

Baby yawned, and I followed suit.

"Both of my patients need their rest," Michael said, picking me up. "I'm taking you both home."

I kissed him.

"I could use a statement before you go," April said.

I told her everything and promised to give an official statement later.

On the way outside, I saw Patrick Dixon handcuffed with his hands behind his back, lying on the floor. He glared at me.

Baby must not have liked the look because he growled and snapped.

Dixon screamed.

I pulled out my phone and snapped a photo.

#CrimeDontPay #TakingABiteOutofCrime #ThisIsWhatJustice LooksLike

CHAPTER 53

News travels fast, and the news that Serafina's killer had been arrested beat me home to the house.

Michael let me walk but insisted on driving. When he pulled into my garage, Miss Hannah and Fiona were waiting.

Miss Hannah pulled me into a hug and squeezed tightly before dropping down and giving Baby a hug. "You saved her again, and I'm glad I bought you a chicken. You earned it."

"She bought Baby a whole chicken?" I whispered to Michael. He shrugged. "Maybe if we beg or do some tricks he'll share."

Miss Hannah stood up and swatted Michael's arm. "Now you know I didn't forget y'all. I got fried chicken for the humans, but Dru Ann roasted a chicken for Baby. It's better for his cholesterol than fried."

Miss Hannah and Baby went into the house, leaving Michael and me alone in the garage.

"She's worried about Baby's cholesterol?" I asked.

"Roasted is better for all of our cholesterol." Michael shook his head and started to walk into the house when I stopped him. "Before you go in, I have a couple of things I want to say."

He waited.

"First." I reached up and kissed him. I kissed him long and thoroughly.

"Wow. What was that for?"

"Thank you. I know that Baby wasn't the only one who came to save me today."

He wrapped his arms around me tightly. "You didn't need saving. You had things well under control by the time I got there."

"Not really. I was terrified when Patrick Dixon pulled out that gun. I just knew he was going to shoot me, and I know this is going to sound crazy, but in that moment, I knew what I wanted."

"What?"

"Love."

He leaned in and kissed me again. "Well, you have that."

"No, I mean, yes, but that's not all. It's not just your love that I'm talking about. It's the love from family and friends and food and people that genuinely care about me. Even Baby."

"That's good because you have that. You've made a ton of friends here in New Bison. Lots of people love you." He pulled out his phone. "In fact, they've been blowing up my phone."

He swiped his phone and started to read. "I have messages from Mr. Papadakis. He heard about what happened and is bringing a floral arrangement to brighten your day."

"He's such a sweet man. Did you know he's teaching April how to make floral arrangements so she can one day open her own flower shop?"

"I didn't know that."

"I'm going to have Mr. Papadakis do the flowers for our wedding."

"Okay." Michael swiped. "Here's one from Sister Sylvia."

"Sister Sylvia from church?"

Michael nodded. "She refunded the money for the food. She said it's on her."

"Do you think she and Dru Ann Love would cater the food for our reception? Would you be okay with that?"

"I'm sure they would and absolutely! You know I love Dru Ann's chicken." Michael scrolled his messages. "Troy Lewis has offered to do the photography, free of charge."

"That's so nice, but of course we'll pay him."

Michael grinned. "Of course we will."

"Carson Law is giving us the Carson Law Inn for the reception, and she offered to do my veil. That just leaves my dress."

"Which your dad is buying," Michael said.

"Yeah. He is." I forced a smile.

"What's wrong?"

"Nothing. I just wish . . . never mind."

Michael kissed me. "What do you wish? Today is the day that all wishes come true."

"Not this wish." I shrugged. "It's fine. You can't have everything in life."

Michael got a new text. He glanced at the screen. "It's Alliyah. She wants to know if it's okay if she comes by to thank you."

"Of course."

He sent the response. "Now, what were you saying?"

Before I could explain, Miss Hannah opened the garage door. "Are you two coming? The food is getting cold, and Maddy needs her rest."

We entered the house and went into the dining room. There was a large spread. Smelling the food, I realized how hungry I was. My stomach growled, and my mouth salivated as much as Baby's.

Miss Hannah and Fiona wouldn't allow me to do anything except sit and eat. They filled my plate as though they were feeding a linebacker for a football team.

I was embarrassed to see that I'd eaten just about everything on my plate. I glanced around the room at my friends and couldn't help smiling.

"What are you grinning about?" Tyler asked.

"I was just thinking about how blessed I am to have such good friends. Before I came inside, I was telling Michael how much I appreciated him. Well, I want you all to know that I appreciate all of you, too."

Everyone echoed the sentiment.

"I was sharing with Michael some of the decisions I made about the wedding." I reached over and squeezed his hand. I shared the decisions I'd talked about with Michael in the garage.

"I'd love to help April and Mr. Papadakis with the flowers," Fiona said. "If that's okay?"

"Of course. I'm sure they'd love that."

"And, I feel confident that Dru Ann and Sister Sylvia can come up with a menu that'll be more upscale than their usual collards and fried chicken," Miss Hannah said.

Candy raised her hand. "Can I help? I'd love to work with them on the menu."

"Of course, but I have one condition," I said.

"What?" Candy asked.

"Make sure there are collard greens for me." I turned to Michael.

"And fried chicken for me," he said.

"You got it! I'm sure we can help create an elegant spread that will fit perfectly at the beautiful Carson Law Inn. You just leave it to me."

Carson Law clapped. "I love it. I'm sure the chefs will help, too."

"And thank you, Mrs. Law, for allowing us to have the wedding at the Carson Law Inn. And for offering to design my veil."

"It's my pleasure, dear," Mrs. Law said.

Michael got a text. He read it and then leaned over. "There's one more thing we need and our wedding will be complete."

"What's that?"

"Your dress."

"Oh, well . . . my dad is taking care of that. Although . . . well, never mind."

"What's the problem?" Michael asked. "I'm sure the Admiral will gladly get you that fancy Hanifa dress you fell in love with."

I paused for several beats. "I don't want a fancy dress. I want to marry you, and I want to wear my mother's dress."

"But I thought your mother's dress got ruined," Michael said.

"It did." I sighed.

April walked through the door carrying a large box. She handed it to me.

"What's this?"

"I had a feeling you might change your mind about the dress, so I asked Tyler if he could fix it."

I reached for the box, but April snatched it away at the last moment. "Unfortunately, he wasn't able to fix it."

"I'm sorry, Maddy," he said. "The unraveling was just too much, and I wasn't able to salvage it."

"Oh." I forced a smile. "But, what's this?"

April passed me the box. This time, she let me take it.

Michael cleared the dishes away so I could set the box on the table.

I lifted the lid and pulled back the acid-free paper and stared. Mouth open, I felt my eyes flood with tears. "My mom's dress. But, you said you couldn't fix it."

Tyler came over and lifted the dress from the box. When he held it up, that's when I saw that he had altered the dress.

"I had to cut the bottom and then I removed the sleeves because . . . well, they just didn't seem to match your style." He hurriedly added, "They were snagged, but I can reattach them. It'll just take a long time and—"

I flung myself at him, catching the dress between us. "I love it!"

After a few moments, Tyler pushed himself away. He fanned himself and wiped invisible sweat from his brow. "Thank God. I was so afraid you'd be upset with the alterations."

I took the dress and looked at it more closely. "Are you joking? I absolutely love it. It's my mom's dress, but with my style. It's amazing. I can't wait to try it on."

"Me either," Michael said.

"You're not supposed to see the bride in her wedding dress, so sorry, soldier. This is all you get until the wedding."

Michael leaned closer and whispered something in my ear that sent heat up my neck and a shiver up my spine.

"It looks like you've made a lot of decisions in one day," April said.

"I learned a lot about myself today. But, most importantly, I learned that making decisions isn't hard if you follow your heart."

Later, after everyone was gone, I sat up in my bed and stared at the short, crocheted dress that my mom wore when she walked down the aisle to marry my father, which now hung on my closet door. Knowing that it was the same dress that I would wear when it was my turn to walk down the aisle filled my heart with joy.

Baby was sprawled out across the bed next to me snoring and drooling like a . . . well, like a mastiff. On the dresser was the quilt that had been passed down in my family from mother to daughter for close to two hundred years. I longed to snuggle up underneath the fabric that had been touched by so many of my ancestors, but I knew it was too fragile. Just thinking about those things brought a smile to my face. These were the things that brought me joy. These were the things that mattered. My wedding day would be special because, just as my mom had found the man of her dreams, her soulmate, I'd found mine. It wasn't the chairs or the napkins that would make our wedding perfect. It's the people and the love.

RECIPES FROM
BABY CAKES BAKERY

Rob's Apple Cake

Recipe courtesy of Melinda Bandy

Ingredients
3 cups all-purpose flour
2¼ cups sugar, divided
1 tablespoon baking powder
½ teaspoon salt
4 eggs
1 cup vegetable oil
⅓ cup orange juice
2½ teaspoons pure vanilla extract
4 medium baking apples*, peeled and thinly sliced
2 teaspoons ground cinnamon

Directions
1. Preheat oven to 350 degrees. Butter a Bundt pan.
2. Combine flour, 2 cups sugar, baking powder, and salt in a mixing bowl. In a separate bowl, combine eggs, oil, orange juice, and vanilla. Add the liquid ingredients to the flour mixture and mix well.
3. Toss the apples into a bowl with the cinnamon and remaining ¼ cup of sugar.
4. Spread ⅓ of the batter into the Bundt pan. Top with half of the apples. Repeat. Spread the last ⅓ of the batter over the apples.
5. Bake for 55–65 minutes or until a toothpick inserted near the center comes out clean.
6. Let cool in the pan for 15 minutes and then remove to a wire rack.

*Baking apples are any variety that is firm enough to stand up to the baking process and won't give you a mushy tart, pie, or cake.

Apple Cider

Ingredients
10–12 medium apples (try mixed varieties like Honeycrisp, Gala, McIntosh, etc.)
2 oranges, peeled and sectioned
$1/2$ cup light brown sugar, packed
4 sticks cinnamon
1 teaspoon ground allspice
1 tablespoon whole cloves

Directions
1. Cut apples into quarters and place in a large pot with oranges. Add water to cover the apples by 2 inches when the apples are fully submerged.
2. Stir in the remaining ingredients and bring to a boil. Allow mixture to boil uncovered for one hour.
3. Reduce the heat. Cover and simmer for two hours.
4. Let the mixture cool a bit and then strain through a cheesecloth. Press gently on the solids and get as much of the liquid into your container as possible. When done, use a second cheesecloth and strain a second time.

Spicy Ginger Cookies

Recipe courtesy of Patricia Lillie

Ingredients
¹/₄ cup vegetable shortening (must be vegetable shortening, not butter or margarine)
¹/₂ cup sugar (plus 2 extra tablespoons for rolling)
1 egg
¹/₂ cup molasses
2 cups flour
1 teaspoon baking soda
¹/₄ teaspoon salt
2 teaspoons ground ginger
1 teaspoon ground cinnamon
¹/₂ teaspoon ground nutmeg
¹/₂ teaspoon ground cloves

Directions
1. Cream the shortening and sugar together until fluffy.
2. Add egg and molasses and beat well.
3. Combine the flour, baking soda, salt, and spices in a separate bowl. Gradually add to the shortening mixture and mix well.
4. Cover the dough and refrigerate for at least 6 hours or overnight.
5. Preheat oven to 400 degrees and grease cookie sheets.
6. Form chilled dough into 1 tablespoon balls (or use a 1 tablespoon cookie scoop).
7. Roll the balls in the extra sugar and place on the prepared cookie sheets, about 2 inches apart. Bake for 10 minutes.
8. Remove from oven and immediately transfer the cookies to wire racks to cool.

Grandma Fischer's Apple Walnut Cake

Recipe courtesy of Kay Lillie

Ingredients
Cake:
4 cups apples, chopped
1$\frac{1}{2}$ cups sugar
2 eggs
$\frac{1}{2}$ cup vegetable oil
2 teaspoons vanilla
1 tablespoon frozen apple juice concentrate
2 cups flour
2 teaspoons baking soda
2 teaspoons ground cinnamon OR 1 teaspoon ground cinnamon & 1 teaspoon ground nutmeg
$\frac{3}{4}$ teaspoon salt
1 cup walnuts, chopped
1 cup raisins

Cider Sauce:
2 cups apple cider OR apple juice*
$\frac{1}{4}$ cup packed brown sugar
1 tablespoon cornstarch
1 tablespoon butter
2 teaspoons vanilla

Directions
Cake:
   1. Preheat oven to 350 degrees. Grease a 9 x 13-inch cake
   pan.

*Apple juice can be made from remaining frozen concentrate

2. Mix chopped apples and sugar and let set for 30 minutes.
3. Beat eggs. Add oil, vanilla, and juice concentrate and blend well.
4. In a separate bowl, combine the flour, baking soda, spices, and salt.
5. Add dry ingredients alternately with apples to egg and oil mixture and stir well after each addition.
6. Add walnuts and raisins.
7. Spread batter in prepared pan.
8. Bake for approximately 45 minutes or until a toothpick inserted in middle of cake comes out clean.
9. Let cool in pan. Make the cider sauce (below) while the cake cools.
10. To serve, cut the cake into squares and put on plates. Spoon cider sauce over cake and top with a healthy dollop of whipped cream or a scoop (or two) of ice cream.

Cider Sauce:

1. In a medium saucepan, whisk together cider or juice, brown sugar, and cornstarch until blended.
2. Bring to a boil over medium-high heat.
3. Boil 1 minute or until thickened.
4. Remove from heat and add butter and vanilla. Stir until butter melts.
5. Let cool until just warm or refrigerate until serving.

Optional but recommended: Whipped cream or vanilla ice cream

Bourbon Apple Cider Cake

Ingredients
Cake
2 cups apple cider (see recipe above)
$3^1/_2$ cups all-purpose flour
1 tablespoon baking powder
1 teaspoon salt
8 ounces unsalted butter (two sticks)
$2^1/_4$ cups sugar
3 large eggs
1 cup whole milk
2 teaspoons vanilla
$2^1/_2$ teaspoons ground cinnamon
$^1/_2$ teaspoon ground cloves
$^1/_4$ teaspoon ground nutmeg
$1^1/_2$ teaspoon allspice
2 Honeycrisp apples, peeled and cored, and then pureed

Icing
8 ounces cream cheese
1 stick butter
5 cups powdered sugar
$^1/_4$ cup plus 3 teaspoons bourbon
$^1/_2$ teaspoon vanilla

Directions
Cake
1. Heat the apple cider in a small saucepan on medium heat until it reduces by half, making 1 cup
2. Preheat oven to 350 degrees, grease three 9-inch cake pans and prepare ingredients.
3. Whisk flour, salt, spices, and baking powder together in a large bowl.

4. Cream butter and sugar together in a stand mixer until light and fluffy.
5. Add eggs one at a time, beating completely before adding the next egg.
6. Mix milk and vanilla together. While the mixer is on low, add $1/3$ of the flour mixture, followed by $1/3$ of the milk. Keep alternating wet and dry ingredients until all are incorporated.
7. Pour in the pureed apples and reduced apple cider and mix to combine.
8. Divide the mixture evenly between the cake pans and bake for 25 minutes.

Icing

1. In a stand mixer with a paddle attachment, beat the cream cheese and butter together.
2. Slowly add in the powdered sugar one cup at a time.
3. Add in the vanilla and bourbon and mix until combined.
4. After frosting the cake, add 4–5 tablespoons of caramel as a glaze.

Caramel Apples

Ingredients
6–8 large apples
1 cup brown sugar, packed
1 cup sugar
1 cup light corn syrup
14 ounces sweetened condensed milk
1 stick butter

Directions
1. Wash the apples to remove any waxy film and place a popsicle stick into the center of each apple.
2. Heat the remaining ingredients in a pan over low heat until the caramel reaches 225 degrees. Stir occasionally.
3. Allow to cool for approximately 5 minutes.
4. Dip the apples in the caramel while slowly twisting, then place on a baking sheet lined with parchment paper.
5. Place the baking sheet in the refrigerator to chill the apples.
6. Sprinkle with desired toppings* (Optional)

---

* Drizzle apples with melted chocolate (dark or white), dip apples in chopped nuts, chocolate chips, sprinkles, toasted or untoasted coconut, chopped candy pieces, or crushed Oreos.